Soul Of Power

C.D. Schrieber

Bloomington, IN   Milton Keynes, UK

AuthorHouse™
1663 Liberty Drive, Suite 200
Bloomington, IN 47403
www.authorhouse.com
Phone: 1-800-839-8640

AuthorHouse™ UK Ltd.
500 Avebury Boulevard
Central Milton Keynes, MK9 2BE
www.authorhouse.co.uk
Phone: 08001974150

This book is a work of fiction. People, places, events, and situations are the product of the author's imagination. Any resemblance to actual persons, living or dead, or historical events, is purely coincidental.

© 2006 C.D. Schrieber. All rights reserved.

No part of this book may be reproduced, stored in a retrieval system, or transmitted by any means without the written permission of the author.

First published by AuthorHouse 2/22/2006

ISBN: 1-4208-9186-3 (e)
ISBN: 1-4208-9185-5 (sc)

Library of Congress Control Number: 2005909131

Printed in the United States of America
Bloomington, Indiana

This book is printed on acid-free paper.

For Katherine, for the courage to try.

For Sarah, for lending a hand along the way.

For Caroline and Dennis, for giving me a chance.

Author's Note:

It is important to note that the president in this story was invented through my imagination, not actual facts. Nor was the character based on any real person who is living or has lived in the history of mankind. Any resemblance to persons living or dead was purely coincidental.

It should also be noted that there is not a random boarding school out in the middle of the pacific ocean - so don't go looking for one. I also have no knowledge to date of an under sea armed base- this is all purely fictional, meant for your enjoyment.

And now without further ado, I hope you find this story as intriguing to read as I found it to write.

Sages: those born with extraordinary gifts. The main foundations of the world – fire, earth, air and water – can easily be controlled by one's will. Our minds: no longer a safe haven. A look could mean death, and not every appearance is as it seems.

Every twenty centuries, ten are born; their birth so great, the parents cannot subsist. They can live for thousands of years, and abstain from death until met with a mortal wound.

But you perceive me wrong; sages just want to live. In peace. Unbothered. They are not evil... Not all of them.

PART 1

A Different Life, A New Perspective

~ 1 ~

"COME BACK 'ERE YA LITTLE RUNT!"

Cody turned around and ran backwards so he could face the two bullies, he grinned, stuck out his tongue, and crossed his eyes. "You'll have to catch me first!" He yelled back. Then he whirled around, and disappeared around the corner.

The two bullies pulled to a stop as they rounded the corner, watching in amazement as Cody ran down the street at top-notch speed; and for the time they rested, he was already miles ahead of them.

"How does he... run so - fast!?" one of the boys gasped, placing his hands on his knees as he caught his breath.

"I don't know... but we can get him - tomorrow... c'mon."

"How old?"
"Fifteen."
"Is he aware?"
"No."
"What's his name?"
"Cody."
"What level?"
"Three."

~

"Hey, Alexander! Gimme your lunch money!"

Alexander grimaced, and turned around in his chair, "Listen Andrew. I don't have any money. If you'll just-"

"Gimme your lunch money!"

"I don't have any!" he repeated, exasperated.

"GIVE IT TO ME NOW!!!"

"I CAN'T!!!"

Andrew, his temper lost, reached down and picked up the small boy by the shoulders, shaking him viciously, "I'm gonna pummel you- ARGGGH!!!"

Suddenly, a blinding flash of light occurred between the two, and Alexander took that moment to squirm out of Andrews grip. He then dropped to the floor, and scuttled away."

"How old?"
"Fifteen."
"Is he aware?"
"No."
"Name?"
"Alexander. Alex."
"Level?"
"Three."

~

"Now class, in today's lesson we will be planting geraniums, if you will look to the instructions on the board, you may begin." The teacher gestured at the board, than began to walk slowly around the room, observing the progress of her class.

Soon she stopped beside a brunette with daring green bangs, "You're going to have to take those gloves off, Ivy." She told the girl in a toneless voice, one accustomed to being obeyed.

The girl raised her head, but didn't meet the gaze of her teacher. "No." she said, quietly.

"What did you say?"

"I said NO." the girl repeated, a little louder.

"March yourself straight down to the principals office, young lady. And you can explain there why you were sent down." The teacher told her in the same toneless voice as before.

The girl scooped up her books, and walked swiftly out of the greenhouse, clearly relieved to be leaving.

The teacher watched her go, then, turning to clear the girls pot and soil from the table, was surprised to find a fully grown plant in the girls pot, where only moments before a seed had been planted.

"Age?"
"Fifteen."

"Is she aware?"
"Yes. But not of her full potential."
"What's her name?"
"Ivy."
"What level?"
"Six."

~

"Hey Alex! Alex, over here!"

Alex turned and walked over to the other girls, "Hi guys." She nodded, "What's up?"

"Nothing much," a girl with frizzy red hair droned, "Mr. Heiishi is setting another quiz for this afternoon – hey! Alex... earth to Alex!"

Alex wasn't listening, she was staring at a blond over on the other side of the room, "Amanda, what a show off!" she mumbled under her breath as the girl flirted with Alex's crush, Brian. Her eye's narrowed.

Abruptly, a window directly across from Amanda blew open, and a gust of wind wracked the room.

When the window was finally forced shut by one of the lunch supervisors, it seemed only Amanda had been affected, her blond hair was now a rat's nest, her clothes hung off her, and she wore an expression of the greatest shock etched upon her wind-blown face.

"How old?"
"Fifteen."
"Awareness?"
"None."
"Name?"
"Alexandra, Alex."
"Level?"
"Five."

~

"No you shut up! I don't give a DAMN if she was just thanking you, it looked to me like you enjoyed it!!!"

"Look, Kim. It was just a kiss."

"Fuck you, Jason! We're through!" and with that, she turned on her heels and walked swiftly down the hallway.

"Kim!... Wait! Ahh, who needs her!"

"Age?"
"Fifteen."
"Is she aware?"
"Nope."
"Name?"
"Kimberly. Kim."
"Level?"
"Five."

~

"Common, give it back you guys!" Kelsi whined.

"No! This little pink watch suits me. Don't you agree girls?" Carla asked her friends, who quickly nodded in agreement, afraid to disagree.

"NO! GIVE IT BACK!"

"No. If you want it so much, why don't you come and get it?"

Kelsi started to cry. That watch had been a gift from her late grandmother. It meant the world to her!

Kelsi suddenly looked up, directly at Carla, staring her straight in the eye, and between them the air shattered like glass, and Carla was thrown backwards, the watch flying from her hand into Kelsi's.

Kelsi grinned.

"Age?"
"Fifteen."
"Is she aware?"
"Yes."
"Name?"
"Kel-see."
"Level?"
"Four."

~

"Shut up!"

"No, you shut up! I don't give a DAMN if she was just thanking you! It looked to me liked you enjoyed it!"

"Look, Kim. It was just, a kiss!"

"Fuck you, Jason! We're through!"

He stood, stunned, and watched her as she walked swiftly down the school hallway.

"Kim… Wait! Ahh, who needs 'er!" and he turned and walked the other way.

"Age?"
"Fifteen."
"Awareness?"
"Not a clue."
"Name?"
"Jason."
"Level?"
"Five."

~

"So she wouldn't come over to my house for dinner right, because she's allergic to cats. So I'm like, fine, I'll cook something else!"

The boys around the table howled with laughter.

"And what'd she say to that?"

"Oh, you know my grandma. She tried to retort, but her dentures fell out!" Eric cracked, the other boys laughed again.

"Did you guy's hear about the kidnapping?"

"No."

"Yeah, apparently he woke up."

They had to hold their stomach's they were laughing so hard.

"Hey Eric."

"Yeah?"

"Did you hear about the church that burned down?"

"HOLY SMOKE!"

"Ahh man! You already heard it!"

Eric grinned as the boys dissolved into a fit of laughter once again, "I'm telling ya' man, there ain't no joke I don't know." He grinned.

"Age?"
"Fifteen."
"Is he aware?"
"Nope."

"Name?"
"Eric."
"Level?"
"Five."

~

His shoulders hunched against the chill wind, Matt walked slowly down the gloomy street, his thoughts buried deep.

"Hey, Matt!"

Matt looked up, "Oh, hey Kyle."

"What're ya doin' tonight?"

"Nothin'."

"-What's the deal between you and Ashley?"

Matt spun around, his eyes blazing, "It was nothing, ok?! She tripped, and I caught her, end-of-story!" Matt turned on his heel, and walked back down the street.

"Come on, man-"

"I don't like her! Ok! So just get off my back about it!"

"OK! YEASH! You know, you're to touchy."

"You wanna keep with this conversation? Or shall I pummel you right now?"

"Ok, ok! Ashley's off topic."

The boy's continued down the street, in silence, shoulders hunched, hands in their pockets."

After a while, Kyle opened his big mouth, "So what about Rachel?" then ducked the fist aimed at his face.

"Age?"
"Fifteen."
"Awareness?"
"Only of the basics."
"Name?"
"Mathue. Matt."
"Level?"
"Ten."

~

"You've got nowhere else to run, Ally!"

"We've got you cornered!"

"Down an alley, how ironic."

Ally turned around to face the three bullies, a slight grin tugging at her lip, her head bowed so her bangs concealed her eyes.

"Aren't you even going to plead?"

"Tell me, boys, do you like fireworks?"

"Huh?"

Ally raised her hands, and out of each of her eight fingers shot a stream of light, each aiming for one of the three boys. And as they made contact, they exploded in a shower of sparks, kind of like mini fireworks, in a beautiful array of color and pain.

When the boys lowered the arms they had used to shield themselves, and looked up, Ally was nowhere in sight.

"Ok... I'm officially freaked."

"What is she?"

"I don't know, and I don't care to find out! Let's just get outta' here!"

"Agreed!"

And as they high-tailed it away from the scene, the sound of shrill laughter accompanied them from the alleyway, resounding, echoing in their heads.

"How old is she?"

"Guess." Dennis rolled his eyes.

"Fifteen?"

"Yeah."

"She's apparently aware."

Brandon nodded, "Her name is Ally."

"Yes..." Miranda thought for a moment, "What level?"

"Ten, but we're not entirely sure..."

"What do you mean?" Miranda swiveled around away from the screen to face her husband, "Dennis?"

"She may be higher."

"That's impossible! How can you be sure?"

"I checked the bio readings..."

"And...?"

"They're off the chart. She may very well be at a higher level than Darius."

Miranda turned wide-eyed back to the screen, and watched the girl as she walked slowly down the street, her hands stuffed into her pockets.

"...*We approach her first.*"

~ 2 ~

"Miss Sholtz, your daughter has amazing math and science ability, to deprive her of this opportunity would be a great loss."

"I *am* sorry, Mr...."

"Dixon. You can just call me Dennis."

"-Mr. Dixon. But we just can't afford a boarding school at the moment."

"That's where you'd be wrong, Miss Sholtz."

"I beg your pardon?"

"We are strictly a non-profit organization. We receive our funding from various sponsors. To send your daughter to this school wouldn't-cost-you-a-cent."

"Uhh... a – well, I-I really think you should talk to my daughter, it is really her choice after – ahh! Ally! There are some men here to see you."

Ally turned to face them at the bottom of the stairs, having just come out of the kitchen, and fixed Dixon with a glare most people would have taken offence of, her eyes contracting menacingly.

Dennis just smiled.

"They've offered you the chance of a life time dear." Miss Sholtz smiled at her adopted daughter.

Ally didn't move.

Miss Sholtz cleared her throat nervously, then continued, "Uh... they – they've offered you a chance to transfer to a high-class boarding school."

Ally was listening now, though she didn't look it. A boarding school meant she didn't have to live in this *dump* any more.

"Well? Would you like to go?"

Ally shrugged, "Sure."

"Think about it honey, this is a big-"

"I'll go."

Dennis and Brandon got to their feet, "All right then." Dennis smiled; "We'll pick you up in a week from now. Have your things ready."

"Uh... wait! What will she need?"

Dennis smiled again, "Only some clothes and personal belongings. We provide the rest."

"Oh... well ok then!" Miss Sholtz shook hands with the men, then showed them out the door.

Outside, after the door had been shut and locked behind them, Brandon frowned, "The others might be harder to convince."

"Naw, they – well, almost all of them, are just as desperate for something new, something just a little different." Dennis answered as they both climbed into the limousine parked outside the house.

~

"You could have at least acted as if you cared, honey."

Ally turned her head partly, "I could have." She took a step up the stairs, "And I'm not your 'honey'. My name is Ally. That's the name my mother gave me," Ally continued up the stairs, "and I intend to keep it."

Up in her bedroom, Ally took a backpack from behind her door, and filled the black bag with some clothes, her Walkman and CDs, her hairbrush, and a few other odds and ends.

Then she plunked down on her bed, and switched on her television.

~

As soon as Matt walked in the door, his dead-beat impression of an adoptive father was on him in an instant, his breath confirming he'd been drinking again.

"Where've you – hic – been! – hic – I've been searching all over for – hic – you!"

Matt rolled his eyes, he highly doubted that.

"You know I've –hic– had it with –hic– you! Some men were here an hour –hic– ago. And –hic– offered you the chance to –hic– go to a boarding school for –hic– they'll be here to –hic– pick you up in a –hic– week –hic– so –hic– get your stuff –hic–"

Matt's foster father suddenly acquired a glazed look about his red face, and stared at a point a few feet to the left of his son, "Hi'ya –hic– mummy." Then keeled over sideways as he passed out.

Matt stepped over the inert form casually, as if drunken foster parents often made a point of fainting at his feet, and made his way over to the stairs that led to the basement, thinking, *'A boarding school huh, hey why not, might learn something-',* "Like how to live with a foster dad who's always drunk!" Matt yelled up the stairs. Then, feeling better, jumped onto the worn moth-eaten brown leather couch, and switched on the T.V.

~

Dennis, biting his lip, quietly closed the door on the fierce screaming coming from within the house.

He let out a sigh of relief, "Whew!" he exclaimed, wiping an arm across his perspiring brow, "Well, I think *that* went nicely, don't you!?"

Brandon rolled his eyes, "Oh yes," he replied sarcastically, "I think that went splendid. Is this before or after your comment on their cute kitten? Which turned out to be a very touchy puppy, who bit you on your as-"

"Yes, well," Dennis loosened his collar as they stepped into the black limousine parked outside on the sun-drenched sidewalk, "Anyone can make a mistake."

"At least that was the last one." Brandon replied, blowing air out through his mouth in satisfaction.

"No. Sorry to disappoint you, but there's one more."

"Oh… which one?"

"Ivy."

Dennis revved up the engine, and drove off down the street.

They quickly left the large city of Bend behind them, and after an hour or so of driving through bare countryside, arrived in the small suburban town of Redmond.

Dennis checked a small roll of paper on the seat beside him, and then drove down a few side streets, until he came to Metolius Avenue. And at number 45, he stopped, parking the car across the street.

The sun was just setting, sending rays of beautifully colored light over the neat row of homes. Kitchen lights and warm enticing smells made the stomachs of the two men rumble, and they drew their jackets closer as the air grew chill.

"Why couldn't she live in Bend with the rest of them!" Brandon complained as he shivered in his thin fleece jacket, looking up at number forty-five with apprehension on his face.

"Stop your griping." Dennis snapped, "You'll be nice and warm and cozy by the fire in an hours time, a half hour if all things go well. Besides," he continued with an air of authority, "Not *all* of them live in Bend, we had to drive all the way out to Springfield just to recruit that jumpy, hyper little kid. What was his name-"

"Cody."

"Oh yeah. And you weren't complaining then now were you?"

"That was because it was after lunch, the air was warm, I was fed, and I didn't have this weird feeling... like I'm being watched-"

"May I help you, gentlemen?"

Dennis and Brandon both jumped two feet in the air as the cool clear voice rang out from the darkness, accompanied by the slim figure of a girl of about fifteen.

"Ahh." Dennis regained his stoic composure, and smiled, if somewhat stiffly, at the girl. "Yes, my dear." He breathed. "Tell me, is your name, by chance, Ivy?"

"Yes..." answered the girl uncertainty, her eyes darkening.

"Ahh, thank god." He said to himself, "May we have a word with you?"

The girls eye's drew together in suspicion, "Out here?... alone?"

"Oh no!" said Dennis quickly, realizing the girls thoughts not a moment to soon, "Inside, along with your mother, or father if they're home." It wasn't a question.

"Alright, come with me." Clearly relieved that the two "gentlemen" weren't there to kidnap her or otherwise, Ivy turned on her heel, and led the way into the warm house.

~

Matt put his chin in the crook of his arm as it rested on the sill of one of the limo's windows. He uttered a faint sigh. He would be leaving his friends for a snobby old boarding school, and for what? A better education? HAH! Matt had never cared much for his "education" so why was he doing this?

'Oh yeah.' Matt remembered, *'this means I only have to see my foster dad every summer break!"* the thought was certainly more comforting than the prospect of never seeing his home again. But then, it hadn't really been his home; it was just a place where he had lived... for pretty much his entire life.

'Well then it's good that I'm leaving!' Matt thought violently to himself, *'I could use a little change in my life!'* and even as Matt thought it, he knew that was the real reason he had agreed to leave, not that he'd had much of a choice – he'd been longing for a change in routine. Something just a little different...

Mathue looked over at the kids seated around him, nine in total, there had been only two in the car when he had been picked up, and since then they had gone around pretty much the entire city of Bend, picking up the other five kids as they went, then they had traveled all the way over to Springfield, which was halfway across the state, just to pick up a loudmouth chatterbox named Cody who wouldn't shut up.

In fact, the kid was *so* annoying that one of the men up front -the bigger one- had finally cracked and threatened to roll the kid's head up in the window if he didn't put a cork in it real fast.

They had then traveled north until they reached Albany, and for a moment, Matt had been sure they'd be traveling all the way to Salem, the capital, until the man named Dennis at the wheel made a sharp turn west-ward, and they drove all the way out to Lincoln City on the Pacific coast.

There they boarded a yacht titled the *R.K. Prowler*, headed out to sea, with – as far as Matt could tell – no apparent destination.

And as he watched the state of Oregon fade into the distance, Matt had the disquieting feeling... that he wouldn't be seeing it again for a very, very, long time.

~

"Isn't this exciting! Isn't it just the coolest!" Cody squealed, jumping up and down in excitement, then he went off with his usual volley of non-stop questions- "I've never been on a ship before! Do you think it could sink? I wouldn't mind if it did, I've always wanted to be rescued by a helicopter. Have you ever been rescued by a helicopter? I imagine it would be loads of fun! Have you ever gone to a boarding school? Have you ever gone to a boarding school out in the middle of the ocean!? I haven't, I assume they put it out here so we can't escape. I've heard of boarding schools, they make awful food, and force you to eat it! And there isn't even any desert! Can you *imagine*!? No desert!"

Matt found it quite amazing that he could prattle on like this for hours, even jumping up and down as he was at the rail, without loosing breath.

As Matt listened to the endless chatter, he started to think it sounded like a static channel on the television you just couldn't escape from, and he half wished the kid would hop himself right over the rail. Matt found himself suddenly with half a mind to do just that. He smiled to himself at the thought.

"-I think it'll be kind of cool, though, going to a new place an' all. I wonder how much longer it'll be before we get there? I'll go ask the captain, or who ever that guy is with the messy black hair. I wonder if he works for the boat company or the school? Maybe he works for both? I'll have to remember to ask him. I hope he's as nice as he looks, I wouldn't want to..."

Matt listened to his voice as the kid jumped from the rail, and walked away, headed for the back of the ship, and the cabin that resided there.

He sighed, and looked back out to sea, it was noon now -according to his watch- and his gut rumbled slightly.

The warm noon sun was beating down on his back, warming him as the cold sea air whipped his face. He watched a couple of dolphins as they raced the ship, mesmerized by their speed and grace as they danced upon the waves.

He looked up, then, and saw a small shapeless black dot on the horizon.

He stared at it, curious, and watched as the dot became larger, and larger, slowly taking on the shape of a large mansion, no – castle. Matt could now make out the high walls and turrets of the castle. He stared in awe; it was HUGE. And it wasn't the modern civilized buildings people called castles these days. Oh no! It was a *real* castle, like one from back in the medieval times, with vines growing along its walls and everything!

And the real eye opener was that it was built in the middle of the ocean, on nothing but a little pile of rock! Matt could see the wall itself disappear into the ocean in some places.

As he stared up at the castle he heard a clear voice sound from beside him: *Its not that impressive.*

He turned his head to face the sarcastic speaker, and found himself facing thin air, "Who..." he peered around in confusion, searching for the speaker.

"Like your new home?" came a much deeper voice from behind him, jarring him roughly back into reality.

For that instant, Matt saw a girl standing beside him. She jerked slightly, at the sounding of the other voice. Her brown hair whipping out behind her in the breeze. Then she slowly turned her head towards him, but just as her face came into view, she shimmered, and disappeared.

From the short period in which he had glimpsed her, Matt could tell she had been about his age, fifteen, and the most beautiful thing he'd ever seen.

Matt shook his head, clearing the girl from his thoughts, and looked over at Dixon, then back at the castle, "This... this is the boarding school?" he asked in awe. Staring up in wonder at the castle looming before him, larger and more magnificent than it had been at a distance.

"Yup. Nice, isn't it?"

"But... we didn't have to pay anything to come! How can you afford it!"

"Ah, now *that's* an interesting question. You see, as we are a non-profit organization, the historical society kindly lent it to us. Providing we keep it neat and tidy, and in good condition. We don't even have to pay the tax on it!" Dixon gave a quick laugh, "And don't worry, its quite warm on the inside."

"Riiiiiiight." Matt raised his eyebrows, then turned back to the castle, watching as the boat pulled up to a drawbridge-looking dock.

Suddenly, as if they had all appeared there by magic, all the other kids, and the other man, Kenith, were on the deck along with himself and Dixon. Clambering and chatting excitedly.

"Alright." Brandon held up his hands to quell the noise - which consisted mainly of Cody's shrill voice- and looked over at Dixon.

"Okay." Dixon smiled at them, "Make sure you have all your things, and follow me."

Matt, backpack already slung over one broad shoulder- waited until Dixon had led everyone from the boat, and onto the dock. Then he followed them silently into the castle.

As they entered, the first thing they saw was a white marble hallway stretching off in either direction, and two large doors right in front of them.

Dixon led them down the hall to their left, and up a small spiraling staircase, down another marble corridor, and into a small room.

Although the castle on the outside looked old and authentic, Matt found himself looking at many modern things inside the building itself, including a small television in the far right hand corner of the room, situated upon a portable trolley.

The rest of the room was pretty much empty, save for a large purple velvet curtain that ran along the left wall, and a small round table beside the trolley.

The room itself was all white, with only the one door, and a window.

As soon as all the kids had dropped their bags in one corner of the room, Dixon brought their attention back to himself, "Now as I was telling Mathue earlier," he gestured at Matt, "this is the boarding school, which the historical society has so pleasantly lent us. We don't really have a name for it, so call it what you will."

Just then, the girl standing beside Matt raised her arm.

"Yes, Kelsi?" Dixon smiled at her.

The girl blushed a deep pink, "Uh, please sir, are... are we the only students?"

"Actually, yes. You ten are the only one's who fit our specifications."

The others were completely baffled by this explanation. How specific did specifications have to be to narrow down the candidates to ten!?

'Ten?' Thought Matt, *'I only counted nine! Including myself.'* He shrugged mentally, *'maybe I miss-counted.'*

"Now if you'll follow me, I'll give you a tour of your new home." Dixon smiled at them, then led the way out the door.

He led them down the corridor, and showed them into the classrooms, which looked surprisingly empty, no desks, or tables of any kind; there was only a blackboard in each, and various odds and ends in different rooms. One even had a table with a large, live, *very live*, crocodile lying on top of it, with two men trying to subdue it.

"Can I touch it?" Cody asked excitedly as they passed, jumping up and down in excitement.

"Only if you want your hand chopped off," a boy mumbled to him out of the corner of his mouth, and after that, Cody kept his mouth – somewhat – shut.

Another room had been filled with glass jars of every size and description, and still more were empty, completely void of even windows.

At the end of the corridor, Dixon led them past another spiral staircase, and out a side door that led to a balcony.

"This is the east balcony, you'll find the slightly larger, west balcony on the other side of the castle."

Before Dixon had even finished his sentence, Cody had rushed over to the railing, and peered down. "WOW!" He exclaimed breathlessly, forgetting his pass of silence, "I can see the sharp rocks over 80 feet below!" he leant farther over the ledge, "I wonder if there are any sharks down there... HEY! You guy's gotta see this!"

The others backed away politely, then followed Dixon back into the castle; pursued by a somewhat saddened Cody.

Dennis led the teens back down the other spiral staircase, back to the "front door," and led the kids through the two double doors there. Into a room large enough to house about thirteen Chevys, give or take one or two.

Inside the room was a long table spanning the entire length of the room, and there were two doors -besides the ones they had entered through- leading off the opposite sides of the room.

Dixon gestured towards the door that led off towards the east, "Through there is the kitchen, you'll eat your meals here." He indicated the large table, "And through here-" he strode purposefully towards the door on his left, "-are your rooms." He opened the door to reveal a short, dimly lit hallway leading before them, and a slightly longer hallway leading away to their right, the dim lamps almost flickering like candles in the darkness.

Dixon indicated the right hallway with another sweep of his hand, "Down there is where the staff and myself sleep; along with the bathrooms. You'll find them about five doors down. And down here," he gestured at the hallway directly in front of them, "-is where you'll be sleeping."

Down the hallway there were five doors in total, each with a shiny silver number nailed into the wood. Three on one side of the hallway, and two on the other, the hallway itself ending in a solid stone wall.

Dixon turned, and herded them back into the 'eating' room, then he led the way back out into the entrance hall, up one of the spiral staircases, and back into the room where they had left their bags.

As they entered, the kids lined up soundlessly against the wall, and turned to face Dixon, who turned in the middle of the room to face them. "Before we go have our rather *late* lunch -which will be ready momentarily- I would ask you ten to-"

"Sir."

Matt turned his head abruptly towards the speaker, who was a strongly built boy with his bangs dyed a bright outlandish red.

"Yes Jason." Dixon answered tonelessly.

"You keep saying ten. Yet I count only nine?"

Dixon's eyes sparkled mischievously.

'*So I was right! There* are *only nine!*' Matt congratulated himself. Only slightly unnerved by the twinkle in Dixon's eyes.

"Ah," Dixon breathed, "But just because we cannot see something, does not mean it isn't there."

"Huh?" Jason, like everyone else in the room, was once again confounded by the logic Dixon seemed to live by.

Dixon smiled again, and turned to the corner Matt was standing beside. A corner where all the shadows in the room seemed to take refuge, "Ally, will you kindly reveal yourself."

For a moment as everyone stared at the corner, nothing happened. Then the shadows seemed to intensify, growing darker still. And then, all of a sudden, the shadows receded, and a small round girl of about eight stepped from the corner.

The girl was slightly overweight, with two red pigtails sprouting out of her head. She had freckles on every inch of her face, and her eyes were a bright, startling green beneath very long bangs.

"In your *true* form." Dixon finished, another smile tugging at his lip.

The girl shot him a glare from beneath her bangs, then her face relaxed, and she closed her eyes.

Matt looked on in wonder, as, suddenly; the girl began to glow, faintly at first, then brighter and brighter, until all they could see was her form displayed in the light.

The form then stretched, and grew tall and thin, until the light had taken on an entirely different shape. Then the light dimmed, revealing an extremely straight-backed girl of about fifteen.

Matt gazed at her in wonder, taking in her slim form, beautifully shaped and curved, perfect in every way. She was only an inch or two shorter than himself, with waist length brown hair, and bangs than grew down to cover the bridge of her nose.

And when she looked up, his eyes caught hers, the blue irises sparkling as she gazed up at him through her long black lashes.

~ 3 ~

Matt was struck completely wit-less as he gazed at the girl; to him; she was the most beautiful creation on the planet. He could feel his heart beating madly in his chest, making him feel sore with longing.

Dixon was now grinning from ear to ear at the sight of amazement mixed with skepticism that was apparent on each and every face.

The boy that had interrupted -the one with the red bangs- backed abruptly towards the door, "What is it!?"

Dixon looked over at him, "*She* is a sage. Like you and everyone else present."

"A what?" the boy asked again, repulsion now visible on his face.

"A sage," Dixon repeated, "A human possessing extraordinary qualities, like shape shifting, which you have just witnessed," he nodded towards Ally, ignoring the baffled look on the boys face, "Now, before we continue, I would like everyone to introduce themselves. When I call your name, kindly step forward. Cody,"

The small talkative boy leapt forward, Matt could see he was easily a foot shorter than all the six-foot teens in the room, wearing a bright red shirt, bronze cargo shorts, and red and white sneakers. "Hey!" he waved enthusiastically.

"Alexander."

Cody stepped back and Alexander stepped foreword, he was blond, but Matt could tell it was dyed; he could see the brown roots. His attire consisted of a black Nike shirt and some ordinary blue jeans. "H-hi." He mumbled weakly.

"Ivy."

A girl wearing a long-sleeved black shirt, black leather gloves, designer blue jeans and green and black sneakers stepped forward silently. Matt looked over at her unusual hairstyle, her hair was a dark walnut, and quite straight, but her bangs were shaggy and uneven, one side was so long it covered the entire right side of her face, and the other side was short, but dyed a bright offending green. Her face still emotionless, Ivy stepped back against the wall.

"Alexandra."

A happy go-free girl in a bright tangerine colored shirt stepped forward, "Hi." She waved. She was wearing bright pink bellbottom pants, and tangerine rubber shoes.

"Kimberly."

"Hey. Call me Kim." Kim said as she walked forward in her tight purple skirt, which reached down to cover her large pink platforms. She wore a skintight bikini top with the brand *WAI* printed on it in yellow, and other than her walnut bangs, all of her hair was captured up in a purple bandana, which was tied about her head like a turban.

"Kelsi."

Kelsi stepped forward; her hair was draped over her shoulders with part of it tied behind her head in a red ribbon. She wore a light pink shirt with yellow sleeves and her name embroidered on the front. Pearl white pants ran down to cover her pink Sketchers

"Jason."

The boy with the red bangs stepped foreword, and Matt noticed that as he did so, he shot Kimberly a venomous glare, who likewise gave him the finger.

Jason was wearing a tight undershirt, which clearly defined his muscular torso; and black shorts that reached past his knees. Looking down, Matt could see Jason wore the new style of boots; which were at least two sizes larger than he would have needed them to be, with the large red covers that worked as the laces over the white boots themselves.

"Eric."

At first glance, Matt could tell Eric was as carefree and loose going as Cody, though maybe not as talkative. Obviously thin, Eric wore a HUGE black sweatshirt, and large baggy blue jeans that draped themselves over his black and white skater shoes. His brown hair looked like someone had taken a hair blower to his head; it was combed forward and fell about his face at different angles. "Heya peoples!" He grinned, flashing them all 'live long and prosper' with his left hand.

"Mathue"

Matt, startled for a moment at the mention of his name; stepped forward with a shrug, "Call me Matt."

Ally looked over at him curiously, his hair wasn't *that* long, but it was long enough to be tied into a ten-inch horsetail at the back of his head. His bangs were almost as wild as Jason's, draping over his nose in wild sheaves that reached down to his chin. And he had a single silver earring in his right ear-lobe.

He wore a weird kind of shirt - one without sleeves - like a tank top, but with a large loose turtleneck. The shirt, though loose as it was, couldn't hide his obvious six-pack. He looked to be even stronger physically than Jason.

He also wore a pair of blue jeans, which just covered the top part of his black hiking boots.

"And of course, you all know Ally." Dixon gestured over at her.

Ally's face didn't register her shock at being startled from her reverie; it remained emotionless.

Matt once again looked over at her sharp profile. She was wearing a pair of long, loose, gray sweat pants, which draped over her blue sneakers, and Matt was amazed to notice that she wore the same weird shirt as him! In the same shade of blue as well!

Matt wasn't the only one, Eric had noticed the shirts also. "Hey! Look everybody! We've got twins!"

Everyone laughed, and for the briefest of moments, Matt noticed Ally's eyelids flutter. Then, abruptly, Matt recognized her face; she had been the girl on the boat!

Pushing this fact aside, he looked around once more at all the kids, and couldn't help but notice some uncanny similarities - for instance, every one of the teens had the same startling dark blue eyes; the same wavy brown hair. None of them had any blemishes, pimples, or freckles of any kind, and they all seemed to be about fifteen. It was almost as if the kids were all twins- which was of course preposterous...

After the brief relaxation that had been gained from Eric's comment, the teens, Jason mainly, went back to being very wary of Ally; shooting her different looks of suspicion. Ally, however, appeared not to notice - though Matt noticed her eyes darting here and there about the room, as if searching for means of escape...

"And now that we all know each other," Dixon continued - startling all of them - causing Kelsi to jump a few inches off the ground. "I believe it is time to explain to you all why you are here. Yes, I know you all believe this to be a boarding school where you will be receiving an extended education, and in a way, you are correct. However, this school is not meant to teach you mathematics and nonsense such as that, you ten have no need of such trivial cognition, you are here to learn how to control your powers; and to improve upon them. Do any of you not understand what I have just said?"

All the kids, excluding Matt, Ally, Kelsi, and Ivy, raised their hands uncertainly into the air.

"Ah. I knew, of course." But what Dixon knew, he did not elaborate upon; instead he turned to Ivy. "Will you kindly step forward?"

Ivy stepped forward without hesitation, her face as cool and emotionless as Ally's - though without the slight glower.

Dixon then walked over to the door, and pushed a small round black button by the frame; and a scant few moments later, two men walked into the room; both wearing black uniforms of the same make. One was carrying a full-length ornate mirror, the other, a potted plant. Which looked as if it hadn't had water for quite a while.

The two men deposited the items on the floor beside Dixon, then turned, and left the room.

Dixon turned back to Ivy, who was looking at the dead plant with a mixture of pity and longing on her face. "Do you know what plant this is Ivy?"

Ivy nodded, "Poison Ivy." She replied, so quietly that Matt had to strain his ears to hear.

He couldn't see how in the world she could tell what the plant was- it's leaves being as brown and crumpled as they were.

"Will you take off your gloves?" Dixon asked her calmly.

Ivy stiffened then, her hands clenching at her side, "I- I'd rather not, sir."

"Please."

Ivy looked at him, then looked over at the others, biting her lip.

"I assure you that no one in this room will think any the different of you."

Ivy looked back at him, then gave a curt nod, and removed her elbow-length leather gloves, placing them into her pockets.

Matt heard the unmistakable sound of many breaths being drawn in sharply, and could see why, the tip of every one of Ivy's fingers were a light, lush green, as if she had dipped them into a can of watery paint.

Eric couldn't contain himself; "Now I've heard of green thumbs - but this is ridiculous!" he cracked. Only a few people laughed.

Ivy, ignoring the gasps of shock behind her, turned once more to Dixon, who nodded. Then she walked over to the plant, and stroked one of its browning leaves.

Dixon turned back to the class, "Ivy's fingers each contain a poison that is deadly to humans... but to plants..." Dixon broke off as he turned back to Ivy.

Matt gazed in wonder as the once brown plant was now a lush, fertile green. It was at least twice as big as it had been before, and was getting bigger...

As he watched, the plant shivered as if it had been touched by a strong breeze, then stretched and reached out, growing longer and longer, spitting off many little shoots and sending them into all areas in the room.

Matt backed away from the on-coming plant hesitantly, keeping a firm eye on as many of the shoots as he could at once. Prepared to fight back if necessary...

"IVY!" came Dixon's strangled voice from a corner of the room, "Ivy! It- it's too big! IVY! REVERSE THE PROCESS!!!"

Looking over at Ivy through the tangle, Matt saw her start, then place both her hands on either side of the plant's main stem, and a soft green glow surrounded the plant; which began to shrink back to it's original size.

As Matt strode forward, he noticed out of the corner of his eye that the rest of the teens had likewise backed off - in fact, it seemed as if the only person who hadn't moved at all, was Ally. She'd stayed resolutely in her place while the vines seemed to avoid her.

Dixon stepped forward once again, wiping his brow on his sleeve, looking as if his birthday had come early, "Well! That was exciting, wasn't it!"

The feeling wasn't mutual.

He then turned to Ally, who still hadn't moved a muscle, "Now, Ally, are you willing to risk seven years bad luck?"

"Why not?" Ally replied in a quiet voice; one only heard by Dixon and Matt.

Then everyone jumped as suddenly the mirror directly behind her shattered, sending glass shards everywhere.

Matt - shielding his eyes with his hands - watched in amazement from between his fingers as the glass shards heading for Ally hit the air two feet from her, and fell to the tiled floor with tiny *clinks*.

Dixon now turned to Kelsi, as if this sort of thing were to happen everyday; "Why don't you give it a try?"

Kelsi looked around at the others, than up at Dixon, "I-I don't know how to do anything fancy, l-like them," she admitted, looking down at her feet.

"Just do what you can."

"Umm... Ok." Kelsi stared straight ahead, seemingly at the wall, until the air before her shattered.

Kelsi looked back over at Dixon.

"A bit slower, if you can." He smiled at her.

Kelsi nodded, then turned back to the wall. She closed her eyes, squinched them tight, concentrated, then opened them.

Matt watched in concealed amazement as the air solidified into a sphere before her, then watched in mounting curiosity as the sphere grew larger and larger, exploded into a million tiny pieces which flew out in all directions, then turned back into a gas, making it look as if nothing had happened.

Kelsi stumbled backwards, than fainted to the floor.

For a moment, everyone just stared at her inert form. Then they all looked over at Dixon, who was looking at Ally, his eyebrows raised.

Ally stared back at him, "Why?" she asked, "She'll wake up eventually."

Dixon inclined his head towards the body, his eyes now cold and almost angry.

Ally rolled her eyes, "Fine." She breathed, then walked swiftly over to Kelsi, and knelt beside her. Matt watched as she raised a hand, and a pale black light issued from her palm to surround the body.

"Wait! Stop! She's killing her!"

Ally, the light still issuing from her palm, looked over at Kim's frightened face, "What make's you say that?" she asked her calmly.

Kim stepped back a pace, apprehension apparent on her features, "It's...the light's black." She tried to explain, her mouth continued to open and close there after, but no words came out, and finally, she shut it with a snap.

Ally continued to gaze up at her through her lashes, "Just because it's black, doesn't mean it's evil." She spat calmly. Then, as the light faded, she withdrew her hand.

For a moment, nothing was said. Then Kelsi stirred and Matt walked swiftly forward to help her to her feet.

In a moment of elation, Matt caught Ally's eye. Then she turned away as Dixon walked forward, and Matt looked over at the wall.

Kelsi blinked, and opened her eyes, looking up at Matt as he supported her. Then she looked over at Dixon who smiled at her, "You expended yourself to far, you used up all of your energy. Ally here," he gestured a hand towards her, "was kind enough to lend you some."

Matt helped Kelsi to steady herself, then went over to stand a few feet from Ally.

Seeing the still confused faces of half of his pupils, Dixon sighed, "Each human has a different amount of energy within them," he explained, "When ever you walk, speak or move, you use up a part of your energy reserve.

"When you faint, that is simply a sudden loss of energy, normally caused by shock. And the only way to gain more energy is to rest, hence; sleep. Understand?"

As confusing as this was, they all nodded.

"Good." Dixon continued, "Now you ten," he indicated all of them with one great sweep of his arm, "are not *normal* kids. You have powers and abilities that require a somewhat... *greater* level of energy. Some of you have even more energy then others because you are at a higher level, but that's another topic all together. Mathue, I believe it is your turn."

Matt's head shot up, he had hardly been listening to a word that was said.

Dixon looked around the room, "And I guess the only thing left for you to do is to... clean up." He smiled.

Matt rolled his eyes, then extended his hand towards the pile of dirt in the center of the room, which went flying into the garbage can by the door, along with the pieces of the broken pot. Then he gestured at the glass shards littering the room, and they too soared into the garbage receptacle.

Then he placed his hands into his pockets, and averted his eyes.

Dixon clapped his hands together, "Well, with what you have seen, what have you to say?" he smiled around at all of them, clearly thinking he'd supplied them all with a substantial treat.

Jason stepped forwards, pointed towards Matt, Ally, Ivy and Kelsi, and stated simply, "They're weird."

The others nodded in agreement.

Dixon looked as if he'd been slapped in the face, "So...so then... you...you don't know what...they are? What *YOU* are?" he asked, scandalized.

Jason looked at the teens on either side of himself, then back at Dixon, "Nope." He shook his head.

"This is some kind of joke, right," Kimberly stepped forward, "I mean, it was fun an' all in the beginning, but now... I think most of us just want to go home."

The others nodded again.

Dixon gaped at them like a landed fish.

Matt stepped forwards, "So then you guys think that we're all," he gestured at Ally, Ivy Kelsi and himself, "just a load of crap?"

"Pretty much." Jason nodded.

Matt threw up his hands, "Fine."

Suddenly, Ally's eyes flared. She raised a hand in Jason's direction, and the arrogant teen was thrown into the air.

Jason griped at his throat where he could feel something squeezing his air pipe, cutting off his oxygen.

"Where's the joke now?" Ally asked him in a whisper, watching as his feet flailed and kicked two feet from the floor.

Jason couldn't answer, whatever it was that was squeezing his throat, was getting tighter, and tighter. He gasped for breath and his eyes grew wide in fear as he realized this *was* no joke.

Dixon ran up in front of Ally, "Drop him! Drop him now!" he commanded.

Ally looked at him, and Dixon backed up, though her gaze was emotionless as always, and as everyone watched, he began to turn a sickly green before their eyes.

Matt ran to interfere, "Ally, just stop okay? I know that he deserves it," Matt pointed over his shoulders at Jason who's face was rapidly turning purple, "But what will you gain by killing him, or turning Dixon into a green blob or whatever it is your turning him into?"

Ally looked at him for a moment, then dropped her hand to her side, and averted her gaze.

Dixon turned back to his regular color, and Jason fell to the floor with a thump.

Ally said nothing, simply glanced at him nonchalantly.

As Jason gasped for breath, he pushed himself to a sitting position, "Okay." He coughed, "I believe you."

~

Ally was still glaring at Jason by lunch, and just for safe measure, Dixon set them at opposite ends of the table.

They were just finishing up the tuna-fish sandwiches and orange juice, when a tight-lipped woman and a very tall man entered into the cafeteria.

"Ahh," Dixon got to his feet, and wrapped an arm around the woman's waist, "Everyone, I'd like you to meet my wife, Miranda Dixon, and Brandon Kenith," he gesture towards the tall man, then pointed to himself, "And of course, as you know, I am Dennis Dixon."

Eric snickered.

Ally observed the new teachers, Mrs. Dixon, unlike her husband who had dark messy hair, wore her reddish-brown hair up at the top of her head in a neat, tight bun, which made her look like the stern library-type. She wore a tight leather zip-up dress, small black high heels on her pointed toes, and she had the palest skin of anyone Ally had ever met. In fact, the only color on the woman, besides her hair, was the pointed purple glasses situated over her sharp nose.

Matt looked over at Brandon; he looked like a stern business-man kind of guy, wearing black pants and shoes that looked to be at least twenty years old and faded, with a white shirt and tie. His face betrayed him to be at least forty, his brown hair slicked back against his skull. In his arms he was holding two large ice-cream buckets...

But that's as far as the assessment went as Matt tuned back into the conversation as Dixon continued, "They, along with me and two other women, will be your teachers for this year. You will be taught depending upon your level, which we will be addressing tomorrow, for now I am sure you are all anxious to get to your rooms and deposit your things-"

At this, Brandon strode forward, and placed the two buckets he had been carrying onto the table, then he stepped away as Miranda moved forward.

"We have a simple way of deciding your roommates," she told them as one; in such a sweet high-pitched voice, they were sure she had stolen it from somebody else. "We have all the girls in one bucket, and all the boy's in another, and we just draw your names from them. Unfortunately, as you may or may not have noticed, we only have five spare bedrooms, which means, of course, that two of you, of the opposite gender, will, be sharing a room. We do hope that you understand." She smiled weakly.

With that said, Dennis reached his hand into one of the buckets, "Eric," He said pulling out a torn peice of paper "will be pared with..." he reached into the bucket again, and withdrew another slip, "...Jason."

Miranda reached into the other bucket, withdrawing two other torn peices of paper, "Kimberly... with Kelsi."

"Alexander with Cody."

Alex looked apprehensively over at the small chatterbox, Matt knew how he felt; he probably wouldn't get any sleep with *that* kid around.

"Alexandra with Ivy" Miranda read as she drew two more slips of paper from her bucket.

Kelsi looked over at Kimberly apprehensively, but Kim didn't notice, she was to busy glaring at Jason on the other side of the table, who was frequently making rude hand signs and faces at her.

Matt and Ally exchanged glances.

Dennis and Miranda both withdrew the last two slips of paper from the buckets, Dennis looked up at the two leftovers, "Ally... Matt. I'm afraid you'll have to share a room."

Eric nudged Matt hard in the ribs, "Aren't *you* lucky!"

Matt couldn't decide if he was lucky or not. Ally didn't seem to hate him for having to share a room with him; but on the other hand, she wasn't even looking at him.

"Now then, you have your roommates, it's time to pick your rooms," Miranda continued explaining to them, "Eric, Jason, since you two were the first one's out of the buckets," she chuckled to herself, "Why don't you choose first."

Seeing their baffled looks, Dennis elaborated, "Just pick a number from one to five."

"Uhhhm... how about two?" Jason asked.

"Naw, three." Said Eric.

"Three it is." And as Miranda scribbled onto a clipboard that she had pulled from seemingly nowhere, Dennis gave them each a small silver key with the number 3 engraved upon it.

"Kelsi, Kimberly?" Dixon continued.

"Ummm..." Kelsi looked over at Kim, who said promptly, "two."

Matt saw Jason glare at her as Dennis gave them their keys with tiny silver 2's on them.

"Alexandra, Ivy?"

"Four." The two girls said together, and took their keys from Dennis.

"Alexan-"

"One!" piped up Cody before Dixon could finish his sentence.

"Is that alright with Alexander?" Dennis asked, holding out the keys. Alex nodded, and Miranda scribbled once more onto her paper. "Ok, and that leaves room five for Ally and Matt." She smiled at them. "We have extras of all your key's, just in case, and I am hoping we will not need to use them." She glanced over the alignment of kids that stood before her.

"You'll find your bags in the hall," Dennis continued, handing Matt and Ally their key's "Take them to your rooms and get settled, we'll call you in about two or three hours for supper. If you get bored before then, or just fancy a stretch of your legs, feel free to explore the school." And with that, Dennis, and Miranda left the cafeteria with Brandon in tow, and went off into the kitchens.

For a moment, nobody moved. Then with a yelp of delight, Cody rushed out into the hall, and came tearing back a moment later with his duffle bag slung over one shoulder.

When he saw everyone just standing there, he looked surprised, "What're you all waiting for? C'mon! Won't this be fun?!? I can't wait to see my room; do you guys think it will have all those new inventions in it? I wonder-"

Instead of asking what he meant by, 'all those new inventions,' which would probably have gained them a good half-hour response or longer; the teens all said in unison, "Shut up, Cody." and went to get their bags.

~

Ally, as the first into the room, quickly found and switched on the light, a large decorative ball in the ceiling, which could be dimmed if the occupants found the necessity. The rest of the room was painted a light baby blue, with identical dark-blue quilted beds on either side. Beside each bed was a desk that looked as if it had been combined with a dresser, with multiple drawers to put their clothes and belongings in.

Matt threw his backpack onto the bed closest to the door - as Ally had already chosen the one furthest from - and went to investigate the door on the right-hand side of the room, beside which stood an ornately carved full-length mirror, that looked to be real silver. Inside was a bathroom, roughly the size of a car, maybe larger, with all the usual things like a toilet and a sink, but what really astounded him was the bathtub. No, the Jacuzzi, except without the jets.

Walking over to it Matt could tell that if it were full, and he stood on the very bottom, the water would come all the way up to his elbows.

As Matt strode back into the main bedroom, he saw Ally shoving all of her things into one of the drawers of the desk closest to her bed. Then she jumped onto the bed with a magazine, picked up the Walkman that was lying there, put the headphones over her ears, and acted as though she were completely unaware of the oddity of her situation.

Mentally pushing this aside, he went over to his own bed, and emptied his bag. He had even less personal doo-dads than Ally. Folding up his clothes and placing them into one of the drawers, he turned back to the rest of his belongings - not much. A Walkman, black and silver like Ally's, a yo-yo, a few sports magazines, some utensils, and a photograph of his foster father.

Wondering how the hell *that* had gotten there, Matt crumpled it up in a fist, then, finding the garbage can, chucked it over.

Score!

"Nice."

For a moment, Matt thought he had imagined the voice, then looking over at Ally, found her gazing at him with her piercing blue eyes, making him feel naked. His heart skipped a beat.

"You didn't by chance-"

"No." Matt said at once. He didn't know why he was so touchy about the subject. He used to think it was cool, to be able to make things fly. He could also create illusions, and small amounts of energy, but he couldn't shape-shift, or make a mirror shatter without even looking at it. He wasn't jealous. No, he couldn't call his emotion that. It was just that, he felt... venerable, around her. Weak.

Ally stared at him for a moment longer, then said, "Do it again."

Matt blinked at her.

"Here." Ally ripped a page out of her magazine, crumpled it up, and tossed it over to him. Well *'tossed'* wasn't exactly the right word, *soared*, was more like it.

He caught it deftly, gazed at her for a moment, then tossed it into the wastebasket.

Ally smiled, "you're good. You hardly even glanced at the can that time."

Matt felt his face go red, "I used to play basketball."

"On a team?"

Matt couldn't be sure at this point if it were possible for his face to get any redder, "No, just after school, with some friends, you know."

"Oh. I never played sports much. I guess you could call me a loner."

"What? For not liking sports?"

"No. Never mind." She turned back to her magazine.

It was clear to Matt that the convo was over, so he turned, and was about to jump onto his own bed when he heard shouting from out in the hall.

Switching direction in mid-step, he turned, opened the door, and looked out.

Kimberly and Jason were arguing, both were red in the face - from shouting, evidently - and both were spluttering as if trying to say every horrible thing they could think of all at once.

Some of the things coming out of the their mouths were words Matt had never even heard of, and some he would never have cared to use. (And he was a pretty free curser when his mood hit a high at that.)

When the verbal argument turned physical, Matt closed the door, and went back over to his new bed. He normally would have tried to stop the fight, but right now, he felt it would be better if he just let it be.

The muffled sounds from out in the hall grew loud, then quiet, then loud again. Then after about a half hour, there came the unmistakable sound of two doors slamming. Hard.

Matt turned back to the article had had been reading about new mountain bikes. He didn't really care what the hell any of these magazines had to say, he had only brought them because he had had tons of room left in his bag when he'd packed. They had been given to him by his friend, Kevin; who told him that he needed to have *some* interests in his life. If truth be told, Matt didn't really have any interests - unless you counted basketball. But he only played that on the streets once and a while with some of his friends. It wasn't really a hobby, and it defiantly wasn't an obsession. He didn't even like girls - well, he liked them, of course, but he didn't moon over them like most guys. He was fifteen now, and he hadn't yet had a serious girlfriend. He just couldn't find anyone he liked, no one who shared his interests... what interests?

What he really wanted was a girl who just wanted to be with him, who loved him for who he was. Not for what the guy next door is, but for who *he* is. Was that too much to ask? In this century, maybe. In 2013 all girls wanted was a guy who bought them presents every off day, and made out with them on occasion. That's not what Matt wanted, that could *never* be what Matt wanted. He wanted a girl he could trust, whom he could share his innermost secrets with, whom he could show his 'powers' to.

Whom he could just hang out with.

In short, he wanted a girl like him.

~

Two uneventful hours later, Dennis came around, and called them all to supper. Matt couldn't have been happier. Lunch seemed ages ago, at the time he hadn't been able to eat anything, his mind had been too full of unanswered questions; but now, he didn't really give a damn what happened to him. All he cared about was shoveling down the lasagna as fast as chewing would permit; it was amazing he didn't choke himself.

There were two new people sitting at the table besides Miranda and Brandon; a straight-backed sharp-featured woman of whom Dennis had introduced as Joanne Thomas. And a kind looking, frizzy-haired woman named Ileena Johnson.

When the plates were finally cleared by one of the cooks, (a stout woman with hardly any hair) Dennis got to his feet, shortly followed by the other adults at the table. He motioned to the kids to remain seated.

"Before we head off to bed, we need to explain one other thing: your classes." He gave them his usual twinkle-eyed lopsided smile and continued, "You will be taught depending upon your level. Different sages have lesser or greater talents depending on that little fact. Most sages have telekinesis-"

"Telekawhat!?" Eric raised his eyebrows.

"Tell-ah-kin-ee-sis," Dennis smiled, "The ability to move things with your mind. Most sages can also create illusions and such, but will, of course, be limited by the amount of energy their body can hold. Hence, the levels. Now Eric, Jason, Kim and Alexandra. All of you are at level five, you will be taught by my wife her." he nodded to Miranda, who gave a stiff jerk of her head in acknowledgement. "Alexander and Cody, you are both a level three, you'll be taught by yours truly." He pointed at himself.

Cody punched his fist in the air, "YES! You an' me Alex! All the way!"

Alexander seemed less than overjoyed, "Yippee." He replied in a dead voice.

Dennis continued his tirade, "Kelsi, you're a level four. You'll be taught by Miss Thomas here. Ivy, you're a level six, you'll be taught by Miss Johnson."

"You'll all come in here for breakfast as you'll do for every morning, and you'll leave with your designated teacher when it is time for class. Understood?"

Everyone nodded, and Matt raised his voice, "So where does that leave us?" he called out loudly.

"Oh yes! Sorry Mathue-"

"Matt."

"You and Ally are both a level ten, you'll be studying with-"

"Wow!" there was an eruption of noise within the cafeteria, everyone looked around at Matt and Ally.

"Ten! What's the highest level?" Matt heard Cody ask Miranda in an excited voice." He couldn't hear her reply, but judging by the new wave of noise that issued forth after the relayed answer from Cody - he could only assume that ten *was* the highest level.

Matt pushed his way over to Dennis, "But, sir. There's been a mistake, I *can't* be a level ten."

Dennis smiled down at him. That same irritating twinkle-eyed smile. "And why not, Mathue?"

"Matt. Because, because I can't do half the things that she can!" he explained, exasperated, gesturing over at Ally.

"Oh but you can. Just because you have never done something, does not mean you never will." He smiled again, and his eyes twinkled. Matt was getting fed up with that twinkle, he wished he could just reach up and throttle Dennis until the twinkle was gone.

Dennis raised his hands for silence, "As I was saying; Ally, Matt, you'll be studying with Mr. Kenith here. Have a nice rest, I bid you all a good evening." And without another word, he and part of the staff turned and walked out into the hall, leaving Ileena and Miranda to the staff room on the other side of the cafeteria.

Matt watched as everyone slowly dwindled out of the hall, and stood there until Cody's pratter could be heard no longer. Then he walked slowly over to the door that led into the bedroom hallway, as he now called it, and pulled it open.

He stopped, then, and turned back. He stared at one of the four bowls of fruit on the long table, and summoned over a pear.

Biting into it, and feeling the sweet liquid wash down his throat, he smiled, and let the door close behind him as he walked towards his bedroom. *'Ten...'*

~ 4 ~

Ally woke up the next morning to a new world. She knew where she was; it was not like in the movies when people wake from nightmares to find it's reality. No, she was happy to be here. These covers were softer, warmer, and felt like more of a home to her than her foster mother's house had ever been. Would she stay? That would be a question only time could answer.

She looked over at Matt, sleeping on his back on the other side of the room, in an identical bed to hers. As he had slept, his cover had slipped down to his waist, showing that he wore only his black boxers and a white undershirt to bed. He had taken his horsetail out the night before, (she had watched him come in after supper eating a pear with a slight smile tugging at his lips) and now his hair was spread all over his pillow; his bangs draped over his face as always, waving softly as his breath passed over them.

She herself slept on her side, she found it more comfortable. No matter how hard she tried, she couldn't sleep on her back. It just didn't suit her.

Ally raised her right hand and looked at her watch, 6:32AM, it wasn't *that* early, breakfast was only in an hour or so. So she got up, grabbed her shirt and pants from the floor beside her bed, and stepped into the bathroom.

Taking off her pajamas, (she couldn't stand nightdresses, they made her feel too girlish.) she ran some water for herself into the Jacuzzi-like bathtub, then stepped into the warm water, and sank onto the seat. Breathing deeply. Content.

The soothing water felt nice, she felt as if she were washing away her old life, creating a clean slate to start anew.

When she was finished she got out, dried off, and got dressed. Then she wrapped her hair in a towel like a turban, and stepped out of the steamy bathroom.

Matt was awake. Sitting on the edge of his bed, stretching.

When he saw her looking at him, his face grew red again and he mumbled an almost incomprehensible, "Morning." Before turning and rummaging around in one of his drawers.

Ally didn't know why, but whenever she looked at his handsome face and strong build, she felt a keen twinge in her heart that hurt.

Shaking her head at such nonsense, she went over to her dresser, grabbed her hairbrush, and jumped back onto her un-made bed. Then she rubbed the towel all over her head to get it as dry as possible, and ran her brush through it to get out the tangles.

~

Matt watched Ally out of the corner of his eye as he rummaged around in an empty drawer for who knew what. He watched her brush out her hair until it shone, then watched her graceful form as she walked out the door and into the hall.

Matt looked at his watch, it was now 7:16AM; he had roughly fifteen minutes before breakfast. Loads of time to get ready.

He took a quick shower, dried off, and got dressed within twenty minutes. Then he ran a brush through his hair quickly, and tied it back in his usual horsetail. People often asked him why he didn't just chop it off, Matt really didn't know himself, he really didn't mind his image, he thought he looked kind of hot, himself. And if people didn't like his image, they could turn their heads. Who really gave a damn.

With that done, Matt clipped his silver earring into the hole in his right ear, and left the room; not bothering - like Ally - to make his bed.

~

When Matt entered the Cafeteria, Ivy, Kim, Cody, Jason and of course - Ally, were already there, and digging into scrambled eggs and bacon. With glasses of orange juice or milk to wash it all down.

He sat down as far as he could from Cody, who was chatting non stop about how good the eggs were, and piled some of the breakfast onto his plate, just as Alex, Alex, Eric and Kelsi entered the room, yawning, and rubbing the sleep out of their eyes, before sitting down at the table, and digging in like the rest.

"Morning." Yelled Cody across the room.

Soon they were all listening to Eric as he acted like a morning radio talk-show-host "And at the world domino championships," He announced in his fake, deep, news-mans voice, "one champion accused his opponent of cheating, and punched the guy, who knocked into the guy behind him, who knocked into the guy behind him, who knocked into the guy behind him, who knocked into the guy behind him-"

Everyone howled with laughter, and as Matt wiped fresh tears from his eyes, he caught a glimpse of Ally, who was clutching at her chest, doubled over with laughter.

"And now... for the weather!" Eric continued, "We will be expecting some heavy showers due to the mud this season, and we should all bring out our sunglasses because Renee Fernesca has taken to sleepwalking in the nude!"

This time Cody fell off his chair he was laughing so hard.

"Why is everyone so giddy?" came a high pitched, girly voice from the doorway that led to their rooms. Matt had forgotten that it was where the staff slept as well.

Miranda walked swiftly into the room, and folded her arms across her chest. But she wasn't frowning - she was smiling. Evidently she'd heard Eric's last joke.

"Ahh... Mrs. Dixon!" Eric bowed to her from his perch upon his chair, "Would you like some eggs? I'm sorry to say they were beaten."

Matt could see that Miranda was trying her hardest not to laugh. There was a slight twitch at the corner of her mouth that betrayed her. And so giving up entirely on her image of the stern, reprimanding teacher, she sat down and began to eat as Eric went on with his show.

By eight, everyone had eaten, and were just getting to their feet. Dennis smiled at them, "Well then, everyone to their teachers."

Matt stood, and followed Ally over to Brandon.

"We're gunna wait until everyone else has left," he told them, "For today we're going to see what you can do - so it just seems more reasonable to stay put."

Ally watched as the rest of the staff and students slowly filed out of the room, then turned back to Brandon, who was scrutinizing them both with his pale brown eyes. "Alright," he said finally, "Can you two first move this table out of the way?"

Ally looked over at Matt, who had raised his eyebrows at her. Then turned with him to face the table, which went soaring across the room.

"Now I'm sure either of you could have done that yourselves, am I right?"

They both nodded.

Brandon nodded back, then tuned towards the staff room, "Bring it in!" he hollered.

Matt looked startled over at the staff room door, where twenty cooks and mid-servants came out, each bearing a part of a giant metal wall, which was about six by seven feet in diameter, and about two feet thick.

They watched as they brought it over, and placed it in front of them, just like a wall. And Matt and Ally's eyebrows arched as they walked back into the kitchen; like zombies.

"Right." Brandon turned back to them, "Ally, I've seen you do this a hundred times over. Matt - would you kindly melt this for me."

Ally looked over at Matt, who looked shocked at being asked to melt a sixty-ton block of pure steel.

"M-melt? Sir, I – I don't think…I've never…I can't-" Matt stuttered, his face was going red again, and he looked as if would really like to disappear on the spot.

"Sure you can." Brandon smiled - it was the first smile Ally had seen him wear since she'd met him. "You just have to concentrate."

Matt swallowed, and looked over at the metal barrier.

Ally watched as he took a deep breath and closed his eyes, then he stared straight at the wall without blinking.

Ally then glanced over at the metal wall. She had melted things before, and blasted walls out of her path - but nothing this big before. She watched as the top of the barrier started to melt, watched as the hot liquid metal ran down onto the floor.

Within a short period, half of the metal had melted into a giant puddle, and Matt was getting tired. Finally, Brandon told him to stop.

Gratefully, Matt sank to the floor. His breathing heavy.

"Ally," Ally jumped at her name, "Do you think you could finish?"

"Maybe…" Ally wasn't too certain, she stared at the cold metal, and concentrated on raising the temperature around it. Immediately it began to melt, and within moments, there was nothing left but a big puddle on the floor.

"Excellent, Matt," Brandon turned to him, "You've got what it takes, you just need to concentrate more on the task, instead of on yourself, then you'll put more of your energy into what's needed, instead of wasting it. Understand?"

"No."

"You will in time. Now both of you take a moment to rest, I'll be back in a moment." And with that Brandon left the cafeteria, and walked out into the hall.

Ally sank down to the floor beside Matt, she looked wasted. When Matt had watched her melt the rest of the metal block, she had appeared cool and collected. Now, however, she looked as if a soft bed was all she desired.

"I didn't think I could do it." She whispered.

"What?" Matt's gaze shot towards her. Both of them were breathing hard, but he had been positive that he had been the worst off.

"I've never melted anything *that* big before," she confided, "Only small things, and the occasional *wooden* wall." She looked over at him, and smiled. Matt felt his heart melt; the gaze was too much. He quickly looked away.

Luckily, Ally didn't take it personally. She just went back to catching her breath.

A few minutes later, Brandon walked back in with an armload of cushions, and placed them in a pile by the door.

"Ignore those for now," he said as he came over to them, "For now, I'm going to test you on how strong your shields are."

Matt looked up, "Our shields?"

Ally looked over at him, "You know, something that protect-"

"I know *what* a shield is!" Matt said defensively.

"You know how to generate yours then?" Brandon asked him bracingly, as if he were afraid of the answer.

"Yeah... sure."

"Alright then." Brandon rubbed his hands together, "Have you two caught your breaths?"

They nodded.

"Good. Than take your positions on either side of the room."

With Brandon off to one side, Matt faced Ally from across the room. Their faces stoic.

"Alright then," Brandon cleared his throat, "Raise your shields."

Matt had only used his shield once, by accident, when his stepfather had had one too many drinks, and had come at him with a shotgun. But none of the bullets had hit him. Only later did he conclude that he could generate an invisible barrier to protect himself.

Matt concentrated hard; convinced he couldn't do it. Then he saw it, like a shimmering clear blue wave of water, washing up and over him to form a sphere.

For a moment it shimmered around him, then grew transparent, then invisible. He looked over at Ally; she didn't even look as if she'd done anything.

"Now," Brandon continued, "When I say *go*, I want you two to throw miniature, *emphasis on miniature!* -Orbs of energy at one another, got it?"

They both nodded.

Brandon raised his arm then, "Ok! One... two... GO!" his arm came slashing down through the air, and before Matt knew what had hit him, he was thrown back into the wall with such force, that the air was instantly knocked out of his lungs.

~

Ally watched Matt as Brandon counted, then as soon as she heard the word '*go*', she raised her right hand, and flung a solid sphere of energy straight towards him. It hit his shield, and shattered it effortlessly, but the shield prevented Matt himself from getting hit, and was instead flung backwards by the force of the blast.

She watched as he coughed, and got back to his feet, leaning against the wall for support.

Brandon walked over to him, "You all right?"

Matt nodded, his back ached pretty bad, but he was alright. He wasn't shaking, he wasn't suffering any trauma, and nothing was broken.

"I take it you've never created a shield before?"

"I have," Matt croaked, "But only once."

"Really?!" Brandon raised his eyebrows.

"By mistake." Matt admitted. He decided that, if he was going to be telling him the truth, he better make it good. But to his surprise, instead of thinking Matt weak, Brandon looked impressed.

"And this was only your second time!?"

"Yes..."

"Extraordinary! Just extraordinary! Ally!" Instantly Ally was there, she had probably walked over when Matt had been catching his breath. He scowled.

"This puts us back a bit, but not by much - he'll get the knack of it fast enough. What I want *you* to do, is simply fire smaller sphere's, got that?"

"I can't get much smaller that I did before-"

Matt's scowl deepened. To think he'd had a crush on her!

"-But I can try."

"Excellent. And just keep making them stronger, until Matt can throw them off just as well as you."

Ally nodded, and went back to her original spot across the room.

Matt followed her with his narrowed eyes the entire way, hating her for everything! Her slim, graceful body. Her emotionless façade. Her tempting lips. Her crooked smile. Heck! Even her slender fingers! Matt hated her through and through.

But then, when she reached the opposite wall, and turned to face him, he met her gaze, her deep blue eyes boring into his, like she was reading his thoughts, like she knew what was in his mind.

He immediately replaced his mental barriers, angry at himself for letting them grow so weak in her presence; angry at her for making him believe he had found her, had found the girl of his dreams. He couldn't forgive her for that. He would *never* forgive her for that.

He raised his shield so fast and so fiercely he startled himself. Then he faced Ally across the room; looking anywhere but at her eyes.

~

Ally raised her hand for the second time that morning. She caught Matt's eye just before she fired, and what she saw she didn't like.

His eyes were cold now; she saw none of the warmth she'd seen there before. He looked as lost and as shielded as he had on the boat, as though living was just something he did, and he only continued to see what would happen next.

Ally shook her head. Matt wasn't suicidal; she knew that much. But he *was* depressed, she could see it in his eyes.

Without another thought, Ally aimed, and fired. The small marble of energy flew straight towards Matt, rebounded upon his shield, and came streaking back at her. Leaving her with only enough time to drop to the floor. She looked up, startled - her arms still draped over her head - at Matt - who looked just as stunned as she was.

~

After only a surprisingly short time, Matt had mastered his shield - he could deflect all but Ally's strongest blast of energy. Which she herself couldn't even fend off from him when he took his turn firing at her.

Matt wasn't bad at creating energy orbs, he actually found it quite simple; and after a while, it became clear to the both of them that he was slightly if not *much* stronger in that field, than her.

Lunch had consisted of some tomato soup and crackers with water or milk, along with a show put on by Cody and Alexander, which had started when Cody had accidentally flung a spoon of soup into his face. (How this could be *accidentally* done, Matt never knew.) and had ended with Alexander blasting him with a small speck of energy, which cut a slice into Cody's arm, and had completely knocked out Alexander.

Miranda said that it was amazing he had even managed to make any form of energy at all, seeing as how he was only a level three, and even level seven's sometimes had troubles with transferring their energy from a gas inside them into the form of a plasma of which they could control.

And even with Ally's help, Alexander was still unconscious for quite a while after.

Matt had found out then, after asking Miranda, that a level one sage was really just a regular human, without any powers at all, and a level two sage is simply a homo-sapient with a *sixth* sense- meaning that they couldn't do anything abnormal physically, but mentally they just *knew* things...

Therefore, a level three sage has just the basic abilities; like the ability to teleport oneself over short distances, or go faster then normal, i.e.: Cody. Or maybe to create illusions - but not even those lasted long.

All sages had the ability to create shields about themselves, even normal level one's, but their shields only deflected *verbal* blows, nothing physical; and normally they never even knew they were doing such a thing. On a very rare occasion, normal humans *would* find out that they were exceptionally good at ignoring people, but nothing closer than that.

After lunch, Matt was still holding a grudge against Ally - even though he couldn't remember why. All he knew was that he hated her, and would do all he could to beat her in *any* contest. That included their social life.

And that's how Matt found himself mentally stepping further and further from her as they stood side by side three hours later, listening to Brandon's next set of instructions.

"-and you've come a surprisingly long way in only a morning, so now I'm going to test your reflexes, power level, and your shields all at the same time. I want you to each stand in front of a pile of cushions," he gestured over at the two piles he had set on either side of the room. (The table had once again been removed to the opposite end of the cafeteria) Then looked back at them seriously, "And I want you to fire at each other. The first one to be hit, loses. So basically it's like a game - try your hardest, but be fair. And *do not* get overly zealous. Like I said, it is just-a-game." he said each word separately and slowly, as if making sure they remembered them - like teaching a six-year-old to spell.

Matt suddenly found himself thinking about what he'd be doing now if Dennis and Brandon had never come to pick him up. As it was September - he'd be at his first day of *normal* school; pretending to write and take notes on what the teachers said whilst doodling and daydreaming...

They nodded again, as they did to all of Brandon's instructions, then went off to stand in front of different sets of cushions; facing off across the room.

"Do not raise your shield or do *anything* until I say 'go!' ready..."

Matt braced himself; he knew Ally could be quick, but he also knew he could be quicker.

"And..."

The key word there was 'could.' It was all down to chance
"GO!"

Ally raised her shield immediately, and raised both her hands; charging her energy, then threw it at Matt - well 'threw' doesn't exactly describe how you hurl energy at someone, 'push' is closer - and missed.

Then she charged another one, which collided with his shield and exploded.

At the same time, Matt began to hurl sphere after sphere at her, all of them hitting her shield in unison - one after the other - until she noticed that he was firing them all in the same place; his aim was ten time's better than her own and she knew it. She swiftly fixed the break in her shield, and deflected the last two of his shots back at him, which he handily dogged, and fired again at him.

Matt could tell it was all a matter of who got weak first - which wasn't going to happen anytime soon; all the same, Matt wanted to end this fast. He was desperate to prove he was better than her, that she was only human.

Ally was no quitter herself. She couldn't believe this match was almost even; *'almost,'* she was better than him, she was better then everyone, she always had been.

And with those thoughts of superiority, both opponents knew what to do.

At almost the exact same time, both of them dropped their shields - they would need all the energy they could scrape from their very being - and raised both their hands before them, charging up their next attack.

Matt kept his eyes on Ally the entire time, though his mind was completely focused on the task at hand. He not only wanted to beat her now in body, he wanted to hurt her in ego as well. And his sphere grew larger still.

Ally's ball of energy was now the size of a computer. If that were to collide with human flesh, it would be instant death! But with a sage at level ten, even an immature one, there would still be some life left; it had to be bigger!

With all their hate blinding them from the obvious truth, Matt and Ally poured everything they had into their weapons. Then without pausing, shoved them out before them with all their strength; hoping... Hoping.

And the outcome surprised them both.

Matt watched in fascination - then growing fear as both spheres collided in mid air - but the battle wasn't over. The sphere's didn't explode - nor did one overcome the other and continue on its present path as would normally have happened.

They were even.
Completely.
Utterly.

They had two choices, they could let the spheres grow weak without a power-source, and simply let them fade away. Or they could continue the battle.

There *was* no choice.

Each opponent grabbed a hold of their own sphere, and fed it more energy, urging it to grow stronger, to overcome the other.

Already Matt was feeling weak, he had put too much energy into his original attack, and now he was feeding it more... But he wouldn't give in. He wouldn't give up.

On the other side of the room, Ally was feeling the same. She was weakening, growing faint, but she still had energy left, and she would not give in so easily! If he could do it, she could do it ten times better.

After a while, about maybe twenty minutes as far as Matt could tell, they were still struggling with the stalemate, neither willing to give in.

Matt abruptly heard voices near the door to the hallway, and realized startlingly that everyone had come in for supper.

What a shock *they* must have received!

His eyebrows drew together in concentration, and focused on the wave of energy he was supplying to the sphere; both of which were now roughly the size of a human male - about the size of Brandon. It was getting harder and harder to control the power.

Then Matt felt it; his sphere grew transparent, and flew straight through Ally's. Though without anything to hold it back, Ally's sphere came pelting towards him, and he had time enough only to shield his face with his arms, and raise his barrier.

The ball of ebony energy struck him hard, and he flew back and up into the wall. Slammed into it so hard he was sure to have broken something. Then, his arms still clasped around his face, he fell to the floor with a deafening *thump*.

Then... black.

~

When everyone came into the cafeteria for supper, an unbelievable sight met their irises: Matt and Ally were battling. Fighting to overcome the other.

They watched both faces as they screwed up in concentration, watched the final wave of energy transfer into the spheres - then both balls of energy turned almost transparent-translucent - and flew off through each other towards the opposite person.

Both Ally and Matt threw up their arms and shield's just before the sphere's made contact, and the teens all around the doorway watched in fear as they hit. The shields shattered, and both competitors were thrown up against the wall. Missing the piles of cushions altogether.

Matt hit the floor *hard* and they could all tell he'd instantly blacked out. Ally hit the floor at the same time, rolled over, and coughed up a reddish, viscid liquid oddly resembling blood...

She looked over at Matt; saw him lying on the floor across the room... still.

In her mind she begged *No! Please no*! Before blacking out as well.

~

Brandon hurried over to his charges, Dennis close on his heels. They examined the bodies, and explained to the frantic Cody that they'd be all right; their shields had stopped most of the blow- so as not to be fatal.

"But what possessed them to do such a thing!" Kelsi sobbed.

"It was my doing... I should have seen it sooner."

Dennis turned to Brandon, his eyebrows raised.

"I wanted to test their battling skills, so I had them try to hit one another, but they realized, all too soon, that to hit one another, they'd need something powerful enough to get through each others shields, and still be powerful enough to reach the being behind it. In short: loads and loads of pure hatred transformed into energy.

"After a while it became clear that they not only wanted to hit each other, they wanted to kill each other, too."

Kelsi gasped, and her hand shot to her mouth.

Brandon continued, "But they knew - as did I - that to kill the other, they would have to kill themselves. Both were an even match - though Ally appeared stronger at first."

For a while there was silence as everyone thought this over. Then Dennis cleared his throat, "Seeing as how we have no one 'awake' who can lend some energy to them - they will undeniably be unconscious for about a week, maybe two. We'll just have to see."

Miranda strode forward as the men bent to pick up the bodies, and watched as they carried Matt and Ally off to their room. She turned back towards the other kids, "I know it will be difficult - but when they awaken, I want you to act as if nothing happened, alright? Like you didn't see a thing."

They all nodded, and Miranda looked back over at the door that led into the bedroom hallway, "Who knows how deep they hate each other..." she whispered, more to herself then any of her audience.

~

Ally awoke in the dark recesses of night, or at least, she assumed it was night - as the room was pitch black.

She sat up quickly, and looked around. It was definitely her room, she could see her Discman lying on the desk beside her bed. She looked over at the door, and saw the hall light streaming under the door. She looked closer - yes... it was certainly artificial. So it was definitely night, but there were no windows in her room, so she couldn't tell how late or how early.

The light coming from the hall illuminated a figure by the door.

Matt was standing with his back against the wall, but his head was turned, and it looked like he was staring into the silver mirror on the wall by the bathroom.

Matt looked over as he glanced her movement from the corner of his eye; she beckoned him. He gazed at her for a moment, the pushed himself from the wall, and walked over to her. Dropping down onto her bed where she patted it.

"How long have you been awake?" she asked him in a whisper.

"Only an hour... not long." He answered silently. He was again avoiding her eyes.

"Do you know how long we were out?"

"According to my watch - about five days."

"Almost a week!" She hissed, her voice still no louder than a gasp.

They were silent for a few moments, than Matt turned his head towards her - still not meeting her gaze, "Ally... I'm sor-"

"Shh." Ally placed a soft hand over his lips, "There's no need to apologize, we were both mad." Matt hurriedly changed his laugh into a cough. "Stark raving mad. We should have realized the fight was pointless, that we would have *both* ended up dead.

Matt looked back down at his feet; she was right, of course.

His anger, his frustrations were gone. Replaced - once again - by admiration and physical - if not emotional - attraction. He did not know how he could have felt so much hate towards her... but he never would again.

He looked back over, this time his gaze meeting hers, and he felt the usual twinge of pain in his heart when he saw what was in them: pain, loneliness, hurt. He realized now how alone this girl must feel. He didn't know anything about her past life, but by looking at her, he could tell she must have hated it.

Looking back at Matt, Ally saw that there, in his eyes, she had at long last found a friend.

~ 5 ~

When morning came, Ally and Matt got off the bed, where they had stayed for the rest of the night in silence, and went out into the cafeteria.

As they entered, everyone stopped their usual chatter, and looked up at them.

Miranda got up hastily from her seat - knocking over her chair in the process - hurried over, and began checking them over from a distance. Since Matt had raised a semi-transparent shield about himself so she could see it and had refused to lower it; and Ally had glared at her so fiercely when she came near, that she backed away quickly.

"But you should still be out!" she exclaimed, still gazing over them, "The force you withstood should have killed you at that!"

"Well, we're alive." Sniffed Matt, "And there's nothing you can do about it so you may as well live with it."

Eric snickered.

Ally looked at Matt with new reverence. She'd always thought him shy, but no - he stuck up for himself. He reminded her of... herself.

Quiet, but fierce.

Miranda stammered, her high-pitched voice sounding hurt, "I didn't mean-"

"Neither did I." Matt assented, and walked over to the table and the pancakes lying in wait for him.

Over the course of the next week, Matt felt as if he couldn't have been happier. All of his friends throughout elementary and junior high had not really been his friends, they had just stuck around him because he... well... he didn't quite know why he'd had any friends at all in elementary. But in middle school, guy's hung around him because his bad-boy appearance seemed to attract girls... a lot of girls. And he never really knew why at that.

Before he'd left for the boarding school, Matt had been dreading his switch to high school; he found it all pointless. Everything they learned. All *he* needed was common sense. That's all he'd ever needed.

Ally was his first and only 'true' friend. She was the only one he'd been able to trust, though he still couldn't bring up the nerve to tell her his deepest secrets - those were for his mind only. And though Matt didn't know it, Ally felt the same about him.

They had moved from the cafeteria, and had started taking their "classes" in one of the rooms on the second floor. In the, 'velvet curtain room' as Matt so cleverly called it. And after five days in that room, Matt had started to feel an impending desire to just take a peek at what lay beyond the curtain - even though it looked as if it were just covering the wall.

Today Brandon was slightly late, but when he finally came ambling into the room, he was wearing a broad smile, and beckoned them into the corridor.

They followed him down the hall, and into one of the other classrooms. This room was long, and housed over a hundred glass jars. There were all kinds of jars, tall jars, fat jars, short jars, colored jars, plastic jars, jam jars – every kind of jar you could imagine. They stood on the many tables, on the floor, and some jars had even been hot-glued to the ceiling and walls!

"Sorry it took me so long to set it all up." Apologized Brandon as he surveyed his handy work, clearly pleased with himself. "Today I'll be testing your aim, so Matt will fire first, then Ally, then Matt, then Ally – you get the point. The catch? Your shots can't be any bigger than a marble." He smiled at them, "Go on then, Matt."

Matt stared at one of the glass jars. He'd gotten so good at controlling his energy, that for the minor amounts of it, he didn't need the support of his hands. Nor did Ally.

He concentrated on taking the energy from himself, drawing on it like drawing air for breath. Just a tiny amount, then he aimed, and released the small sphere, watched as it shot away from him and smashed into one of the glass jars on a table.

Bull's-eye!

"Ally."

Ally knew her aim wasn't as good as Matt's, but she was better at controlling her energy than him; and within a second, a glass jar on the wall had shattered.

Ally missed a few jars in the beginning. And at one point or another Matt had panicked, charged his energy too much, and had ended up smashing the entire contents of one table - not to mention the table itself.

Though by lunch hour their aim was vastly improved; even Matt had had room for improvement.

They left the room slightly exhausted, but extremely pleased with themselves.

When they got to the cafeteria, everyone was already there; sitting down and eating, with Eric doing his usual mealtime stand-ups.

They sat down side-by-side as usual at one end of the table, and started to eat the tuna-fish and PB & J sandwiches. Neither saying a word to the other. Listening quietly and laughing occasionally at Erick's jokes – "Why did the chicken cross the road? ... To get to the chicks on the other side! ... Get it? Chicken? Chicks? ... Never mind."

This was the way it always was. Matt and Ally never spoke to each other in public unless it was absolutely necessary - and even when they were alone, in their room together or somewhere else, their conversations were somewhat short, and to the point, as there weren't many topics. Since the fight, they'd both been rather reserved around one another - more than before. And around the others especially.

Besides Eric, Matt found himself somewhat entertained by the antics of Kim and Jason. Apparently they used to go out. But now they just hated each other's guts because of some girl Kim had found Jason cheating on her with.

Matt watched them from across the table as they argued over their plates. Spitting food from their mouths in their fury...

Ally was hardly listening to anything that was going on around her; she was simply picking at her food whilst watching Matt out of the corner of her eye... Thinking.

Abruptly, movement caught her eye as Matt got to his feet. And following his gaze, she saw that Kim and Jason's verbal argument had become physical, and they were both firing small sparks of energy at one another across the table.

Ally stood beside Matt, and though his eyes were on the fight - as were everyone else's- she knew he was watching her.

"Should we intervene?" she asked him quietly.

-*Wait*. Matt answered, without moving his lips.

Ally glanced sharply at him, doubtful of her own inference. "What did you say?" She asked him quietly.

Matt turned partly toward her before turning back to the fight. "Nothing." He answered succinctly, then raised his hands, and shot a clear beam of light straight across the table.

Ally watched his every move, they had just learned to do that, to raise or move their shields to places besides around themselves. But she wasn't thinking about his shield, she was thinking about what he'd done before - what she had done.

The shield gone unnoticed, Kimberly and Jason continued their animated battle. Firing ever increasingly large orbs of energy at each other. But they were fast growing weak, and when their next attacks rebounded back upon them in mid air; they crumpled to the floor instantaneously.

Ally cleared her head of her previous thoughts, and followed Matt around the table.

Everyone else had seen the beam of light as it shot across the table; and all eyes were now trained on the two of them as they stood before the inert forms. Ally to Kim. Matt to Jason.

They healed the incomprehensible amount of tiny cuts and slashes on their bodies. Mended their clothes. Then got to their feet, and walked towards the door that led to the bedrooms; in unison - as if reading one another's thoughts. Neither was very hungry anymore.

"Wait!" came a voice from across the room, when they had just reached the doors. It was Kelsi. "Aren't you going to revive them!?"

Matt turned and raised his right hand towards Jason; a blue beam of light gushed from his palm to surround the form. Beside him Ally did the same; and the black light filtered into Kim's body.

Then - as the two fallen teens stirred - they turned, and walked back to their room.

~

"I have to talk to you." Ally said as soon as Matt had shut the door behind her. "About what just happened now."

Matt turned to face her, and for the first time, as she met his gaze, her heart melted.

Ally quickly shook her head. *Stay focused!*

Matt raised his eyebrows, "What part?"

Ally took a deep breath, and sat down on his bed. "Remember when I asked you if we should intervene?"

Matt nodded, and sat down beside her, curling his knees to his chest.

"What were you thinking at the time?"

Matt paused for a moment, than said carefully, "I was telling myself to wait for the right moment to... you know - separate them."

He smiled.

Ally frowned.

"Matt." She whispered.

"Yeah?"

"I could hear you." Ally was now looking down at her feet; avoiding his gaze.

"You want to repeat that???"

"I could hear your thoughts." She breathed, hoping he would take her seriously.

"You mean... you heard what I was thinking.

"Yeah." She looked up at him, up into his handsome blue eyes; so rich and deep with color.

Matt gazed back at her, "You think it's another one of your abilities - one you and Brandon didn't know about?"

"Maybe... listen, Mathue-"

"Matt."

"-I'm sorry I brought this up, I should have just pushed it aside, let it be-"

"No, I don't mind. I'm glad you told me."

"You are?" Her eyebrows arched.

Matt took no notice. "Yeah. Now I know I'll have to be more careful about what I think from now on!" He laughed.

The corner of her mouth twitched, and she smiled. Her first real smile in a long, long time.

Matt met her gaze, and held it.

Ally stared back at him, still smiling, thinking...

He's different, not like regular people; more... understanding.

Matt stared. Had he heard what he'd thought he'd heard... *No!* And he pushed the thought aside.

"Whelp," Matt said, as if the comfortable silence had never been. "I guess now everyone thinks we're crazy."

Ally laughed.

~ 6 ~

"Okay, you've mastered the control of your energy. You've mastered the control of your shields. Your aim is perfect. You've even learned how to transmit your energy to other sages - and all in under two months. I believe soon we'll be starting heating-"

"What?"

Ally turned to face him, grinning, "Heating, you know - like heat... temperature?"

"I know what heat is, I just don't-"

"You will be learning to heat your bodies, to adjust to other temperatures, and to heat other things. But for today, we're just going to have a testing trial for everyone else."

"You mean, like, the others?"

"Besides everyone else. Who else is there in this castle, besides the others?" Ally rolled her eyes.

Matt blushed.

"You two are not the only one's who've been improving, and though you two may be the strongest - the others have gotten stronger as well; today we're going to find out *how* strong."

"So where do we come in?" Matt asked, raising an eyebrow.

"I thought that'd be obvious."

Ally's eyes narrowed in contemplation, then dilated in an instant. "You want them to test their abilities on us!"

"In a word: bingo!"

Ally slapped her forehead.

Matt sighed, and asked succinctly- "When?"

"In about ten minutes, so we'd better get cranking - and don't worry; they probably won't be able to do anything to you."

"I don't doubt that." Matt whispered into Ally's ear.

She giggled; more from his tickling breath than his words.

Ally had changed; she knew it herself. Even if no one else had noticed. She was no longer the brooding shadow that lurked in dark corners. No, she was now open - at least physically - to Matt; he was the only person she felt close to, the only person she trusted.

That's not to go as far as saying she trusted him with her life but - with her soul? Perhaps. With her emotions? Undeniably.

Matt had changed as well. Only two months at this strange and interesting place; and he was actually having fun. For the first time in his life he was truly content.

It was because of each other, that they'd accepted life for what it was.

They walked down the west spiral staircase. Down to the entrance hall, and entered the cafeteria; following Brandon like little lost ducks.

Everyone else was already there, waiting for them.

Matt and Ally immediately forced their faces to become emotionless; they may have been open to each other - but every one of the other teens present still thought them crazy or at least different. They weren't the same.

As they walked through the large room; eyes followed them, boring into them until they came to a halt in the center of the room; and pivoted to face them.

Brandon turned to the other kids; he smiled at them. "I suppose you're all wondering why you're here?"

Matt and Ally exchanged glances.

They all nodded, still looking at Matt and Ally- like they would spring at them at any second.

"Today we shall be testing how good you've become," Brandon continued, looking at each of them in turn. "For some of you; this will be a simple demonstration of your abilities. For the rest of you... we'll see if you can get past these two." Brandon gestured behind him, at the stationary set standing immobile, side-by-side.

Then - leaving them all in suspense - he walked off to stand beside Miranda; who was grinning with pride at all the level five's.

Dennis now stepped forward and gestured at the right wall, "Will all of you - excluding Matt, Ally and Cody - kindly step back against the wall?" It wasn't really a request.

Everyone complied, and for once, Cody looked as if his jaw had been locked shut.

Dixon then turned to Ally. "The table, if you will." He smiled at her.

Ally - her face still void emotion - moved her gaze to the long table, and sent it flying across the room to the right wall.

A few eyes morphed into saucers.

"Right," Dixon turned to Cody, "No need to be frightened - I want you to ignore everyone, and give us a slight demonstration of your powers." He smiled, than moved back.

Cody was now obviously shaking - but he swallowed, and raised both of his hands. His face screwing up in concentration almost so as he looked constipated.

For the longest time, nothing happened; but when Cody was positively rippling with fright; a shimmering image of a butterfly appeared before him - life size - and grew solid. It fluttered around the room sporadically, then disappeared in a whiff of smoke.

Cody shook once more, convulsively. Then his legs lost the desire to hold his weight, and dropped him to the linoleum.

Before he could hit the floor, however, he was surrounded in a bright black light transmitted from Ally's hand. In a moment his eyes had snapped into focus, and he straitened up. Still shaking. But obviously pleased with himself.

"Alexander, your turn." Came Dennis's voice from across the room, and Alex walked forward; looking only *half* as scared as Cody after seeing what he'd be required to do. And in a moment, a pig was galloping around him. Alexander managed to hold the image for a moment, before it, too, disappeared in a plume of colorful air.

Miranda had out her clipboard again, and was once more scribbling madly upon it after each show of talent.

"Kelsi."

Kelsi stepped forward, and stared at the opposite wall, raising her left hand. Then air before and around her shattered a few times in different places - and this time, she didn't faint.

But as she was just turning to go back to her place in the line against the wall, Dennis's voice stopped her.

"Wait a moment, please. Kelsi: stay where you are. Matt: come foreword."

Matt strode forward until he was only a few meters away from Kelsi. Than stopped; posturing despite himself.

"Mathue,"

"Matt."

Dennis continued, "I want you to raise your shield - but not the whole thing. Just about a quarter of it. And make it semi-transparent, so she can see it."

Matt complied, and raised his shield slowly, if not dramatically.

Kelsi stared at the shimmering blue orb around his body, her throat constricting horribly at the thoughts running around her head, chasing each other to see which one was the most horrible.

"Kelsi, I want you to try and break his shield, use any means necessary. And don't worry, he won't do anything to retaliate."

Ally looked over at Matt, grinning. She saw his head shoot over to face Dennis, resentment apparent in his features. *So what? I'm just here to provide something for her to shoot at!?*

Kelsi swallowed again, and closed her eyes.

Matt watched in fascination as the air began to swirl around her – *So that's all that she can do, she can control air, and everything about it.* Matt looked forward to what might happen next. *At level four she can't do much... but it still might be worth watching.* And he gazed at her intently.

Ally braced herself as the wind began to get fierce. She watched as Kelsi's face grew strained - she was weakening fast.

Then the air swirling around them united into a great swirling vortex before Matt - like a mini-tornado, and before he had time to marvel properly at the intensity of the wind and Kelsi's power, the tornado swung forwards, and struck his shield like a bat. Creating a small sliver in the shield; which mended itself instantly.

Kelsi hadn't seen any of this, she'd fallen to the floor just before her tornado struck. Slowly, the wind began to die down.

Matt lowered his shield, and revived Kelsi, who, led by Miranda, returned to the wall. Healthy, if somewhat shaken.

"Alexandra. Try your luck with Ally."

Matt stepped back, and Ally moved forward. Facing off against Alex.

"Ally, same process, except this time raise *half* your shield"

It was all Ally could do to keep herself from smirking at the look of fear on Alex's face, when the shimmering black sphere rose up around her,

"You know what to do, Alexandra."

Alex - eyes still vomiting her fear - raised her arms, and, after charging an energy orb for what seemed like an eternity, fired a marble-sized speck of energy at Ally – which didn't even leave a mark.

"Right. Kimberly."

Kim did the same thing; to the amount of time it took her to charge up, to the fact that she couldn't even dent the shield.

After Kim came Jason and Eric. They fired at Matt. Same results.

"And lastly, Ivy." Dennis announced an hour later, his voice still with the enthusiasm it always sported.

Ivy moved up against Ally, who once again raised only half her shield.

Ivy raised her hands, and sent what appeared to be sunlight streaming towards her.

The beam of sunlight hit her shield with amazing force, and Ally, unsuspecting of such a fierce attack, slid back a few feet over the smooth floor. But then, regaining her composure, she stood with a gleam of menace in her eye. The shield was fine - not even a break - and the attack had caused Ivy to crumple faster than any of the others, her body slumping to the floor in a heap.

Matt - seeing Ally blinking furiously; as if trying to dislodge a particle of dirt or a stray eyelash from her eye - realized what had happened before anyone else; Ivy hadn't attacked Ally's shield, she'd attacked Ally herself. Making her blind. Temporarily, he hoped.

Matt moved quickly, reviving Ivy with a stream of blue energy. He then stepped over to Ally, and grasped her hands - which had been furiously rubbing at her eyes - tearing them away from her face.

Ally struggled a moment in his grip, not knowing who it was. Alarmed, unnerved and downright terror-stricken at being plunged into a world completely void of light.

Stop, it's me. Please stop! Came Matt's voice from in front of her, and she relaxed in his grasp.

Matt sighed in relief, then released her.

Don't leave me!

I'm not. Hang on.

Matt - unknowing exactly what he was doing - stared straight into her eyes. Knowing full well that she couldn't see him through them. And concentrated.

~

Ivy looked up, and watched as Matt grasped hold of Ally's hands - that which were franticly trying to rub away the blindness that had infected them. She watched as he drew her hands away from her face, and as Ally began to tear away from him - then, abruptly, she stopped. As if some unknown force had told her who it was; which Ivy doubted, as neither of them had spoken. Matt then looked straight into Ally's face, and a beam of blue light shot from his eyes, met with hers, and held. Then, after a moment, the light faded, and they both blinked. It was obvious, then, that Ally could see once more. She looked around Matt at Ivy, who shrunk away from her blazing anger, getting to her feet, and moving swiftly back against the wall with the others. Ally's gaze burning into her back the entire way.

Matt shook her slightly, *Let her go, she was only doing what Dennis told her to. And as far as I'm concerned, she did a pretty bang-up job! If she'd been stronger, she'd have probably made you lose your concentration enough to lower your shield.*

Ally glared at him. *There is no 'if' about it; she used a pretty rotten trick if you ask me!*

Ha ha. Well I say you're just a bit embarrassed that she'd managed to get through part of your defenses.

So what if I am!

Just let it go, Ally.

Ally looked away.

"Ally?"

" ... Fine."

They both turned to find everyone watching them, and Matt found the heat rising in his face. He could well imagine how odd it must have looked; them just staring at each other, then abruptly saying words out of the blue which sounded like they'd been carrying on a conversation - which they had, just not one that anyone else could hear.

Now they know we're crazy. Perfect.

Ally shot him a smile.

Dennis cleared his throat then, and broke the uncomfortable silence, "Ah-hem. Well, Matt, Ally; I believe it is your turn."

"What?" Matt and Ally both spun to face him, their expressions full of shock.

"But we know what'll happen!" Ally told him, "You saw before; we're evenly matched, there's no way one of us can defeat the other!"

Matt saw Brandon raise his eyebrows at Dennis; clearly he'd known nothing about this little turn of events, either.

Dennis smiled at them, "Who said anything about defeating each other. I only want a slight demonstration of your powers, like everyone else."

He's crazy. No- worse than crazy; he's obsessed!

A laugh burst from Ally's lips.

"What's so funny?" Dennis grew nonplussed.

Brandon was looking from Matt to Ally, his eyes narrowing. Then abruptly, his expression led them to believe he'd just come to the discovery of the incandescent bulb. And he turned to whisper into Dennis' ear.

He knows.

Greeeaaat.

After a minuet or two, Dennis turned to face them, "Well then... go on."

"Pardon me?"

"Give us a demonstration of your powers." Brandon smiled.

Matt looked over and met Ally's gaze. *Should we?*

We don't really have a choice...

I still say he's crazy.

Ally laughed again as they moved away from each other.

Ready?

You first.

Ally nodded, and Matt raised his shield, his *full* shield.

He watched as Ally quickly charged some energy, and hurled it at him. It hit his shield, and exploded, forcing everyone in the room to duck. It wasn't the strongest of her attacks, Matt knew, it was more like half.

My turn

Ally raised her shield.

Matt charged his energy, and let go of it, watched as it flew off towards Ally.

Duck, she grinned.

What- hah! Ally had reflected his orb back at him, and as it flew at him, he caught it deftly in one hand, absorbing it back into his being.

Ta-da! Matt turned to look back at Dennis, bowing mentally in his head. And out of the corner of his eye, he saw Ally cover her grin with her hand.

Dennis and Brandon both folded their arms, and Matt found himself thinking they were angry with them.

Well what did they expect us to do, fry each other!?

Matt let out a snort, but quickly turned it into a hacking cough when Dennis' fierce gaze shot to his dancing one.

Dennis whirled back to the rest of the kids, his smile stretching back onto his face. "You may all have the rest of the day off, so make good use of it. Matt, Ally... Follow me." And as he turned to face them, the cold frown was back. They followed him hastily; Brandon bringing up the rear as everyone else slowly filtered from the cafeteria.

Dennis led them into the kitchen, than turned to face them as Brandon closed the door. He didn't say anything.

Silence.

After a few moments of uncomfortable quiet, Matt cleared his throat, "So, uh... what'd we do?"

Or what didn't *we do.*

"How long have you known?"

"Huh?"

"How long have you two been able to communicate without the use of your tongues?"

Oh! And I thought he was asking how long we've known we were sages!

Ally burst into an uncontrollable fit of laughter, and Dennis glared fiercely at her.

Ally stopped laughing as soon as she caught his eye. Then she straightened up, and met his gaze sternly, "Oh stop glaring. Truthfully we only just figured it out."

Dennis was taken aback; whether by her tone or by her answer was hard to tell. "You *just* found out?"

"Yes. Why?"

"I think they're telling the truth, Dennis. After all, they only just showed signs of it now."

Dennis sighed, "Alright."

"Besides," Ally continued, defiant. "What does it matter?"

"It matters," Brandon answered, holding up his hand to silence an impertinent Dennis. "Because we'd like to know about everything you can do. So tell us in the future, ok?"

Ally looked over at Matt, he shrugged, and they both nodded.

"Excellent." Dennis' smile was back, as were the twinkle in his eyes. "Now go on, you get the rest of the day off as well."

˜

I wonder why they were so mad at us for not telling them sooner?
Beats me.

It was odd, sitting across the room from someone, conversing with your thoughts. Odd but... strangely normal, too.

They'd both had the same idea once they'd reached their bedroom. Plunking down across from one another on their beds, they sat discussing the afternoon's events - and one extremely pressing matter.

Matt?
Yeah.
You remember when... Ivy blinded me?
Uh huh.
What did you do? You know, to make me see again.
I dunno. I just, focused on your eyes, and, well, you can see now - can't you?
Of course.

They were silent for a long while later, then Matt got up and walked over to the door. "I wonder what they all think of us?"

"Who cares." Ally lay back down on her covers, and rolled over so that her back was to him.

Matt stared at her for a moment longer, then turned back to the door. *Well that's just it, isn't it? Who really cares anymore?*

Ally remained stolid.

~

"Well *I* care!"

"Oh shut up, Jason!"

"You shut up!"

"No you!"

"I said shut it!"

"MAKE ME!!!"

"Hey! Guys! Break it up alright. Fighting won't get us nowhere."

Kim and Jason sat back down at the table, still taking mental target practice at the other.

Eric remained standing; worried the two of them might go at it again. Then after a moment, he sat back down, if somewhat stiffly.

"Alright, let's get back on topic." Alexander, usually shy, said abruptly. "I doubt they're going to fry us. They're just at a different level than us- it doesn't make them any less human!"

"Alex's right. So they blew each other up, that wasn't their fault."

"I *really* hope you were being sarcastic there." Kim raised her eyebrows at Kelsi, who averted her eyes and blushed deeply. Coming to terms with how the statement must have sounded.

"That was Mr. Kenith's fault." Alexandra sat back in her chair and folded her arms." He admitted it himself."

"You mean Brandon? The guy who teaches them?" Cody asked, standing in his chair.

"Yeah."

"But that-"

"Jason, what have they done to us? Huh?" Kim glared at him from across the table.

"Well they... remember when they..." Jason raked his memory for a reasonable variant.

"My point precisely." Kim turned back to the others, "So it's agreed: they're human, and we're going to treat them as such. No more of this glaring at them whenever they enter the room! It's rude and offending."

"Hey, Kim, when did you get a sense of being polite!?" Jason smirked.

"I didn't. I just think that if we keep this up they *will* fry us."

~

"Today, as you know, we're going to start heating."
Matt glanced Ally roll her eyes- and he had to agree with her; Brandon had a knack of sounding corny, stupid, and old-fashioned all at the same time.

"Since I have obviously never done anything like this before, and can't show or tell you what must be done; I can only tell you to try your best, and practice hard. So, Ally, Matt; I'm going to have you start by trying to raise your body temperature. Go on, try it."

Matt looked over at Ally, and she returned his gaze. Shrugging.

He concentrated hard, and closed his eyes, like when he first learned how to take energy from himself and shoot it. He focused on the task at hand; i.e., his temperature.

He was nice and warm at the moment, because of the temperature in the room. But Matt, like every other human being on the planet, knew that when the air grew chill - like it was outside at the moment - his body would also become cold; unless he wore warm clothing, or learned to heat his body.

Nothing happened.

Opening his eyes, he saw that Ally, too, was frustrated.

Brandon smiled, "Don't get disheartened. This is one of the two most difficult abilities to learn. Even for level ten."

Great. That means more fun for us.

Beside him he saw Ally smile.

Brandon continued, unawares of the transition that had occurred right before him, "So then, I'll give you all the time you need to practice. Do you have a place in mind?"

No.

"How about the cafeteria?"

Matt glanced over at Ally, *Why there?*

Ally didn't move, *I dunno, it was just the first thought in my head.*

"Alright then. I'll leave you to your practicing." And he turned, and left the room.

As soon as Matt could hear his footsteps echoing off the linoleum floor no longer, he turned to Ally, who was already looking at him- "Why the cafeteria?" He asked again, calmly.

Ally shrugged, "It's bigger, so we can practice anything there. And it's also closer to our room."

"Alright. I didn't really care, I was just wondering."

Sure...

"You callin' me a liar?"

Ally laughed as they made their way down the hall.

~

Too hot! WAY TOO HOT!!! Matt felt as if his eyes were popping out of their sockets it was so blindly sweltering!

"Oh! S-sorry!"

Ally hastily lowered the temperature in the room, and Matt fell into a chair, wiping the perspiration from his brow. "Nice!"

"Well I tried my best!" she whined, smiling.

"I guess we still need a bit of practice..."

A bit *of practice?*

"Ok OK! We need a *lot* of practice."

Ally laughed, "I guess we should get to it then-"

Too late...

Just then, the doors to the cafeteria swung open, and Cody and Alexander limped in.

Lunchtime.

"What happened to you guys?" Ally asked aloud, an eyebrow raised in amusement.

Cody looked over at her and smiled, Alexander scowled. "We learned how to create *physical* illusions!" he announced, his shrill voice cutting through the air.

Matt glanced at her, and they both smiled; judging by the way Alex kept frowning, it couldn't have been half as fun as Cody made it sound. They could guess what must have happened.

I'll do it.

Matt raised his right hand, and the blue light that washed from it surrounded both Cody and Alexander, refreshing their spirits and healing their bodies.

"Thanks." Alex mumbled, and sat down at the table as the others entered the room.

Matt had noticed a definite change in the attitudes toward them; nobody was glaring at them anymore, nor did they appear to be frightened or apprehensive. They seemed to have accepted them, and even smiled at them occasionally.

He didn't mind this, he didn't really care if they liked or hated him; it didn't matter to him. And he was pretty certain it didn't matter to Ally.

When everyone was seated, and the food lain out on the table, Matt dished some macaroni and cheese onto his palate, and began to eat. Listening absentmindedly to Eric as per usual.

But he wasn't really hungry; all he really wanted to do was get back to practicing his temperate skills with Ally.

He picked aimlessly at his food. The cooks at the school had ways of making everything tasty - and healthy. This macaroni and cheese was homemade, like all the other food, not store bought. It had tasty little bits of spice mixed in with the cheese, and he started to pick these off and eat them one tiny bit at a time.

What's wrong?

Nothing.

"Hey, Mathue!"

Matt's head shot up, this was the first time any off the other kids had ever addressed him - let alone used his full name.

Eric waved again, "Could you pass the sauce?"

Disoriented for a moment, he then stared at the little bowl filled with the creamy white sauce, and sent it flying across the table over to Eric - mumbling silently beneath his breath: "Matt."

"Hey thanks!"

Matt sat back in his chair, and picked at his food for a while longer. Then – finally - he got up abruptly, and left the room.

~

Ally watched Matt from the corner of her eye. Watched him as he slowly picked at his food until all that was left were the mushy noodles picked clean of any spice or sauce.

She watched as he passed the Alfredo over to Eric, then, as he got up to leave, she slowly shrunk back into the shadows, and followed him. By the time she reached their room door, she was exhausted; the little trick cost her more energy than she let on, and she had already been tired after heating and cooling the room all afternoon. But it wasn't for naught; they could heat and cool themselves just fine - it was only when they spread their power to others or to the room as a whole did problems start to arise.

The room door was open. Matt must have accidentally left it ajar when he came through; and she gently eased it aside.

"Holly SHIT this room is hot!"

Matt spun around - almost giving himself whiplash - and instantly the room cooled. His face grew heated instead.

Ally felt her face go red in unison with his "I'm sorry. I didn't mean to barge in on you like this. You just, just left so quickly, I thought something might be wrong..." She let the sentence drift.

"No. Nothings wrong. I just got bored and decided to give the thermostat something to do."

She snickered and hastily clapped her hand to her mouth.

Matt couldn't help the grin that broached his face at having brought a smile to hers.

There *was* something wrong, actually, but Matt couldn't tell her. He wasn't even sure if he could admit it to himself. Instead he shoved the thought from his mind and walked over toward his bed, the door, and Ally, "I'm guessing you're probably going to want me to stop-"

"No, actually." She hastily cut him off, "I wouldn't mind practicing a bit more myself, if... that's alright with you?"

"No. Sure. Why not." He grinned and Ally felt her heart skip a beat.

At either ends of the room, sitting on their respective beds, Matt and Ally warmed up by heating and cooling themselves slowly. Then after saying, *'no you go first'*, nonstop for about ten minutes; they both agreed to do it at the same time.

"Ready?"

Ally nodded sharply. "One..."

"Two..."

"Three!"

The temperature shot up so fast that the combined pressure in the room forced the ornate silver mirror by the bathroom door to spontaneously shatter. Sending shards over the room in a multitude of directions.

Ally quickly stopped, and across the room, so did Matt. Lowering the arms that had flown up to protect themselves.

They both blushed, waiting in silence as the room cooled to its regular degree.

"One at a time?"

"Yeah."

~

A week later, they had it down pat, and Brandon had another little surprise waiting for them in their classroom.

"WHAT!!!!"

"Calm down, Matt. It's harder than it sounds. And its going to take a hell of a lot of practice. -But after only three months and a week, seeing what you have learned in *that* time, I supposed it wouldn't be such a long shot for you to try this. Also, it's pretty much all I have left to teach you anyway; so I thought, heh, what the hey." He smiled at them.

Matt was still gaping at him, the blood drained from his face. His mouth flapped, but no words came out. He looked like a landed fish.

Beside him, Ally, too, was startled. But she was not struck witless - nor was she speechless. She simply gaped at him for a moment or two, then smirked, "Very funny Mr. Kenith."

Brandon became stern. "It's no joke. It's the truth. You can, and you *will* learn to use your eyes as an energy release-"

Matt, then, finally regained the power of speech. "So you're saying we can shoot LASERS OUT OF OUR EYES!!!" he shouted, spit flying from his mouth.

Brandon looked over at him, again smiling. "Yes, and no. The 'lasers' will really only be the regular energy that you would normally 'transport' from your body. By doing it this way, you don't waste *half* as much time *charging* the energy. Instead, you go straight to the attack. Though," he amended, looking thoughtful. "with the amount of energy it will inadvertently take, it would probably make more sense to simply use the regular way... But all the same," he said, looking sternly at each of them, "this way is much more powerful, much quicker, and much easier. It would be best if you learned how to do it before you decided you didn't like it."

"Okay, okay. We didn't say we didn't like it, we were just a little startled, is all."

Ally was back to wearing her usual indifferent mask, and she stared Brandon straight in the eye. "So? How do we do it?"

"Oh it's really simple." Brandon smiled again - it was getting to be just as annoying as Dixon's twinkle; like he knew something they didn't. "You just do the same as you usually do, except this time, you concentrate on brining the energy out through your eyes, got it?"

They both nodded.

"Excellent! I'll leave you to your work then." Then he turned, and started towards the door.

"WAIT!" Ally ran forward, surprising both Brandon and Matt. "Shouldn't we practice somewhere else. You know, where we won't destroy anything?"

Brandon's eyebrows raised, and he smacked his forehead. "Of course!" Ally exchanged glances with Matt, "You can practice out on the west balcony, it's the larger one, and you can shoot out to sea. The snow just fell, so you might have to warm yourselves constantly - but that shouldn't be much of a problem for you two now, eh?" he chuckled to himself, then left.

~

"Hey guys. Have you seen Matt or Ally lately?" Eric asked during lunch on Friday.

"No." Kelsi glanced over at him. "Come to think of it, I haven't seen them since last month - two weeks ago."

"Me neither." Cody jumped onto his chair, the better to be noticed.

"Does anyone know where they are?" Alexandra asked around, her face full of concern.

"I have." Everyone looked over at Jason, who had his arms crossed and his head bent so that his eyes were shadowed by his overhanging bangs.

"Where." Kim folded her arms and smirked at him, assuming an attitude stance.

Jason looked up at her and mimicked her smirk. "On the west balcony."

"What would they be doing up there?" Alexandra half-laughed. "And how would they stand the cold?"

"They're at level ten, remember." Alexander stood up; "Maybe they have a way of staying warm?" he shrugged.

"Well then, lets go see." And without waiting to see if anyone was following her or not, Kim got up from her seat, and strode from the entrance hall. Her lilac skirt rippling about her legs. Jason watched her tight ass for a moment with an intriguing gaze and a sparkle of lust; then got up to follow her, the others following in his wake.

~

Matt stared out to sea, his eyes wide and glazed.

Ally watched him closely, watched as every muscle in his body strained, trying to force the energy inside of himself to do what he wanted it to do.

Abruptly his eyes turned a light blue, growing darker and brighter with each passing heartbeat. Then his eye's widened even further - if that were possible - and the light shot from his irises and out to sea. Out past where the eye met it's limit.

The energy continued to stream from his eyes until Matt wavered, and dropped to the snow-covered stone that made up the west balcony.

Ally watched him fall, slowly, as if I she were watching him fall from a dream. Then she stepped swiftly over, and knelt in juxtaposition. The snow melting at the touch of her warm body.

She'd had to do this more often in the last week; when they had just started. When they couldn't even do it properly. They still had to learn how to do it better - there was always room for improvement - but the main problem was that when they got started, they just couldn't stop. The energy would simply run until it ran out - and they fainted.

But they'd get better, they always did.

She gently stroked his warm cheek with the back of her hand; her heart beginning to beat madly as it always did when she looked at him or drew near.

She looked into his eyes, and remembered how much it had hurt them both when they first tried. How they'd had to keep their eyes shut and covered with a cool, wet cloth before the pain had ebbed.

Eventually, Ally brought up her right hand, and a wave of black energy washed from her fingertips into the inert body lying prone beside her.

She watched his chest rise and fall heavily when he took a sudden deep breath of the chill air. Then his eyes fluttered, opened, and he smiled up at her. "How'd I do?"

She smiled back, "Longer than usual. But, as you can see by the fact that you're lying in the snow flat on your back once more..."

"Yeah, yeah. No need to rub it in." Matt grumbled, taking the hand she offered to him, using it to pull himself to his feet. Then he dusted himself off, and turned to face her. "As I recall, you're not so great at stopping yourself either."

Ally grinned up at him through her lashes. "We will see." She said, then turned from him, and took two steps towards the wall of the balcony, her eyes widening, staring out to sea.

Her eyes started to glow a dark black, then got darker. Then at the last moment, she lowered her head, and the energy shot out of her eyes, blasting one of the rocks below to smithereens. Spraying water ninety feet into the air.

Ally continued to stare, then abruptly blinked, stopping the flow of energy. She stumbled backwards, away from the ledge, and fell into Matt's arms. She stared up at him, shocked.

Matt stared back, his mouth agape.

"WOW!!!"

The sudden voice made Matt start so suddenly, he almost dropped the shell-shocked Ally. Instead, he caught himself, and lifted her back to her feet. Holding her steady for a moment as she regained her balance.

Cody was bouncing up and down on the balls of his feet, positively glowing with pleasure. The others standing behind him somewhat still.

"Did you guy's see that? Did you! Did you! How cool was THAT!!! They can shoot LASERS out of their EYES! I- Phfbit!"

Eric took two steps over to the yapping protégé, his eyes half-mast in lassitude; and clamped his hand firmly over the blaring orifice, effectively cutting off the noise. Then he looked up at Matt and Ally.

At the glance Matt felt his insides unclench somewhat; he was smiling.

"We only came looking for you two to ask you guys where you've been; we haven't seen you at breakfast, supper *or* lunch for nearly a week!" he grinned, "You aren't fasting, are you? 'Cause if you are I doubt Dixon'll be very enthusiastic."

His stomach gave a very ill timed grumble at his neglect, and Matt suddenly realized how very hungry he was; clutching at his stomach as if to create the illusion he were full.

Beside him Ally's face had grown wan. She was still, but shaking imperceptibly; taking in slow shallow breaths of air. Her face a stone wall, normally so emotionless, cold and hard - was now teetering, her facade crumbling; looking as if she would fall at any moment.

As Eric spoke, Matt caught a glimpse of her from corner of his eye, and shifted slightly in the snow just in time to catch her as her legs lost their strength, and her knees gave way beneath her.

Cody squirmed and broke loose from Eric's grip; bounding over to where Matt was laying Ally's inert form on the chill stone, "What happened to her? Why did she fall? Did she faint? Was it a sudden loss of energy?" He had taken that from Dennis. "Will you be able to help her? She looked fine a minute ago," Clearly he hadn't seen her. "Will she be alright? I wonder-"

Matt glared up at him, and Cody's jaw snapped shut.

"She expended herself too much. It just took a few more seconds for the rest of her energy to leave her." Matt told him simply, as he knelt down beside her with a pained look in his eyes - as if seeing her like this afflicted him. Then he raised both his hands over her chest.

The others watched as an even more powerful aura of energy streamed from hands to engulf her body lovingly. For a moment Matt remained stationary, then the flow of energy ebbed, and he stopped. Ally didn't twitch.

Matt sighed, and bent to pick up her body.

"What are you doing?" Cody asked frantically as Matt lifted her form, and moved towards the door. "Can't you heal her?"

Matt didn't stop, but called over his shoulder: "It's not a matter of healing, it's just that we've been practicing all day, and I haven't the energy left to revive her." He continued on into the castle.

~ 7 ~

Ally woke to a world of darkness, and sat up in a panic, her eyes straining against the black in hopes of penetrating the obscurity.

Abruptly she felt something pressing on her just below her collarbone, and fought desperately against it. Her breathing hard and fast, her panic speeding her heart to a frantic tempo.

Stop, Ally. It's me.

Ally's breathing hitched, and she stopped struggling.

That's right, calm down.

Matt didn't remove his hand; for which she was grateful. He kept it pressed up against her body, administrating only a slight amount of pressure to force her back down onto the soft covers of her bed.

Where are we... why is it so dark?

Our room. The lights are out.

She relaxed under his hand, her body going limp in reaction to her shock, her breathing slowly returning to normal.

A sigh of relief escaped his lips, and Matt removed his hand. Already he was uneasy, he'd touched her - and not just like holding her hand; he'd touched her to close to a place he felt was out of bounds to him. A place he made a point of looking away from.

With the warmth of his hand gone, Ally felt suddenly cold again, frightened. She knew she was being stupid - since when was she afraid of the dark!?

'Rest assured, you're not, Ally. You just pretend to be afraid so he'll touch and comfort you.'

That's-not-true!

What's not true?

"Uh... nothing. -Just... Nothing." Damn, she'd forgotten he could read any of her unprotected thoughts.

"Alright." Matt turned his eyes from her once again, and stared blankly at his feet - as gray and shadowy in the dark as they were.

He'd much rather stare at her.

Ally's eyes were slowly becoming accustomed to the dark. She was now just starting to make out his still, muscular outline sitting on the edge of her bed... sitting very close to her.

After a long, strained silence, she asked quietly, "What happened?"

"You blacked out again - right after Cody started up with his usual monologue. I carried you inside. You've been out for nearly ten hours." He looked around at her, and smiled, though he knew she couldn't see him. "Dixon doesn't know. Neither does Kenith."

"You carried me inside? Ten hours... then, it must be-"

"Three in the morning? Yeah."

"And you've been up all this time?"

"Yeah, I didn't have the strength left to revive you out on the balcony, so the only thing I could do was let you rest." He smiled again, weakly, then turned back to his interesting shoes.

Ally's heart did a double take; he'd carried her inside, sat beside her and watched over her for pretty much the entire night... he really cared about her - as a friend, if nothing more.

She slowly sat up, and placed a hand on his shoulder, "Matt..."

He twisted to face her, his eyes meeting hers.

God he's hot.

"I... thank you." She lowered her eyes, "You're a true friend, Matt. You know that. No one else would have done that for me... No one."

Matt moved his body slightly on the bed, and moved a hand up towards her cheek. Then he stopped, and let it drop, getting to his feet from the bed; feeling her hand slip from his shoulder. "I'm sure anyone would have done the same." He said, simply, and walked away from her over to his own bed. Leaving his heart behind.

~ 8 ~

"YES!" Ally punched her fist into the air, and performed a jig that could only be described as a happy dance.

Beside her Matt shook convulsively as he strove to cover his mirth. "Well done."

The two spun to see Brandon standing in the arched doorway to the west balcony, smiling, his arms crossed over his chest.

Matt put his hands back into his pockets; his momentary pride at Ally's accomplishment gone.

Brandon strode towards them, "Can both of you do it like that, or only Ally?"

"Both of us. But we still need quite a bit of practice."

Matt's gaze shot in Ally's direction, startled. He couldn't do it half as well as she could and she knew it.

"Alright then, I'll leave you to it." With that he turned and left.

Matt watched him go, than turned back to face her. A curious expression stretching across his profile. "Why did you say that? You know I'm not as good as you."

She smiled at him, "Course you are, you discredit yourself."

Matt grinned, his eyes narrowed in skepticism. "No, I'm not. And you know it."

"So maybe you aren't, but with a little more practice you will be."

"You know, one day that face-value attitude of yours-"

"Guys, supper time."

"Thanks Cody. –What were you about to say, Matt? Something about my face-value attitude?"

Matt averted his eyes and mumbled something to the stones at his feet, which sounded a lot like, "Murble-dock."

"What was that?" Ally asked sweetly, fighting valiantly to keep the grin from her face.

Matt glanced up at her, "I said: I don't have a clue what your talking about. And can we go in for supper now 'cause I'm starving."

Still grinning at one another, Matt and Ally made their way into the castle after Cody.

~

The sight that met their eyes when they entered the cafeteria was certainly something to gawk at. The entire room hand been decked in fake silver icicles, golden bells, and green holly.

Confetti that had been made to substitute as real snow darted about their feet as they walked across the floor, and over in the far corner of the room was a Christmas tree; awe-inspiring by all aspects of the imagination.

The tree was at least twelve feet high, with golden lights strung all around it. Bright silver and cherry tinsel - draped like rain over the delicate bows of the tree - sparkled in the light like diamonds. And little ornaments of blue and white glittered on every branch. The tree itself representing the whole of peace and all that is good in the world.

And beneath the tree were presents. Each in a different color and style of wrapping paper; cluttered under the tree like little newborn kittens protected by their mother.

Matt and Ally stood stunned.

"When did all this go up?"

"All this morning. Me and Alex got to watch them at it, we even got to help a little. And look!" Cody bounded over to the tree and pointed down to the presents, "Ten of them! One for each of us! But Miranda said we can't open them 'till tomorrow." Cody sulked for a thousandth of a second, then regained his usual jovial attitude, and hopped over to the table. "I can't wait to see what they made for supper, Christmas eve an' all, maybe piggy puddin'! Do you know what that is, I heard about it in a song once - what was it called... silent night-"

"Shut up, Cody." Everyone recited in unison - Matt couldn't help thinking they sounded quite monotonous - and took their places at the table as the cooks came out with the food.

I know this might sound stupid but... I had completely forgotten it was the twenty forth!

Me too. Matt looked over at her out of the corner of his eye, and winked.

Ally felt herself go as crimson as the tinsel.

Looking around swiftly, Matt was relieved to find no mistletoe in sight. That didn't mean Cody hadn't hidden it though - so he resolved to stay on his guard for the rest of the night.

The dinner consisted of many things Matt had never even seen in his life, so he couldn't very well name them all. Later on, Matt would remember the evening as bright, cheery, and loud.

The table groaned under the weight of three chickens, many different deserts including 'Figgie' pudding, many different salads, drinks and breads, and one, very large, candelabra, which covered at least a tenth of the table it was so big.

Holding only three candles, the candelabra was ornate platinum - worth over fifty million at least. It managed to light the entire room with the help of four smaller, fragrant candles placed along the table - one of which was found to be the cause of Cody's indigestion later on in the night...

Matt found he was actually enjoying himself, and when they were offered a glass of white wine each, he made a spectacular show of spitting it back out after the first sip. He was fifteen. Not his foster father - who would drink anything you shoved in his face. But he'd tried it, even if it was only because - and he would never admit it aloud - Ally had been smiling at him out of the corner of her eye, watching his face as it slowly got redder and redder.

Ally herself had declined all offers of wine; she'd tried it before and liked the taste less than incompetence.

By the end of the dinner, most everyone was red faced - either from the wine or from laughing at Eric's new wave of jokes and stand-up comedy – most, if not all, of it very dirty and un-censored as the comedian was truly drunk, and without restraint. Causing even the naïve Cody to blush to his roots and excuse himself hurriedly to the bathroom to compose himself.

And Cody, at one point, had even passed out straight into his pudding, to a new wave of laughter all around.

So it was that when Matt finally fell onto his soft, modest bed in his cool, tranquil room; he found himself with a lot of memories to reminisce.

And later, a lot of giggles to get out of his system.

~

Ally fell back against the side of the tub, exhaling deeply. It was Christmas morning. She knew that of course, but she wasn't wasting all her strength being happy about it. To her, Christmas had always been just another day of the year. A lot brighter, maybe, but no different than the day before.

Like her birthday.

She reached over, and took the soap off the ledge, rubbing it gently across her body, washing away the sweat caused by the heat and exertion of the night before.

She washed, then rinsed out her hair, and stepped from the tub; wrapping a towel about her body. Moving to find her hairbrush, she whirled as the door was suddenly swung wide and Matt stepped in.

Her eyes the epitome of shock, Ally clutched the towel more firmly about her, and fell back against the wall. Trying desperately to disappear, her mind so clouded and muddled by the wave of heat that raced through her skin, it escaped her that she could.

Matt stared at her for a moment, frozen between attraction and horror. Then realized what he was doing, and hurriedly averted his eyes, stepping back and pulling the door with him. "Gawd I'm sorry, Ally. I-I thought you'd already left." Then he tripped back into the bedroom, all but slamming the door, his cheeks afire.

Ally, her heart still slamming into her chest, slowly relaxed her tensed up muscles, and slumped against the wall. Her eyes clenched over her flaring embarrassment. *Why do I always feel like that when I see him!* - she screamed at herself. A tear gently washed from beneath her lashes, trickled down her cheek, and fell to the tile at her feet.

~

Matt slumped back against the door to the bathroom, his left arm flung across his heated visage. *You idiot! You should have knocked first! Idiot! Idiot! IDIOT!!!* He continued to berate himself until his heart stopped it's mad hammering in his chest, and his hands had stopped shaking.

Then he slowly slid down against the door, and buried his head in his arms.

Neither of them showed up to open their presents in the mess hall with the others that morning.

~

"Wow! I think you've got it!"

Matt turned around, and flashed her a winning grin. "Thanks. I couldn't have done it without your help, though."

"Oh stop being so modest! What did I do? Nothing but encourage you."

"That's what helped."

Ally blushed.

After only an added couple of days, they'd gotten the new technique down. They could do it perfectly, without flaw, and they didn't waste *half* as much energy as they'd used to - though it still took a hell of a lot out of them.

And they had to admit - shooting lasers from their eyes was kind of... exhilarating, if not breathtaking.

At breakfast that Tuesday, though, they were all surprised when Dennis came into the cafeteria and announced to them all they'd be having one big class in the morning that day - then would be allotted the day off.

"You've all been working exorbitantly hard lately - and I think you're ready." What they were ready for, of course, Dennis never elaborated upon. He only smiled anew, and his eyes twinkled. "I've got a surprise for you today, then you'll all have the rest of the day off."

"Yay! I wonder what sort of surprise? Is it more presents? I love presents!!! I wonder who invented the present? Hmm... I mean, the present is what happening now, right? But if we get a present, how can we get time? Wouldn't that be the best present of all!? I wonder if you could actually-"

"Shut up, Cody."

They all followed Dennis out of the cafeteria, and as they walked along the second floor landing, Dennis continued, "It's mainly for you, Ally. So you know."

Ally's face grew dark, "Yippee." She replied sarcastically, and looked over at Matt, who was already looking at her. She hurriedly averted her eyes.

Matt stared at her a moment, wondering what this was all about; then followed Dennis into the purple curtain room - except now there was no more velvet, purple curtain.

Matt saw now why it had looked like the curtain was against the wall: the curtain had blocked the opening to another part of the room - and you had to climb a set of stairs to reach it.

The other part of the room contained a large, no - *huge* tank. It spanned at least twenty by fifteen feet around; was about fifty feet deep, and pretty much filled the entire section of the room.

Off to the right of the tank was a stairway, which led up to a three-foot wide ledge that ran around the top of the tank. The tank itself containing a thin layer of sand along the bottom, a large pile of rocks in one corner, a few fish here and there, and some reeds - live ones - scattered in different areas around the tank.

All in all, it looked just like the floor of the ocean. Or as Matt assumed the floor of the ocean looked - considering he'd never seen it.

As Matt gazed up at the tank in honest interest, he abruptly sensed, rather than caught, the movement off to his right side, and turned to see Ally backing away in the general direction of the door.

What is it?

Ally neglected to answer; she just prolonged her fearful stare. Almost angrily glaring over at Dixon. But she'd stopped moving backwards, and Matt took that as a good sign - though he really shouldn't have.

"No... No I WON'T!"

Dennis' face grew austere. "Ally, I am not asking you to perform. Just show them what you can do-"

"NO!!!"

"Ally-"

"NO!!!"

After a while's worth of arguing, Ally finally conceded to do whatever it was Dennis wanted her to do; and climbed up the stairs that led to the top of the tank. Her face set, emotionless as always.

Anxiety followed her from Matt's eyes; not for her safety - he knew very well she could take care of herself. But more for what the others would think of her for whatever new 'trick' she was about to implement.

Not that it mattered.

Dennis was glowing again, and he looked as if it were Christmas all over as he turned to face the others once more. "Ally, as you know, is a female sage at level ten. What you didn't know, was that she is also a *water* sage. I am not going to bother *telling* you what that is, instead

I'll let Ally *show* you." And with that, his and all other eyes turned up to watch the statue before them.

Ally exchanged one last pained look with Matt, than dove head first into the bone numbing water.

Matt watched her with piercing eyes as she moved through the tank. Slowly, gracefully she swam around - seemingly without effort.

It was only when Matt took notice of the gentle rise and fall of her chest did his worry start to lessen.

Then he saw them: three thin slits just below each of her ears and running down her neck in parallel fashion. Gills.

He watched in ever increasing fascination as Ally's shirt appeared to dissolve; replaced by a thin, black cloth tied tightly about her body to cover her breasts. His eyes further widened as her legs fused together - her pants dissolving the way of the shirt to be replaced by scales. Shiny, black, sharp scales which started at her waist - below her navel - and ran steadily down her once long and graceful legs - now one long, pliant appendage resembling that of the tail of a fish. Ending in two beautiful silky fins, which swept through the water like air; the tail propelled her around the tank with awing speed and grace.

Ally darted about the tank once more before coming to a stop at the fore of the tank; her hair fanning out behind her at her sudden halt. She then slowly raised her head, and opened her eyes to gaze out at them strangely, otherworldly.

Matt saw they were still the same piercing dark blue, but different: a thin milky substance covered them, like a second eyelid, and dulled them slightly.

Ally smiled shyly out at them - no, him; and flicked her tail once more to speed to the top of the tank, where she rose from the water, and pushed herself onto the platform.

Matt could see that, out of water, she appeared to be heavy, and clumsy; but nevertheless breathtaking, as her shiny black tail flipped and weaved beneath her as she sat on the ledge of the tank. She blinked once, and the other eyelid was gone.

"Wow..." Cody breathed, "I've never met a mermaid before. Can I touch her tail?" he asked Dixon.

Ally's eyes flashed, and for a heart-stopping moment; Matt feared for Cody's life.

Dixon looked up at Ally, and smiled brilliantly at her majestic form. He looked indeed like a child in a candy shop.

Ally's face relaxed. "You can-"

"Yay!" Cody exclaimed and started for the steps.

"But I wouldn't if I were you."

He stopped. "Why not?" Cody looked genuinely disgruntled.

"Because those scales are harder than diamonds." Dennis broke in. "And sharper then cut glass. To Ally and her kind they're soft and silky to the touch, but if you were to touch them - you'd rip your hand open."

Cody swallowed.

"Now to continue our little lecture." Dixon turned back to the others - but Matt had tuned out. He was much too preoccupied with watching Ally. Watching as her tail flipped gently back and forth along the ledge, her eyes downcast, staring at her slender hands folded over her tail where her lap would once have been. Something in him had snapped, opening the floodgates to his soul. He couldn't tell precisely what it was that made his heart hammer desperately at his chest, but he knew it had something to do with that tail. Something it represented. To him it was more then otherworldly... it was closer then that.

To him it represented something akin to... familiarity.

More aware as to Matt's lack of response to anything around him than he let on, Dixon continued: "Ally, as I said, is a water sage, but there are also air sages as well. They have wings-"

"WOW!" Cody exclaimed, "Am-"

Dixon smiled, "-and I'm sorry to disappoint you, but none here are any of the like."

Cody pouted.

Dennis continued, "Ally has the ability to change back and forth between a water and land dwelling mammal at will. But she is not the only one."

Ally's gaze shot up from her lap to Dixon. Obviously this was news to her.

"Can anyone guess who?" His eyes twinkled.

Ally's head slowly turned to face Matt, and he stared back, his heart racing around his chest. Their eyes locked.

Dennis looked over at Matt as well, and the others followed his gaze. Matt didn't notice, and even if he had; he didn't remove his gaze from Ally's.

"Mathue." Dixon prodded gently, and Matt looked slowly over at him, his mind clearly elsewhere. "Would you like to go up have a swim?"

Someone snickered, but Matt paid them no heed. Instead he swallowed, and forced his body to move. Slowly, step-by-step, he made his way up to the ledge, until - all to soon - he was standing beside her. Staring down at her strange, new form.

Ally continued to gaze at him steadily, than broke eye contact, turned, and dove back into the water. Resurfacing after a moment to reconnect their gaze.

Matt couldn't move. He just stared at her.

"Go on, Mathue."

Hoarsely, he mumbled, "Matt" then bent to slowly remove his shoes and socks. Sitting down on the ledge, so that his feet swam into the water, he then slipped off the ledge, and gasped as the cold water hit his body. Gulping down the air slowly as he treaded the water, he kept his eyes clenched tight. All of a sudden, he felt something soft -like silk - brush by his legs, and his eyes shot open to see Ally inches from his face.

Are you all right?

Yeah... I think - I thought it would rip open my skin if I touched it? It?

Sorry, your-your tai-

It's all right. This just proves that Dixon was right... for once...

Matt swallowed dryly, and took in another deep breath of the soothing warm air.

Abruptly he felt Ally's hands wrap around his, and gently tug him under. Matt panicked, but Ally's grip reassured him, and he took another deep breath of air; holding it before his head was submerged.

It's all right. Just relax, and concentrate.

What if I drown?

I would never allow that to happen.

Ally took her time moving her tail back and forth through the water; pulling Matt gently along with her, until she felt herself hit the soft sand that covered the base of the tank.

Normally she would have remained at the bottom without having to try at all; but since she held Matt, she had to continuously weave her fins to stay at the bottom.

She looked up at Matt, gazing at his clenched eyes. First would come the panic, she knew...

Matt had his eyes clenched tight against the salty water, and held onto Ally tightly. He knew she wouldn't let him drown - whatever reassurance he had other then her spoken word - but he couldn't shove the feelings of panic from his heart.

His chest began to burn with the need for air, and he moved to swim upwards. But something took hold of his hands and held fast; it wouldn't let him go! He'd drown!

Matt started to panic, and struggled with ever increasing hysteria against the force that kept him submerged. He opened his mouth, and the salty water rushed into his lungs. Burning.

He choked on the water, gasping for air, his state of alarm growing critical. Then, suddenly, he had air. It flooded into his lungs and washed out the water; he inhaled in again, and felt the force withdrawn from his wrists and chest.

He breathed once more, but still didn't open his eyes. *So this is death.* It was a logical statement...

No, silly. Open your eyes.

Matt did as the voice commanded; and another choking attack resulted.

Breathe!

I'm trying!

Not through your nose or *your mouth!*

Matt tried and suddenly the air flooded into his chest again, filling it with beautiful, blissful life.

There, see. It's not that hard.

Matt struggled to open his eyes once again - but as before - he couldn't see a thing beyond the stinging salt and his resulting blurred vision. He snapped his eyes hurriedly shut once more.

Close your other eyelids.

What other eyelids!?

Matt...

What?

Just try.

Matt tried, opening his eyes again, blinking in annoyance to try and clear them. Then, suddenly, he could see. He blinked again, and the water stung again. He shut them tight.

He could hear Ally laughing before him, and opened his eyes again, shut them, then opened them, and again, until he'd gotten his 'other eyelid' to close once more.

Blinking, the eyelid remained. He saw Ally sitting before him, her long, slender black tail curved beneath her. Breathing slowly, he moved his hands to his neck to find three thin slits in his skin just below his ears. As he exhaled, he felt a stream of water rush past his fingertips. It didn't take the water massaging his bare torso to tell him he wasn't wearing his shirt anymore. His chest uncovered and revealed. He realized then that the water was no longer cold - but warm and soothing. Just right. He looked down, and stared in wonder. His tail stretched out before him, blue and glimmering like sapphires.

Feeling movement to his right, he jerked himself from his trance and looked over to see Ally had swum above him, and was presently grinning down at him. *What do you think?*

I think I'm about ready to wake up now...

She chuckled

I don't really know... can we talk - you know - regularly... underwater?

Why don't you try?

Matt opened his mouth uncertainly; worried that if he opened it again, he'd swallow more water. It was hard to breath through his gills, it took concentration, but he assumed it would eventually become second nature. He hoped. He felt the water rush into his mouth, and flicked his tongue in annoyance. "Matt." He said into the water, and was surprised to hear his voice come out of his lips. He looked up at Ally to find her still smiling at him. "Neat, isn't it?" her voice sounded hollow, echoing in the calm recesses of the water.

Weird *is more like it.*

Ally laughed. *You'll get used to it.*

I hope.

Try and move.

Matt glanced back down at his tail, and tried to move. All he managed was a searing pain that raced down his spine and left his tail feeling like it'd just been electrocuted. Before he hadn't been able to feel his tail at all - he liked it better that way.

Ally ceased swimming around him, and floated down to rest beside him. Her face strained. *Your body just isn't used to it yet, it might take a while.*

Not too long, I hope. He smiled at her.

She smiled back, and moved to take a hold of his hands once more. Then she gently tugged him up with her to the surface.

As Matt's head broke the water, he felt the air was cold and chill; like the water had been when he'd first entered it. Using Ally's arm to pull himself over, he rested his arms on the ledge of the tank, looking up as Ally climbed from the water; her tail splitting in two, her fins melding back into the firm, taut appendages that made up the human leg. His eyes then darted to the others, staring up at them from below.

Matt put his head into his folded arms, and took reassuring gasps of air through his gills before daring to try and breath from his nose again. It felt as if he were just learning to breath for the first time in his life. It felt... bizarre.

The tepid water lapped gently against his bare chest, his tail now swaying gently in the water. He couldn't help feeling that this was better than walking - so much easier. Refreshing.

Ally looked down at Dixon in scorn, her gaze cold and piercing. She was back to normal, her fins and scales replaced by her usual attire.

Dennis never noticed, busy as his eyes were: speaking to the others. Catching a glimpse of her from the corner of his eye, he hastily concluded his lesson; "-advise you not to. And now the rest of you may have the day off." He smiled.

Talking excitedly, the others slowly filed from the room.

Dixon watched them go, then - when he was quite sure they were all gone - he turned, and walked up the steps around the tank up to where Ally was standing, her arms crossed and her temper blazing.

"Now as for you two-"

Ally's gaze now positively burning holes through his skull, she cut him off; "Why show everyone else!? Why not just show Matt and me?"

"Because I *wanted* them to know, so that when you two start out in the ocean, they wouldn't be wondering at your disappearance. Now to get back-"

"The ocean?" Matt looked up at him through his wet bangs, his mind still hovering in that distracted place somewhere between abstracted, delirium, and preoccupation.

"Never mind." Dixon waved a passive hand. "Anyway, Ally," he said, turning to face her. "I want you to teach Matt everything about his new form. Teach him how to swim, how best to maneuver - you get the point. Will two weeks be enough time?"

Ally looked from Matt to Dennis and back again. *Enough time for what?* "Alright, sure."

Dixon's eyes twinkled. "Great." And he turned to leave down the stairs, exiting the room as the others had.

Ally watched him go with narrowed eyes, then fell back into the water as if exhausted. Splashing water over the ledge and Matt.

Matt rolled his eyes, shaking himself from dreamland and the water from his face. Then he took a deep breath of air; held it, and let go the ledge, sinking down into the water.

As he sank he opened his gills, taking a deep soothing breath of oxygen from the water. He exhaled, and carefully took another breath. Then - when he felt himself hit bottom - he released it and opened his eyes. He had to blink a couple of times, but eventually managed to lower his other eyelids, looking out at Ally sitting before him; smiling at him.

To think I thought I was the only one!

Matt grinned. *Think again.*

Ally settled herself in the sand before him, and looked up into his dark blue eyes. *Alright, first of all, you'll find that your tail is practically pure muscle. I've found I can go up to seventy miles an hour if the need suits me.*

Matt whistled - or tried to. And ended up choking.

When the spasm had passed, Ally continued. *You'll get used to breathing through your gills, and in time you won't even have to think about doing it. Just like when you learned to walk.*

Hey, Ally?

Yes.

How did you find out you were, were a-

A water sage? The bathtub.

The what?

When I was really little, I found that when I had a bath - so, when I was in water - little scales would appear all over my legs. And sometimes my feet would turn into fins. And when we went to a lake of any sort for a vacation, I'd dive down as deep as I could, and remain there, having learned I had gills. Slowly I began to get more and more fish-like, and eventually I was like you see me now. Ally spread her arms to encompass her entire figure.

But what about your... your, uh... Matt blushed.

Ally blushed slightly, but smiled. *I tied it on myself, before I had nothing.*

Oh. Matt looked down, away from her chest, his cheeks heated.

Ally took no notice, and continued with her story. *It wasn't until we went to the ocean that I really came to realize the import of what I was. I was out extremely far - way past the drop off - when I encountered a shark. Before I could swim away, it charged me, and I curled up into a ball by reflex. Next thing I know, the shark was swimming away; blood trailing after it. I looked at my tail, expecting to see a chunk of it gone. But only a couple of scales were missing - it didn't even hurt. So if a shark ever attacks you, let it go for your tail.* She smiled.

Anyway, there's not much I can really teach you. You just have to learn how to swim on your own. After that, though, you can try some different moves or whatever, like dodging - if you like. Maneuvering capability comes with time - its not really taught.

Matt nodded and looked down again at his tail. It was beautiful, yes, and extraordinary in it's own right. But at the moment; to him it felt like a clumsy dead weight. He looked back up at Ally. "Ally?" he twisted his nose at the echoing sound of his voice.

"Emm-hmm?"

"One more question?"

"Shoot."

"How come when we're, you know, regular humans, we float to the surface in water; but now... now we sink?"

"I'm not a scientist, so I can't give you the scientific reason. But I do know that, for a fact, if a human drowns, they'll sink. But if we were to die in the water, we'd float to the surface. I think it has to do with the different kinds of oxygen we breathe." Ally shrugged.

"I guess that makes sense..." Matt looked back down at his glimmering tail, and flipped it up through the water; searing pain washed through his body once again, and he cringed.

Ally watched him with pity. Not sure what more she could tell him, or how she could help him; after all, her transformation had been slow and had taken time. His had occurred so suddenly, his body was going through a considerable amount of changes it had to adjust to in an extremely short amount of time.

Matt flipped his tail again, and clenched his teeth against the pain. Then he flipped his tail so hard in frustration that his body was propelled up swiftly through the water, before sinking back down to the bottom. Matt clutched at his tail in agony, his teeth clenched over a scream.

Ally gazed at him in sorrow. *This... might take a while.*

You said it.

After five days of 'flicking' his tail, Matt could move his fins without causing himself any serious amount of pain. Then he began to swim. At first he couldn't move his tail properly, and shot through the water in random directions with varying erratic bursts of speed. With Ally laughing as she swam alongside - gracefully and expertly - Matt couldn't help but want to improve - if not for the simple desire to rub it in her face.

Soon though, he got the hang of it, and shot through the water at amazing speeds. Flipping his tail and fins through the water in tandem; he could go as slow or as fast as he wanted by changing the movement and length of his tail strokes.

And soon, he completely forgot to think about breathing.

At one point, Ally had had to rescue a spluttering Cody who was to be found one morning in the tank, half drowned as he'd tried to 'change his appearance'. This he told them as they dragged him from the tank. But in all, Matt found it a heartening experience. And one he wouldn't trade for all the Cody-free mornings in the world.

~

A week and a half later, Matt woke to find himself in a very buoyant mood, and he got up and dressed before Ally had even awoken.

Anxious to get going, he silently left the room, and shut the door softly behind him before tiptoeing down the hall and into the cafeteria. Breakfast was already lain out - as always - and Matt practically shoved down the bacon and eggs before racing off to the 'tank room'. The new name in credit to his amazing abilities.

Without sparing a glance, he took off up the side of the tank, and - having reached the ledge - didn't even bother to remove his socks or shoes before diving straight into the water.

Before the water had always felt cold and alien to him. Now it felt calming and welcoming. He felt his gills open along his neck, and inhaled deeply. Already he was swimming rapidly around, weaving in and out of the reeds and chasing the fish to all areas of the tank. Exalting in his glorious freedom.

Then in elation, he sped up, swam around the tank once more, converged upon the center and swam up. Clearing the water he soared ten feet into the air before flipping, and crashing back down gracefully into the water.

Swimming in circles as he slowed his momentum, he eventually became aware of the sound of muffled clapping sounding from behind him, and spun to see Ally floating a few feet from him.

Impressive. She smiled, than raised an eyebrow. "But can you catch me?" and she sped off around the tank with Matt in hot pursuit.

Ally had told him before that - as a male - and because of the fact that he was slightly larger than her; he'd probably be faster than her. Once he got used to his fins, of course. And as he tore after her, he couldn't help but marvel at his own speed. After so much exertion, he wasn't even tired. He supposed it had something to do with the water, or his tail... -More questions he didn't really need answered.

As he slowly caught up to her, he found himself watching her tail as it flipped effortlessly through the water. Up and down up and down; propelling her around the tank... and further from him! Matt suddenly realized he'd been slowing down, too caught up in her beauty to catch her. He clenched his teeth over a grin, and sped up once more, closing the gap between them. Reaching forward, he caught her tail in both his hands, and managed to pull her to a stop. Causing them both to tumble over in the water.

Ally - laughing and hiccupping uncontrollably - allowed herself to be pulled into Matt's firm embrace. She smiled brilliantly at him, exalted. "Well done." *But if I had wanted to get away, it would have been all too easy.*

Matt raised his eyebrows at her. "Are you insinuating you *wanted* to get caught?"

"No, I just wanted you to feel like you were as good as me."

"So you wanted to get caught." He grinned. *And I already am as good as you.*

Ally looked up at him through her lashes, and held his gaze. *In your dreams.*

Matt suddenly realized that he still held her at her waist, and hurriedly let go. Pushing himself away from her and lowering his gaze. "Sorry, I didn't mean to, to..." he let the sentence drift.

Ally bit her lip, and clasped her hands behind her back. She could still feel the warmth of his hands at her waist where her scales started. The tingling caused by them remaining. Her heart was still beating madly after his nearness.

Unclasping her hands from behind her, she slowly swam over to him, and was about to take his hand in hers when she caught movement from beyond the tank. Looking over, she caught sight of Dixon and Kenith as they entered the room.

Never taking her eyes from them, she motioned for Matt to follow her, and together they rose to the top of the tank. Climbing out, they walked down the steps to confront the two men.

Dennis was smiling as always, but today his grin was larger than usual. (Which was saying something.) "Well, it looks as if Matt's as good as he's going to get. So I'll ask for you two to follow us out to the dock." And without a backwards glance, he and Brandon turned and walked from the room.

Matt exchanged glances with Ally. She shrugged.

Dixon led them down into the entrance hall, then out the two front oaken doors and onto the dock. He gestured towards the water.

Matt and Ally were confused, and they looked at Dixon in hopes of an explanation.

Dennis sighed, "Just get into the water, I'll explain."

Matt shook his head, "Explain now." He told Dennis simply, and beside him he saw Ally fold her arms. This was certainly odd, Dennis wasn't even smiling... in fact he was almost cross. Almost.

Dennis sighed again, and threw up his hands. "Alright, fine. You two will be working with Brandon - as usual - but now you'll be working out in the ocean-"

"Doing what?"

"Just getting used to it and such. Here, you'll need these." Dennis held out his hands; on each were two rings about the size of their wrists, with five small different colored light bulbs spaced along the bands. Matt and Ally each took one.

Matt looked closer at his after strapping it on, and found that beneath each little light bulb was a small button and a label. The purple was labeled: *found something*. The blue was: *come back up*. The red: *stop*, the Green: *go*. And the white bulb was labeled: *be careful*. Matt grew even more confused, and more than slightly worried.

"What are these?" Ally asked, strapping hers onto her wrist as she had seen Matt do.

"Those are so you two and Brandon can communicate when you're underwater, got it?"

They looked over to see Brandon wearing the exact likeness on his left wrist. Both nodded.

"Excellent." Dennis smiled, the act of which slightly reassurred them. "Now Brandon will be following you on the surface, in the *R.K. Prowler*" he gestured over at the large boat floating just out to sea. The self same yacht they'd ridden to arrive at the school.

For a moment Matt wondered how Mr. Kenith would get to it - then he saw the small dingy tethered to the dock.

Dennis continued, "because of a tracking device implanted within your wristbands: he'll be able to see your exact location on the monitor in the yacht. Any questions?"

"Yeah. *Why* are we doing this again?"

"You're just going to be scouting out the ocean, looking for interesting trinkets and the like. Basically it's just to give you two the chance to get more acquainted with the ocean, alright?"

Matt had the disquieting feeling that Dixon wasn't telling the truth, - or was at least omitting parts of it - it seemed to him to be a jumbled mass of excuses. But he nodded like Ally, and dove off the dock with her into the chill water.

When they re-surfaced, Dixon bent down as Brandon hopped into the dingy, started the motor, and tore off towards the yacht. "Just swim out to the *R.K.* and Brandon will tell you where you'll be going first, okay?"

They nodded, and swam under once more.

When they reached the Yacht, Brandon bent down over the railing, and smiled at them. "Just head east for now," he told them, pointing east along the port side. "And remember to check your wristbands frequently just in case I need to tell you something, alright? Good. Now take your time - go for it."

Matt looked over at Ally to see she'd already gone down, and quickly followed her beneath the waves.

The day may have been cold above the water - though never the less calm and bright - but under the waves it was warm and soothing, and Matt swam silently along beside Ally. Hardly even flicking his tail.

All they could see for miles was no end to the kelp bed that stretched on forever, and they wove lazily through the weeds, looking around for anything 'interesting'.

Matt was swiftly bored, and looked over at Ally, swimming slowly beside him. A thought suddenly occurred to him. "Didn't you think Dennis' explanation of why we're doing this seemed a little vague?"

Ally looked over at him, "Yeah, but it doesn't really matter, even though this *is* slightly irksome." she laughed. "It's better than sitting in that castle with everyone staring at you like your crazy all the time."

Matt faced front once again. Ally was right. Compared to the new wave of odd stares they'd been receiving since their first day in the tank... this was paradise.

They swam on.

Around midday, when the sun was sure to be high in the noon sky above the yacht - Matt looked down at his wristband to see the blue bulb was flashing. He waved to get Ally's attention, then led the way back up to the surface, where they found Brandon and a rope ladder waiting for them.

Matt swam back slightly to allow Ally to go first, and watched as she grabbed hold of the ladder, and began to pull herself up. She must have had amazing upper body strength; for without the use of her legs she had to literally lift her own weight from the water. As her tail left the oceans currents, it split, transforming back to normal. When she'd risen a ways above him, he too grabbed hold of the ladder, and hoisted himself up.

On the deck waiting for them was a lunch of hot dogs and milk; and they dug in hungrily, absolutely famished. It was nice, eating on the deck and watching the waves float by. Feeling the cool ocean breeze running her soothing fingers through their hair. But though they took their time, before long they found themselves diving back into the water.

By the time Brandon called them back up to tell them they were going back home, Matt guessed they'd traveled at least sixty miles in total that day. He had his aching tendons to prove it.

Matt stayed at the font of the *Prowler* as they were taken back to the boarding school; watching as the sky slowly darkened, and flared in beauty near the horizon. And by the time they got back to the school, he could see the crescent moon glimmering high above the water, tossing moonlight across the waves.

When they entered the castle, the lights were still on - as Ally assumed they always were. But the castle itself was still and quiet, and the two of them found themselves trying to make as little noise as possible as they made their way to their room down the hall.

Ally was so exhausted that she fell asleep the moment her head hit the covers, and was soon wandering in the blissful tundra that was dreamland. Matt looked over at her before climbing beneath his own covers, and as tired as he was, he just couldn't drift off until well after midnight.

~

At breakfast the next day, both Matt and Ally were dreading their return to the ocean - as beautiful and serene as it was; and were immensely relieved to hear from Dixon that they'd be having another review session that day.

Once the breakfast dishes had been cleared from the table, and the table thrust up against the wall, the teens all lined up along the opposite wall as before, and waited for Dixon to call them forward. Dixon motioned for Cody to come forth, telling him to 'let loose'. Which Cody did: ending in the compete wreckage and absolute dismantlement of the double doors, and the complete and absolute lecture on Dixon's behalf once Cody's inert form had been revived by Matt.

Once the doors - or what was left of them - had been cleared away; Dixon gestured towards Alexander, who - like Cody - hadn't quite gotten the hang of creating physical illusions, and sent a wild stag galloping straight into a wall, creating one hell of a dent.

After the two lowest sages came Kelsi, who literally blew Matt away... before he planted his feet firmly, and sent her own power back at her by accident.

Of course, once he'd revived her; Matt got a big lecture on the meaning of the term: Don't retaliate! Yelled out for him in big bold letters.

Then came Eric, Jason, Kim, and Alexandra, who - upon instruction from Dixon - all fired at Matt at the same time. He had to admit that they were a bit stronger than last time, but still not strong enough to get past only half of his shield. They hadn't even forced a weak point.

Then came the highlight of the morning - a climax Ivy would rather have circumvented.

"Ivy." Dennis smiled at her. "Let us see you try your luck against Ally once more."

Ally stepped forward upon hearing her name. She raised no shield, but stared Ivy straight in the eye. Her face more unimpassioned than Matt had ever seen it.

Dixon looked over at Ally for a moment, wondering if perhaps he'd simply missed her raise her shield, then shrugged. "Go on then, Ivy."

Ivy swallowed, and shut her eyes for a moment. Then she raised her hands, and aimed.

Matt saw it all in slow motion: Ally smiling, and staring at Ivy. Ivy not looking at Ally's eyes, but at her chest, where she aimed the vines that shot out of thin air at her command.

The vines caught Ally and tightened around her body, raising her from the ground. But Ally didn't stop smiling - no: grinning. And as the vines got tighter, Matt was suddenly enlightened to what should have been obvious.

"NO, ALLY- DON'T!!!"

He raced forward into the vines, slashing at them with his hands infused with energy - just as Ally sent a wave of power straight down the vines towards Ivy. Finding the vines cut, the energy went directly into the next best thing: Matt.

The energy surged into his body like lightning – shocking, destructive. He clenched his teeth and fists against the onslaught; but despite the pain, knew he'd be fine. The amount of energy Ally had meant for Ivy would seriously harm the 'insignificant' level six sage. But to Matt, it really only singed his insides a bit.

Ally gasped and stopped the flow of energy at once. Watching in horror as Matt clutched at his chest and collapsed to the floor. Gasping and choking for breath.

"No!" she breathed, and stumbled over to him. Skidding on her knees the last few feet before she reached his suddenly still body. *Please no!*

Matt, forgive me! I'm so sorry! She rolled him over, and was relieved to see him breathing hard; but still smiling.

He grinned wider at her look of intense relief. "It'll take a lot more than that to do *me* in."

Suddenly, without cause, Ally wanted to crush him to her chest. But even as the thought passed through her mind, she knew it was crazy. Instead she smiled sheepishly at him, and offered him her hand.

Matt took it gratefully, than clutched at his heart convulsively as a new wave of pain shot through it, threatening to throw him off his feet. But he stood tall, and kept his teeth clenched against the pain. *I found a cure for heart attacks...*

Ally struggled to keep her laughter to herself.

Dennis was positively brimming with fury as he marched over to them. His fists and jaw clenched to cover his anger - though he wasn't doing that great a job of it. He fumed silently at the two of them for a moment, forced himself to calm down, and turned towards the others. "Take the rest of the day off." He told them stiffly, almost snappishly, then turned back to glare at the two level tens.

"You... you... you- you- ARGH!!!" he let out a deep breath. "Alright! I can understand why you want revenge on Ivy, Ally, but if Matt hadn't intervened I... I- Just go to your room!"

Ally raised her eyebrows at Dixon, but obeyed nonetheless; and walked stiffly towards the hall. Matt following on her heels; though he was sure Dennis had meant the punishment for Ally only.

Closing the door behind him, Matt turned to find Ally standing motionless in the middle of the room, her back facing him. He gazed at her for a moment, than walked slowly over, placing a hand on her slender shoulder; noticing in concern that it was shaking. "Ally..."

Whatever it was he'd been expecting - it wasn't anything like the reaction he got. As soon as her name left his lips, Ally whipped around and buried her head into his chest, her hands clutching at his shirt, her sobs racking her body.

Matt wasn't exactly sure what she was crying about - surely not what had happened just now? But he knew that the best thing he could do for her was to let her get it all out. So he placed his arms around her in assuagement, and let her cry into his shirt. His heart thumping in excitement or panic at her nearness - as per usual.

~ 9 ~

Miranda smiled around at them all seated at the breakfast table. Looking over each of them in turn. "Whom here knows what day it is?"

Matt glimpsed Jason roll his eyes.

Seeing no answer forthcoming, Mrs. Dixon prodded her audience, "Aw, c'mon. Such an important day to *all* of you - I'm sure *one* of you at least knows what day it is? ..."

"It's the twelfth." Kim said, her voice toneless.

"What?" Kelsi looked confused.

Jason leant towards her across the table. "Listen, Kelsi, what day is it tomorrow?"

"The... thirteenth."

"Of...?"

"February..."

"Exactly." Jason sat back and tilted his chair; folding his arms as if he'd just answered the great question.

Kelsi was still flummoxed. Then abruptly her face lit up in realization, and exclaimed: "It's my birthday!"

Jason smacked his forehead.

At that moment, Dennis entered the room through the now doorless entryway; his face shining. "It's not just your birthday, Kelsi. It's also-"

"MINE!" Cheered everyone around the table. The girls in particular squealing and shrieking wildly in ululation.

"-as well." Dennis finished, somewhat deprived.

"And since it's all of your birthdays at once," Miranda continued, her face the epitome of pride and excitement "we've decided to throw a party for all of you-"

"What do you mean: all our birthdays are at once?" Eric stood in his chair, he and the others looking bewildered and more than a little perplexed.

Dennis smiled; the twinkle back and shining. "Funny you should ask that, Eric. You were born on February the thirteenth at precisely one in the morning - am I right?"

Eric nodded.

"Well, everyone else here was born on the exact date - just at different times: Jason was born at two in the morning, Kim at three, Matt at four, Ally at five, Alexandra at six, Alexander at seven, Ivy at eight, Cody at nine, Kelsi at ten, and of course, Eric was born at one. Making Eric the oldest, and Kelsi the youngest." He smiled around at them all.

Alexander blinked, "That's *too* weird!"

"Bizarre." Echoed Alexandra.

Cody whooped. "COOL!"

"Anyway." Miranda called their attention back to herself, "The theme is miscellaneous; so you can wear whatever you like." she smiled at their looks of relief - it wasn't as if anyone had anything exotic or otherwise to wear anyway. "The party starts at ten this evening, and there will be no chaperone-"

A cheer went up from the surrounding kids.

Miranda smiled, and shouted to be heard above the ensuing noise and discussion. "So we expect you to behave yourselves!"

Brandon looked then as if the pronouncement went against all his better judgment.

Dennis then fixed each of them in turn with a stern glare; the intended effect somewhat belayed by the twinkle in his eyes. Silence reigned. "To make it better for everyone, you are *all* required to attend - though you may stay for as long as you wish. That sound reasonable to everyone?"

They all nodded happily, and Dixon beamed.

As everyone set off to their different classes for the day, chattering excitedly about the party; Miranda made her way over to Matt and Ally. She smiled sweetly at them, and asked carefully: "If it's not too much trouble, can I ask you to give up your ocean outing for today and come help me with my class?"

Ally and Matt exchanged glances - what more could they have wished for!

Miranda, however, took their silence as rejection. "All I need is for you to-"

"We'll do it." Matt said simply, and then he and Ally followed a happy Miranda to her level-five class on the second floor.

The classroom was the one right beside the tank room, Matt noted - but was baffled he'd never known. The entire room was covered all over with little craters - in the walls, in the door, on the ceiling... Everywhere Matt looked was another hole."

Miranda looked around gloomily. "As you can see, they desperately need your help." And she led the way into the room with Matt and Ally in tow - both of them trying their best not to laugh or grin.

Eric, Jason, Kimberly and Alexandra were already there and waiting at the back of the classroom. Kim and Jason already in a heated argument.

"Settle down, settle down you two. Now today, Matt and Ally are here to provide you all with something less fragile to shoot at."

Oh great. Once again we're *the targets!*

Ally snorted.

Miranda spun around, "What's so funny?" She asked, her eyebrows narrowed.

Nothing, just your high-pitched squeaky voice - were you a mouse in a past life?

She couldn't help herself; Ally started to laugh, but stopped when she saw Miranda's serious visage. Holding her stomach, Ally wiped a tear from her eye, and struggled to meet her gaze without cracking up. "Nothing, Mrs. Dixon. Just something Matt thought."

"Matt... thought...? Oh yes! Brandon told me about that new ability of yours. Up 'til now I hadn't believed a word of it. Now, if you two will go stand at the front of the class room," she gestured yonder at the dented blackboard at the front of the class, "we can begin."

Matt walked over to the blackboard that more closely resembled a battlefield, with Ally beside him. Turning, they raised their shields - but only half of them, as usual.

"Oh! Raise the whole damn things!" Miranda spat, suddenly infuriated.

Ally looked alarmed, "But Mrs. Dixon, at their level-"

"Oh just do it! Now," she said, turning sweetly towards her pupils, "go ahead."

Ally looked over her shoulder at Matt, as if seeking support. She was disappointed, however, when he shrugged, and raised his entire shield. "We warned you." He hissed quietly, staring pointedly over at Miranda.

But Ally wasn't going to give up. "Mrs. Dixon, if they shoot at us with our *full* shields up - there will be dire consequences. For them!"

"Oh tish-tosh. Ready, and... go!"

Matt saw Ally close her eyes tightly, and he felt a strong desire to do the same. But curiosity to see what would happen overwhelmed him, and he looked up at Jason; the only one brave enough - either that or the only one arrogant enough - to fire at him and Ally.

Jason smirked at him, and charged his energy. Then he aimed the small marble at his shield, and fired.

What happened next happened so fast, Matt wasn't entirely sure it had even happened at all.

He watched in fascination as the small sphere pelted towards him, and made contact with his shield. Unsurprisingly, the barrier absorbed the attack; but extremely surprisingly, the shield then - completely of its own volition - shot a stream of energy back at Jason; who crumpled instantaneously.

Miranda rushed over to Jason to feel for a pulse, than whirled on Matt, who looked her straight in the eye without feeling. Her voice faltered at her lips.

Matt lowered his shield, but refrained from breaking eye contact. Finally he opened his mouth, and chose his words carefully, "We did warn you. At this level, they're not strong enough to attack our full shields without stopping their attack from multiplying and being fired back at them." This he ascertained through inference. Not even he could have predicted what would happen. "I don't think even Ally could have stopped that. But he's probably not dead; his attack was to weak for that." He smirked inwardly. And without another word, Matt raised his right hand, and shot a stream of sapphire energy over to the motionless form that was Jason; who was abruptly sent gasping for breath. Jerking into a sitting position he proceeded to hack and choke, struggling to regain his breath.

After Kim had stopped laughing at and heckling Jason; Miranda agreed to let Ally and Matt put their shields to half strength. And they spent the rest of the day standing up at the front of the classroom as targets. With no place to sit and no breaks to cool their fastly broiling tempers.

~

Matt slammed the door malevolently behind him without looking at it; the force he used shaking the room to its foundations.

"I know." Ally sat up on her bed and met his gaze with understanding, "Just try not to think about it."

He fell down angrily onto his bed, "I'm starting to think that a boring day out in the ocean would have been preferable to that!" Still fuming, Matt threw one of his pillows into the air and blasted it venomously with a fist-sized orb of energy, sending feathers everywhere, like feather fireworks. She watched them float back down for a moment, then brushed one from where it'd landed on her leg, and got softly off her bed. Walking across the room to sit beside Matt.

He felt her sit down beside him, but neglected to roll over to face her; already her nearness was intoxicating.

Ally reached over him, and took one of his hands, gently pulling him over to face her, she smiled warmly, "Got that out of your system." She said succinctly, "Feel better?"

Matt met her gaze with equal warmth. *I do now.* "Yeah."

~

By supper, Matt still couldn't get Ally's face from his thoughts. And as the dishes were cleared from the table, he found himself leaving before desert. He walked aimlessly down the corridor, and found himself before the silver letter five before he even realized where he was.

Staring at the door for a moment, he stood trying to figure out just how he came to be there; and attempting in vain to sort out his thoughts. Before long he gave up, however, and pushed the door open, stepping inside.

Closing the door, leaving it unlocked; he leapt onto his bed and drew his knees in close to his body, rolling into a ball and burying his head into his arms.

He had so many thoughts – emotions - to sort out. If only he could think straight. (Or at least on one track for more then a minute.) But every time he tried, her face swam into his thoughts, smiling and blinking slowly at him. Her eyes shining gently with an inner beauty, a warmth and understanding.

Matt shrunk away from the image, unsure of its meaning, its portent. Dubious of his own feelings. Un-trusting of his emotions. All this time, it had been hovering in the air; since the very first he'd lain eyes on her - that day sailing to the school on the *R.K. Prowler*. Through all the time they'd spent together; all of their diminutive adventures. Through the hurt and joy. Throughout it all he'd been shielding himself from the inescapable truth - and all the while it had been furiously slapping him in the face, trying desperately to get his attention.

And now it laughed at him, mocking him for a fool. And he was finally able to see past that velvet curtain of obscurity - finally he could come to terms with what he'd hidden from even himself - his love for her.

~

Ally watched Matt leave, his face blank, though revealing an inner turmoil.

She respected his privacy enough not to go after him - but she longed to go after him. To feel his arms wrapped protectively around her body, comforting her, shielding her; like that night after the practice session.

She'd always been independent - strong and unallied. Now... Now she felt weak, helpless. Like a part of her was missing. She felt vulnerable; and now she knew why.

It wasn't just physical attraction, she knew - it was him. His being. His smile. He'd always been strong where she'd been weak... in mind, and in correlation. He trusted his instincts - she trusted logic. That's where she'd met her downfall; always coming to the conclusion people were out to get her. Never bothering to find out more, always believing she knew everything. Matt went out of his way to understand others, to find a diplomatic means of resolve to dispute, whereas she'd use avoidance or force. He wore his heart out on his sleeve - she kept hers hidden away and locked in a ten-volt vault.

She loved him for who he was; not for who everyone else wanted him to be - or for who they perceived him to be; but for whom *he* was. For the simple fact he was her other half, the equilibrium to her treacherous soul. She couldn't remember a time - bar the time they'd first met - when he'd met her gaze without that same look in his eyes: of friendship, of trust.

And now - as she came to terms with the full import of this realization - she was uncertain as to his feelings for her. He was kind and loving in a brother-like fashion; but that was something of an entirely different nature.

Her mind brimming with unanswered questions and inquisitiveness, Ally sat and waited – impatiently - until everyone else was through eating and the dishes were cleared. Then she got stiffly to her feet, and walked softly down the hall to their room. Pushing lightly on the door as she reached it, she walked unobtrusively into the room.

Her heart beating fast, she looked around to see Matt lying face first on his bed, reading a sports magazine.

He said "hi" without even looking up.

For a moment she found her courage worthless. Then she padded softly over to his bed, and sat down on the edge, as far from his warm body as she could without falling to the floor. Looking over at the ornate silver mirror on the opposite wall, she swallowed hard. "Matt, I... have something to tell you."

Matt looked up then, and caught her gaze. The beat of her heart sped to a frantic tempo.

Her mouth worked soundlessly for a moment, then she managed to croak out a sound, faint, as if coming from the pit of her heart. "I... I lov-"

"Shh..." Matt rose up swiftly, and placed his fingers gently to her lips, effectively halting any further sound. Then he reached up with his other hand, gently tracing the simple curve of her jaw; the flesh of her flushed cheeks. Always maintaining eye contact, keeping her still, entranced. He then gradually lent forward, bringing their lips into near-contact, his breath ghosting across her sensitive flesh-

Breathing hard, Ally jerked up into a sitting position. Finding herself above - and quite by herself - the covers on her bed. Her heart beating madly, she could feel the warmth of his breath still on her cheek, she'd been so sure...

She dared a glance over to find Matt still on his chest, reading the same stupid magazine.

As her breathing returned to stasis, Ally returned to her pillow. She must have fallen asleep as soon as she'd hit her bed - she'd been so tired lately... She was just being frivolous.

~

A gasp caught Matt's attention, and he looked up to find Ally breathing hard on her bed, her eyes wide and staring. She'd been sleeping just a moment ago... she must have had a bad dream. Telling himself it was none of his business, he turned back to his magazine.

He wasn't really reading, he wasn't even looking at the pictures; he just flipped erratically through the pages, aimlessly - her gaze lying in wait beneath his eyelids.

Heedless to how long he'd lain there, distracted, Matt found himself desperately trying to remove her face from his mind. Seeing her smile every time he closed his eyes was... doing things to him. Making him squirm. Finally he glanced up at the clock - desperate for any means of distraction; and found it was already ten twenty.

"Awe crap!" Matt jumped off his bed, still staring at the digital clock above the door.

"What?"

Matt tilted his head over his shoulder to look at her, and grinned sheepishly. "Nothing." *Just the time.*

Glancing up at the clock, her eyes popped and went rolling across the floor, "We're late!" she screeched.

Guess we'd better get going, huh?

Ya' think!?

~

As they stepped into the cafeteria, unpunctual, Cody bounced over to them with a plate loaded with cake and other sweets and goodies, "Hey Matt! Ally! We thought you guys weren't coming!"

Matt couldn't help the grin that infected his face, "Yeah well, the clock in our room is kinda... off." He shot Ally a look from the corner of his eye.

She stifled her laugh behind a hand, it coming out as more of a strange squeak-like choke.

Cody nodded enthusiastically, and bounded back over to the buffet table - much more interested in attaining a sugar-high then learning about too-slow-clocks - his mouth too busy being stuffed to talk.

Matt took in the liveliness of the room; filled with balloons and confetti of every shape and size. He saw Eric trying to persuade Kelsi and Ivy to dance with him, and Jason and Kim were doing a weird sort of waltz in the middle of the room; Kimberly slapping him across the face every once in a while when she caught him looking down her shirt. Alexandra was over in a far corner of the room - trying to teach Alexander to waltz - keyword there: trying - while her feet got more and more damaged by the minute. And of course, Cody was over by the buffet table, stuffing his face with anything and everything that looked good or was certain to give him root canal, which - as Matt noticed - was pretty much everything on the table.

His ears perked up as the song changed, and he listened closely. It was an average song - not too slow or too fast. He'd never discovered exactly what it was about...

He abruptly felt a gentle touch to his skin, and looked down to find Ally's graceful fingers resting on his arm. Her lips twitched, and she began to tug him out onto the dance floor. Behind them Kim shoved Jason out of the room for trying to get his hand down her pants.

Matt gave her a hesitant, lopsided sort of grin. *I've never danced.*

Neither have I - just go with it. She couldn't help the thump of her heart, and the smile that spread to her eyes.

He gave in, and allowed her to pull him onto the floor. His body remaining fixed, he simply watched as she took his hands in hers, placing them at her waist. Then she looked up, caught him staring at her, and smiled. *Just go with it.*

Moving her hands to his neck for lack of anything else to do with them - she then swayed her hips a little, and with them, his arms and thusly his upper torso. He laughed at the mental image. Gradually they began to move in time with the music; swaying gently, gracefully - erotically. Matt found the task of keeping his hands fixed at her waist to be challenging. He could feel the warmth radiating from her body, the pulse beneath his fingers; the creamy flesh barred by her clothing.

Heat slowly radiated from his form, and he felt his visage growing heated.

Swallowing he struggled to remain in control, to enjoy the scenario - not fear it.

Attached to him, - literally - Ally was having similar problems. Being so near, practically rubbing against him, her arms linked about his neck; she could feel the rhythmic beat of his heart. His breath danced across her cheek.

Unnoticed by both, her form shifted unconsciously nearer to his.

The music had faded to a soft hum, the voices and shrieks around them dulling to a murmur. All that remained was the feel of their bodies entwined. All that mattered was the mutual gaze remained. Their dark, sapphire irises reflecting the disco ball above and their mutual feelings in volume.

Perhaps that was what spooked the rabbit.

Gazing into his eyes, she abruptly felt him shift closer, and lent reflexively into his embrace; practically hanging off him. Her arms tightening about his neck, his fingers digging ever so slightly into the tender flesh at her waist. He blinked, and their eyes were inches apart; she could see the affliction, the love - the lust.

His breath warmed her nose and her heart pounded against her chest until it hurt.

He tilted his head, his eyes half-mast, and brushed his lips to hers. A tingling sensation that could only be described as joy shot through him excitedly.

The touch of his lips on hers shocked her jarringly back into reality. Her breath hitched, the music came back in volume, and the voices of the people around them thundered in her ears.

She panicked, and pushed away without thinking.

Staring at him fearfully for a moment, she dashed from the room.

Matt was shell-shocked.

Stunned.

That had gone completely over his head.

He stood frozen for a moment longer, then wandered slowly over to the wall in a state of delirium; sliding down to the floor in confusion. His eyes overflowing with emotion.

What had he done? He'd thought... he'd thought she felt the same. Her eyes so clear - so full of fire - of affection. The way she moved against him - he groaned. He wasn't helping his situation. Forcing himself to think this through, he came to two reasonable conclusions - she wasn't attracted to him in any way shape or form. Or... she just wasn't ready for a relationship of such.

Sighing, he raked his fingers through his hair. Give her time or... does she want to talk?

A shrill whine shot from his throat, lost to the noise in the room - females! Why did they have to be so utterly complex!?

Knowing he really had only one choice, as her room was his and he truly could not avoid her; he pushed himself to his feet, and made his way out into the entryway. *Besides.* He thought, *I'm too damn impatient to wait.* He grinned.

He turned, debating in which direction to head first; and caught a glimpse of Jason and Kim arguing inches from one another down the hall a bit. Swallowing his irrational anxiety, he moved in their general direction. "Hey... guys?"

Jason turned away from Kim to glare at him, his eyes practically blazing with fury.

Matt stepped back a bit, "I don't mean to intrude, but did Ally - by chance - come by here?"

"Someone did, I'm not sure if it was Ally though. They were in quite a hurry; ran that way." Kim pointed down the hall.

"Appreciate it." He called over his shoulder, and ran down the hall towards the opposite end of the corridor. Behind him he heard a muffled gasp, and then a loud *SLAP!* that resounded upon the walls.

He hit the stairs three at a time, than looked around uncertainly when he reached the landing. *Would she be in the tank?*

After a moment's deliberation, he headed down the hall, and entered the tank room. *Well that's a definite no.* He bit his lip. *Where then? ... Maybe the balcony...*

He raced from the room, back down the hall, and out onto the East balcony. His footsteps echoing eerily off the walls.

The snow swirled around his feet as he slowed at the ledge, the evening breeze causing his horsetail to fly and his clothes to billow about him. Looking around the undeniably empty escarpment, he sighed. *No... This was pointless-* if Ally didn't want to be found, he wasn't going to find her.

Stuffing his hands into his pockets, heating himself slightly against the cold, he made his way back into the castle. Resigned to wait for Ally 'til she was ready on her own time.

A pair of deep, sapphire eyes watched him from her hiding place. A trillion thoughts and emotions raced around through her mind, but her eyes and heart remained fixed permanently upon his back; watching as he slowly turned and started back into the castle.

Suddenly, her heart came to its decision.

Who are you looking for?

Matt spun around, his eyes darting - his hands flew from his pockets to balance himself as he slipped slightly on the frozen stone.

Then he looked up.

He saw her, sitting lightly on the top of one of the towers. He raised his eyebrows. *How the hell did you get up there?*

Ally couldn't help her smile, gesturing at the side of the tower. Following the sweep of her arm, Matt noticed the vines growing up along the stones. *You have got to be kidding.*

The distance between them as it was; Matt could still hear her silent laughter as it broke through the chill night air - warming him far more than his energy ever could. He took once last look at how high the tower was, swallowed - made a show of rolling up sleeves that weren't there, and hen turned back to the vines. Walking stiffly over to the base of the tower, his hands clenching and unclenching at his sides, he took a hold of the frozen plants, and pulled himself up.

He wasn't afraid of heights, but he avoided looking down all the same. The vines were icy, and hard to get a hold of - but were strong and more then capable of holding his weight when he did. This didn't stop him from slumping over the shingles in relief when he'd finally reached the top, of course. Gazing half-drunkenly up at Ally in accomplishment.

You did that on purpose. He accused, taking her offered hand, and pulling himself upright, still too diminished and lost for breath to attempt speech right at that moment. *There was probably an easier way, you just wanted me to suffer!*

Ally smiled, but made a point of avoiding that topic. "So, who were you looking for?" she asked instead.

Matt looked up at her, grinning stupidly, "I've found her."

Ally blushed, and looked down at her feet. Twiddling her fingers.

Matt gazed at her for a moment longer, than turned his face up towards the moon. Soaking in its brilliance, pondering his next move.

She'd called out to him - she wasn't avoiding him... give her a bit more time.

The silence they lapsed into was slightly uncomfortable, but not intolerable - and they both remained silent for a while after; sitting still and awkward on the chill shingles.

After a time, Matt drew a shallow breath, exhaling deeply. "Nice night..."

Her gaze shot to the heavens, "Yes its beautiful..."

He looked back at her. "...Like you."

She turned to face him slowly, her breath drawn through parched lips. "Matt I, I want to apologize. I had no right to shove you away like that. Its just that, that..." she paused, struggling to find the right words.

Matt swallowed and moistened his lips. The sheer beauty of her body caused his heart to stop; caused it to cower in the pit of his chest. He knew where he stood - now where was she?

He started carefully, "Perhaps all you need is... to try again..."

She looked at him carefully - searching for an ulterior motive, an intension of harm. Any reason at all for her to back away. Were second chances really given that easily? He met her gaze calmly, and all she saw was love - pure and simple. Doubt and uncertainty fled her in an instant, leaving her cold and alone, afraid, and in need of comfort.

She started to shake, but not from fear.

Gazing at her steadily, he brought his hand up to stroke her cheek, smooth and warm against his fingers; flushed from the cold. His mind in stasis, he gazed into her eyes; cool and sparkling in the light of the moon. He didn't have a choice. If he didn't, he'd regret it for the rest of his life... And she'd never trust him again. - not that he had even the slightest intention of backing down now.

He looked into her mind as he shifted his body towards her; leant forward, then stopped; staring into her clear, blue eyes - searching for any sign of fear or rejection, stroking her warming cheek softly with his thumb. She didn't jerk away, flinch, or cower. She knew what she wanted, now - and would have it.

Before she could react, he'd closed the distance between them, and touched his lips to hers - kissing her deeply, demandingly, but gently - ever careful of that timid coney ready to bolt.

For a moment he just waited for her to slap him, or push him away, and he braced himself for the blow. But she had absolutely no thoughts left of running. He felt her wrap her arms tightly around his neck, and kiss him back; her breath drawn warm against his neck.

Moving his hands to rest at the small of her back, Matt slowly pulled back - releasing her bottom lip gently. And opened his eyes to find her gazing at him, her smile reaching past her eyes into the stars. Falling into his arms, her breath ghosted across his ear; "You've no idea how long I've wanted you to do that."

Matt was sill taking deep breaths from his emotional landslide, clutching her desperately to his chest. "I love you, Ally." he swallowed, "I've loved you... since they day I saw you - on the *R.K.* coming here."

Ally smiled, fastly growing weary. *I know. Your kiss told me everything.*

The bright, crimson harvest moon grinned down upon them from the heavens. The stars winking to one another as they watched the two trembling figures seated below on the tall castle turret. The only witnesses that night to the admittance and acceptance of something difficult to understand, but unbelievable to undergo.

Part 2

What Amity Can Achieve

~ 10 ~

Matt and Ally stood near the forward rail on the *R.K. Prowler*, staring calmly out into the open water. Brandon was taking them back to the place they had ended at the last time they were out in the ocean; he still hadn't told them *why*. The salty sea spray and the wind in their faces served to chill them before they were severed to the warm, apathetic ocean.

Distracted from their thoughts by sharp footsteps heard on the deck behind them, they turned to see Brandon approaching them from the cabin. He was holding up their communicators, and was accompanied by an extremely severe looking woman with hard black eyes and tightly bound hair; who held herself ridged and stiff as a board.

Her face could almost be described as angry, and her expression told them quite plainly she didn't wish to be standing there.

Holding out their communicators, Brandon introduced her. "This is Miss Gilbertson, Ally, Matt." They nodded politely as they took the devices from his hands and strapped them to their wrists. "She'll be accompanying you two today - for you will be reaching the trench, and we don't want you to get lost now do we?"

Matt raised an eyebrow, "Trench?"

"Yes, the Juan de Fuca trench-"

"And what makes you think we'll get lost and *she* wont?" Ally asked in subordination; not liking it much.

"Because she's spent her entire life exploring the trench, and you two should listen to her." He left it at that, eyes narrowing.

Matt tilted his head slightly, his lips quirking, "How much have you told her?"

Grinning, Brandon replied, "Only what I've just told you."

Matt and Ally exchanged glances; twin smiles etching across their faces.

"Now," Brandon continued, struggling to keep his expression under control. "I know you two can talk just fine under water, but you'll have to speak up a little so Miss Gilbertson will be able to hear you-"

"Are you implying I have bad hearing, Mr. Kenith?"

"Not at all Miss Gilbertson, not at all." He winked at the other two.

Gilbertson stared daggers into his back for a moment, then turned to the two teens, her eyes narrowing further. "Alright then, Mr. Dixon has paid me very well to be a tour guide, and you wouldn't want his money to be wasted now would you? So I'll expect you two to listen carefully to every word of mine. I don't want two dead kids on my hands-"

Matt and Ally rolled their eyes, "Miss Gilbertson, I think there is a very slim chance of us dying in the ocean." Matt offered her a fake smile.

"Oh." Miss Gilbertson raised her eyebrows, "And what makes you so certain-"

"Now," Brandon interjected quickly, "You two, as you know, can swim much faster than Miss Gilbertson, so you'll-"

"I *do not* appreciate insults Mr. Kenith-"

"-Have to swim a mite slower, alright."

"Will do." Matt saluted him.

Ally giggled, and behind Brandon, Miss Gilbertson mumbled about unappreciative children.

Ally looked around Brandon over at her, *Oh, and one more thing Miss Gilbertson, we're not children - we're sixteen - and you are* way *out of our league.*

Matt hastily turned his laugh into a hacking cough.

Brandon's speech completed, Miss Gilbertson turned back to the 'kids', "Now, let's get you two suited up - why are you rolling your eyes at me?"

Ally looked over at her, "We'll wait for her at the bottom." Then she and Matt turned, and dove over the railing into the water.

Miss Gilbertson ran to the railing, "Foolish children! How far do they expect to get? They'll freeze!" then she whirled as she felt a hand on her shoulder.

Brandon was smirking broader than ever. "Watch the water." Then he reached over to his left wrist, and hit a button on the band that resided there.

~

"What do you think she'll do when she sees us like this?" Matt asked, looking up at the hull of the boat as it floated over their heads.

"Hopefully she'll throw herself overboard." Ally swam up over him, and tousled his hair, tugging out the band that held his hair at the back of his head in a horsetail.

Matt smiled sarcastically, reaching up to tug her down. Holding her tightly, he lent forward to capture her lips with his; distracting her while he pried her fingers away from his elastic; taking it back from her.

Pushing herself playfully away from him, Ally wrinkled her nose at his new look, "It doesn't suit you." she said, watching his hair as it fanned out behind him in the water.

Matt smiled at her as he tied his hair back, "Better?"

Ally swam back into his arms. "Much." She smiled and moved to nuzzle him lightly - then she noticed his band, fastened loosely about his wrist, and looked at her own. The blue light was blinking. She stared back up at the haul of the boat, "He wants us to come back up…"

Matt, - her body still pressed against his - followed her gaze, "Why?"

Ally shrugged, then swam out of his arms like a greased fish, heading for the surface.

Rolling his eyes, he followed after her.

~

"Well, that's that then, they've been under for *far* too long. If they haven't frozen, they've drowned - foolish children!" Miss Gilbertson fumed, "I want to make it clear I am not responsible-"

"Shut up, will you." Brandon snapped, for once actually loosing his temper, "Just watch the - ah."

Ally's head broke the surface, her hair plastered to her face, and Miss Gilbertson looked on in wonder, "Why, she's not even shaking…"

Matt came up beside her, and raised his eyebrows up at Brandon, "Why'd you call us back up?"

"And what's taking *her* so long?" Ally nodded her head at Gilbertson, displeasure clearly visible in her eyes.

Both were waving their arms in the water - acting like they were actually treading. As if they needed to.

"She thought you were dead." Brandon called down, "Would you two kindly show her what you're capable of in the water, and that your not about to drown for her pleasure."

Matt glanced at Ally and smirked. They both halted the movement of their tails and sank back beneath the waves. Then, once they were far enough down, they flipped their powerful flukes and sped up towards the surface, cleared the water in tandem, flying five feet into the air; splashing back down into the ocean with grace.

There they winked at one another, and came to rest once more at the sandy floor of the ocean.

Back on deck, Miss Gilbertson was staring dazedly at the water, an expression of the deepest shock etched upon her wrinkled visage.

Brandon patted her on the back, "They're waiting, better get going." And he walked back towards the cabin, his hands stuffed into his pockets - smiling.

~

Matt swam beside Ally, following a ridged Gilbertson along the ocean floor. She'd put their 'abnormality' aside for the moment, and persisted to show them the Juan de Fuca trench.

Swimming behind her was no easy matter, as they had to practically crawl along the sand to remain behind her.

Matt watched her flippers stream trough the water for a moment longer before his annoyance took the better of him, and he swam up beneath her.

"So..." he smiled, coming up in front of her from behind, and nearly startling her out of her wet suit. "How close are we?"

He heard Ally laugh as she swam up beside him, and he grinned even broader.

Miss Gilbertson scowled, "Another twenty miles, at least." He voice sounded muffled from behind her mouth piece - and echoed almost as if she were speaking through a long hollow tube.

Matt groaned, "Let us carry you, it'd be *much* faster." He begged. The tendons in his tail had already stiffened up from the strain and lack of movement.

"Absolutely not! I will *not* be towed across the ocean by a pair of fishes!!! Besides," she said, sticking up her pointed, weathered nose. "I doubt you could go any faster. We are currently traveling at two miles per hour - you can't get much faster than that without a machine!"

Ally looked at Matt, "Oh we can't, can't we?"

So swiftly Gilbertson had hardly anytime to react at all, Ally and Matt had taken an arm each and had torn off with her in tow. Moving at full speed just inches from the sandy floor, leaving a trial of spinning sand in their wake.

Between them they only just managed to keep their hold as Miss Gilbertson screamed bloody murder and thrashed in their grip; almost loosing her mask as she was dragged along through the water at almost sixty miles per hour. Fish, reeds and bubbles flying past her unnoticed, her life accompanying them.

Above the waves, Brandon watched the monitor with amusement as the white dot representing the slow moving Gilbertson was caught in-between the two red dots - which had previously been meandering through the water behind her, moving back and forth in boredom.

Now the three inter-locked dots moved across the monitor twenty times faster than before, and Brandon grinned as he sped the Yacht up to keep pace with the three figures directly below him.

He was most pleased to see Ally and Matt take charge; it would have taken them the rest of the day to reach the trench if they hadn't taken matters into their own hands - or fins as it were.

~

Matt's tail was feeling much improved; he swung it up and down through the waves, elated in the thrill and feel of the water as it coursed smoothly along his powerful, sleek body.

Suddenly, the ocean floor dropped from beneath them, and all Matt could see was black.

He and Ally stopped their forward pull abruptly to gaze down into the darkness; amazed that such a thing could exist. Trying to gauge the distance to the bottom - this being no easy task as they couldn't even see it.

Miss Gilbertson tugged herself free from their arms. Catching sight of their bemused expressions, she smiled; pleased to see they were speechless. She gazed out over the trench like a mother would appraise her children. "The Juan de Fuca trench." she said slowly, "About a mile wide, and a hundred and ten miles long. Gary, eat your heart out."

Ally looked over at her, "Who's Gary?'

"My partner. He always used to say that nothing could beat the Grand Canyon - well, here's proof he was wrong!"

"Was? ..."

"He's dead, fell out of a hot air balloon when he tried to catch a hawk with his bare hands. At least the hawk got a free meal; all they found was the bottom half of his body, and even then almost all of his flesh had been stripped from the bones."

Ally was stricken, she glanced over at Matt with horror pooling in her luscious blue orbs. *How could anyone talk about their lover in such a way!?*

He shrugged. *Though I know I could never go on living if I lost you.* He gazed at her steadily.

Ally blushed and adverted her eyes - her heart hammering.

Not having heard the exchange, Miss Gilbertson started down into the trench. "Well enough chit-chat, I've been hired to show you the trench - and tour guide I'll be! At least it's not bad work for fifty thousand."

Fifty thousand! Ally's head shot back over to stare at Matt. Forgetting in her shock, her embarrassment. *How'd he get that much money?*

Matt shrugged, again, and followed Gilbertson down into the darkness. His eyes troubled.

~

After five minutes of swimming through the black inkiness that was the trench, the significant awe had worn off; leaving a boredom more cumbersome than before. Made especially stifling because of Gilbertson's insistence to swim by herself - at her crawling, slothful pace.

A while passed, and the boredom grew more oppressive. Eventually Matt and Ally started to drift; wandering off here and there, exploring the small caves and overhangs found at the sides of the trench. Soon they forgot the 'mission', and commenced a game of tag over and around Gilbertson - until she lost her temper and exploded with a barrage of expletives neither had heard before in their life. They had there after remained swimming inch by inch behind a sill fuming Gilbertson.

~

It had been close to an hour - as close as they could tell - of swimming endlessly through the trench, and Matt was starting to drift asleep; when he saw a recede to the darkness lying just up ahead. A breath escaped him in alleviation.

Thank god! I was beginning to feel as if my fins had fallen asleep!

Matt looked over at Ally and grinned. He could relate.

They swam out of the trench, and back into open water. But instead of the feeling of relief he'd felt a moment ago - all Matt now felt, was foreboding. "Something's not right." He said quietly, so only Ally could hear. "I don't know... I just feel... Something's not right." He repeated, backing up through the brine.

Ally was looking around her fearfully, her eyes darting like minnows before the ravine. "I can feel it too - I just don't know what's causing it!" she hissed angrily in a stream of bubbles.

Jittery and panicked they swam together, back to back, each scanning the water all around for proof and rationing to their fear.

"Now what are you two doing?" Gilbertson snapped, watching them with skepticism - and a slight amount of interest.

"Go up to the boat." Matt said quietly, his eyes everywhere but her.

"Pardon me?"

I said: go-up-to-the-boat! Matt glared at her, and shot her up to the surface.

Ally watched the woman's old form as it sped upward through the water like a torpedo, fish and bubbles scattering in her abrupt appearance. "Gee, I hope the force doesn't kill her when she breaks the surface..."

"I do." Matt went back to scouring the ocean.

He couldn't explain it, and that scared him more then the time his foster father had come at him with a shotgun. An elusive shadow at the back of his mind, darting constantly and staying just beyond his reach. Warning him - yet not offering an explanation.

I suppose it could be defined in one simple phrase: animal instinct.

Brandon watched the monitor with an inquiring mind as the two red dots drew close, the white dot growing larger and larger. He puzzled silently to himself as to why Miss Gilbertson was rising... and the other two weren't.

Then his curiosity gave way for concern. "She's rising too fast!" He yelped out in sudden realization - then whirled impulsively from the screen when he heard a great SPLASH from behind him. Turning to see Miss Gilbertson fly from the water and up into the air. Flying about twenty feet above the Yacht, screaming to the heavens and beyond.

"There!" Matt shouted, choking on the water in his hysteria. Not fifty feet from their current position, one could see a large black form making its way steadily in their direction.

Ally moved from where she held her back to him, and squinted into the murkiness that appeared to have followed them from the trench. Then her eyes widened, "It's a shark!"

"Traveling alone! Weird."

"Logic later, life first! I think it intends to make us its next meal!"

Indeed, the Great White came charging towards them; its massive, angular flukes propelling it through the water they could only hope but try to outmatch. They only *just* managed to avoid it by swimming frantically in aimless directions - anywhere where the shark wasn't was good enough.

They turned in time to see it pelting back towards them, and tore off in sync towards the relative cover of the trench. Thinking only to get away, fear overriding their natural judgment, they powered their fins in wide swirls in a maddening desire to out-pace the beast.

They could feel the beast behind them, the water streaming in its wake.

Matt glanced over his shoulder, and swerved headlong to his left as the shark came up behind him; bringing its immense teeth to crash together where his torso had once been.

Well at least they had one advantage over it; better maneuvering capability.

And probably brains as well...

Twisting to keep the shark in his range of sight, he saw to his horror that his dodge may have saved him, but Ally was caught in the gapping maw, her tail completely enveloped, her arms and hands pushing back violently against the sand-paper skin; striving to dislodge herself.

"ALLY!!!" He bellowed, racing back to her, his teeth set in a snarl born of anger, hatred and fear.

Before he could so much as touch the assailant, though, the shark suddenly whipped around in the water at breakneck speed; its tail catching him squarely in the chest as a baseball bat might meet a ball, winding him effectively, and sending him to crash into the far wall of the trench.

He gasped as he hit, his nerves reacting by attempting to force his body into a ball. The sheer force of the impact sending rock and rubble cascading down upon him, as he sank boneless towards the sea bottom.

Matt gritted his teeth as rock upon rock hit him on every part of his body - assuring him multiple sores and bruises. His temper at its end, he clenched his fists, and sent a barrage of energy out in all directions, like a starburst; blasting the rocks away from him.

Once he'd pulled her over the rail Brandon helped Miss Gilbertson to a sitting position, removing her oxygen tanks. He then looked her squarely in the eye, "What - happened!?" he demanded, his breath drawn. "Why did they force you to the surface!?"

Gilbertson just mumbled incoherently, her head lolling onto her shoulder. Still much to shocked in body after her impact with the surface of the water - both going up, and the coming back down.

Brandon shook her in his frustration "What happened to them!!! Why did they send you back up!? I must know…" his voice trailed off as millions upon millions off rocks came pelting out of the water. Making it seem as if gravity had just turned upside down.

He stared in wonder for a moment at the shower, his eyes widening, than ran back to the monitor - almost crashing into his chair in his enthusiasm.

Matt groaned, and shoved a boulder off himself with his forearm, the knowledge of his energy bypassing him entirely.

Then, after catching his breath for a moment and registering the ache of his body; he glanced about for any sign of Ally or the shark.

He saw the White - lying motionless at the bottom of trench not twenty feet from him.

Swimming silently over, his heart in his throat, he came up over the massive form of the shark and gazed in confusion at the motionless body. Movement caught his eye and he glanced sharply to his left. Ally.

With her tail and most of her chest still locked in the shark's gaping mouth, Ally persisted to struggle and push herself uselessly from the orifice that held her captive.

Matt glided over her, and tried adding his strength to hers - to no avail. The teeth that had been clenched about her waist were strong -

stronger then brute force could mollify. So, leaving one hand to support the small of her back, he raised the other and blasted a few of the teeth away with small marbles of energy; shattering the enamel like glass. Then, taking a hold of her beneath her armpits, he tugged once and she fairly flew from the fishes hold.

Flipping his tail up to stop their backward momentum, he swam until they were a relative distance from the monstrosity, and laid her down upon an outcropping of rock. Void save a crab, clicking the cheliped on its forearms in annoyance as it backed away from them, and off into the shadows.

Hovering above her, Matt touched the skin at her waist delicately, almost afraid of it peeling away as he gingerly checked her over. He was beyond relieved to see she wasn't hurt overly bad. Recalling what Dixon had said about their scales being stronger than diamonds, he was sure the shark had gotten the biggest surprise when he'd snatched her into his mouth. Sure enough, when he looked back at the shark, blood was washing freely into the water; a dense cloud that hovered darkly over the carcass. He was fairly certain this wasn't because of a couple missing teeth.

His hands skimmed over her flesh, hardly touching, and she shivered beneath him; watching those hands attentively. Fingers coming to rest sympathetically over the large cuts that ran along either side of her waist like scars, bleeding into the water steadily. A blue glow was emanating from his palms, and within moments the jagged gashes had faded, and sealed. Leaving no trace as to their previous existence.

Ally's eyes darted to his face and carefully gauged his expression; his eyes focused and attentive as he closed the wounds, his bottom lip somehow becoming wedged between his teeth. Tracing a hand down along his torso, he discovered the miniature bruises and cuts dotting his body like an illness. She looked up to see him gazing down at her with glazed eyes. "You're hurt." She told him softy.

He smiled, than winced. "Not bad, I just got caught in a landslide."

A small laugh squeezed its way from her constricting stomach, before she tilted her head upward to catch his lips in a demanding kiss; a soft black glow reaching to encompass his entire body from where their lips melded. Stroking, caressing him - mimicking the motions of her hands along his lower abdomen.

Breathing was suddenly a far less demanding process. Tightening his arms around her waist, drawing her up so skin rubbed against skin' Matt deepened the kiss. Elating in the after glow of the battle, he allowed his relief to sweep over him, brushing away his anxiety and fear, removing the tension from his limbs. Eventually they parted, their faces slightly flushed, and Matt proceeded to lift her bridal style into his arms - one hand around her shoulders, the other beneath where her knees would be were she breathing air. Then, powering his firm lower appendage, he swam them both toward the surface, and the hull of the boat.

His head breaking the surface, Matt lifted Ally up with his mind, floating her gently over the rail; watching as her tail and gills slowly dissolved to be replaced by her regular attire. The small effort drained him unsympathetically, and it was all he could do to drag himself up the ladder thrown over the side for his convenience.

Despite this, however, he still couldn't help the feelings of spirited victory coursing through his very veins.

~

"What was it?" Dennis asked frantically as they stepped languidly the castle, scrutinizing them from head to foot as they stood in the entryway - checking them over for injuries or bruises in an almost distressed way.

"A shark." Matt said simply.

"A very hungry shark." Ally added.

"A great White." Brandon enlightened them - but no one was paying the least amount of attention to him. They were far more interested in a little chatterbox; or to be more specific: they were far more interested in shutting up a little chatterbox.

"COOL!!!" Cody pocked his head out of the door-less cafeteria, than scampered over to them, and started to bounce up and down on the balls of his feet; unable to keep his body (or his mouth) still. "Did it bite you? What did it feel like? Did it hurt? It probably didn't get any where near you, right!? You probably blasted it out of the water as soon as it charged you! Didn't you? Didn't you?" He bounced in one spot until that particular spot of linoleum lost its appeal - then proceeded to leap in circles around and around them. "Man I wish I could be attacked by a shark! What kind was it? A hammerhead? A Tiger Shark? A bloodthirsty mammal ready to rip you to shreds!? Or maybe one of those little tiny one's that come up behind you and bite you where the sun don't-"

Brandon made his voice heard over the scattered conversations, discussions, and Cody. Speaking in a soft, booming voice that echoed along the hall. "Please - for sanities sake, Cody. Will you seal that gapping aperture in the middle of your face!!!"

"And a shark isn't a mammal, Cody - it's a fish." Miranda smiled sweetly at him.

Cody seemed not to have heard her; instead he blatantly replied to Brandon, continuing on what he obviously assumed to be a conversation. "I don't think I have an ape- apetule- akakature- whatever it was you said, Mr. Kenith. I'm pretty sure that that's the term you use for when you decapitate someone." His eyes lit up almost scarily, "Have YOU ever been decapitated – no, I suppose not. But it would probably be really exciting! You'd be able to look back at yourself and go- oh! So THAT'S what I look like. I wonder-"

Jason effectively cut him off. Ending the tirade with one simple - though blunt - comment. "He means your mouth, Cody. Shut your god damn mouth."

Extremely put out, Cody wandered off in search of Ivy, who was still in class with Mrs. Johnson, and would undoubtedly be wanting to hear all the gruesome details of Matt and Ally's battle with a bloodthirsty fish.

Once he'd disappeared up the west staircase, a feeling of something a lot like agitation seemed to have lifted from their shoulders. Grinding of teeth subsided. Clenched fists relaxed. And the look that said, 'I'd like to wring his neck', was wiped from a few people's faces.

An exasperated sigh of relief washed from Dennis' lips. He turned back to Brandon abruptly, "Where's Miss Gilbertson?"

Brandon looked over at the duo behind him, trying desperately to push down his grin without success. "As soon as we reached the dock, she jumped ship. Muttering something about 'the gods of the sea' and a guy named Gary... and how he'd come back to haunt her - whatever that means. She took the dingy for shore - though we might have to send someone after her with the *Prowler*."

Ally and Matt exchanged glances, trying their hardest not to smile... but failing dismally.

~

Ally sunk into the warm water filled bathtub, breathing a sigh of content. Her waist ached a little, and she was quite positive it wasn't because of the shark. It was because of him.

His lips always felt so soft and comforting against hers, she wanted him to touch her, to comfort her, to feel the warmth of his hands around her waist once more.

She sighed again, and reached over for the soap.

~

Matt gazed up at the ceiling from his position on her bed, unseeingly, thinking about her: her smile, her touch, her lips. He loved her, and it was always a powerful experience to kiss her - almost monumental. But he was only human; he couldn't help but desire more. He wanted their relationship to go beyond simply touching, wanted her to feel all his love for her in one all-consuming act - wanted to express it so there wasn't a doubt left in her mind of his feelings for her.

Sometimes denying that... hurt.

His heart still ached with pain whenever he saw her, but it hurt more now that he had her. It burned whenever he touched her, and it exploded in ecstasy when he kissed her. He knew of only one way to ease the pain.

Though even as the thought entered his mind, he chased it out again with an iron rod. *You don't need too, Matt. You'll do it if she wants you too - when she's ready. Got that!?*

Suddenly, the door to the bathroom swung wide, and Matt lifted his head to watch as Ally walked out, rubbing her head with a towel, like she always did after a bath.

Besides the one being used to dry her hair, she'd also slung another towel about her body - held up only by her breasts. It revealed her strong, shapely legs. Smooth, pale skin the result of lack of sunlight. These thoughts and more swam around inside Matt's head, providing him with scenarios and possibilities that sent blood rushing to two very distinct parts of his anatomy - one being his face.

Ally looked up, then, and caught him staring at her from the bed.

He was sure she knew the heat in his face hadn't been caused from the steam still issuing from the bathroom; and this only caused his blush to worsen.

His face was void of emotion, blank; but his eyes were shinning in the light from the bathroom, and wavering with such a strong emotion, her knees almost gave out beneath her. She knew this was it, she'd waited so long - she couldn't decide whether or not to cry in euphoria or scream in joy.

She compromised by smiling at him, and dropped the towel from her head onto the carpet with a wet *fwump*. Wrapping her arms around her waist lightly, as if to create the illusion of modesty, she walked with measured steps over to him. Taking her time. Delaying the inevitable to come. Sitting down precariously on the edge of her bed, she was careful to sit as far from his warm body as she could - without actually falling to the floor

Matt gazed at her a moment longer, then propped himself up onto his elbows so he could be at eye-level with her. His body at once noticed her face - pink from the heat of the bath, her lips full and slightly parted as she gasped in the chill air of the bedroom that caused goose bumps to rise along her exposed skin.

Still smiling steadily, she shifted slightly to face him better on the bed. "I guess, today was better than the last time we spent together in the ocean." She said in an effort to conversation.

A small, humorless laugh escaped his lips. "Yeah, if that shark hadn't come along, I'm sure we both would have died of boredom." They were silent for a moment, then, "Ally... I love you. You know that. And I just want you to know that I-"

"Shh..." Ally touched a finger to his lips lightly - the action alone stopping any further sound, as her finger obviously wasn't exactly sufficient. "Before you... speak. I have a few things I've been wanting to tell you." Gazing at him meaningfully, she removed her hand from his lips.

The movement of lunging forward so rapidly to hush him had forced her body into an ungainly sprawl across his legs, her other hand planted firmly in the covers to keep herself aloft. Now she forced herself back upright, and moved so she was sitting less awkwardly to his right, her legs folded neatly beneath her, her hands clasped in her lap. "This year - these last five months have been... enlightening. I never realized... what I mean - just let me get my words straight." She paused to suck in a deep breath, her gaze fixed on her hands, her visage burning. Exhaling slowly, she tried again, "I'd never known people like you existed." She glanced up at him then, it was quick, fleeting, but it conveyed all her anxiety and appreciation in volume - before she fixed her gaze back to her lap. "People... I've always seen as selfish. Self-satisfying. But then I met you and... you're pure - at least in mind. You care for yourself, sure - I'm sure everyone has to be selfish sometimes. But you also manage somehow to care deeply for other people along the way - you give them a chance.

"First impressions aren't often enough; and you know this. I'm just... I guess what I'm trying to say is..." She looked back up at him once more, this time catching and holding his gaze, her entire body shaking. "I'm grateful you gave me a chance - I'm grateful you let me in, let me see the real you. And I'd... I would like to thank you..."

Matt's torso contracted painfully as she leant forward and straddled his lap gracefully. Her body was shaking - but her eyes were calm, assured in her decision. Fixed on his as she tilted forward to catch his lips up in an earth-shattering kiss.

A tremor raced down his spine and down to his toes - giving him the impression they'd fallen asleep. *I guess... she's ready then.* His heart exploded into little shards of joy, causing him to gasp against her mouth; allowing her tongue to dart in. Twisting around, tasting, exploring this new - previously unknown - territory. Concentrating on the feel, she moved up her left hand and traced two fingers down his chest; feeling his muscles spasm beneath the fleeting touch. She grinned against his lips, delighting in this control - this superiority - she held over the other. She pushed on his chest lightly, and Matt dropped his arms from beneath him, causing them both to fall onto the covers, the kiss never breaking. Their bodies flush.

She writhed against him, rubbing against his flesh in an increasingly stimulating manner. Pressing down onto him so he was finally forced to groan openly against her mouth. His hands clutched desperately at her waist, pulling her down onto him. He thrust his hips upward, grinding into her with growing passion.

She pressed back just as eagerly, then gently withdrew. Releasing his lower lip slowly, temptingly, as her eyes fluttered open and caught his with ease. Still slightly parted, her mouth quirked upward in a grin. "Besides," She told him in a low voice dripping with lust, her hot breath ghosting across his moistened lips. "Knowing you... I doubt you would have ever made a move without being prompted."

True as that were, he wasn't about to let her get away with it.

His eyebrows arched, and he mirrored her grin. Lifting his left leg, he pushed up, and in one sudden movement had flipped them both over so he was effectively pinning her down with his own body, his knees on either side of her hips. The sudden action caused the towel clutched about her to slip free; it now lay pooled at her waist and tangled around her thigh. Leaving her upper torso bare. Exposed to roaming eyes.

Her hair was spread-eagle all over the pillow, the wet strands wavy and gleaming in the light, darker than her usual shade of brown - almost black. Her chest heaved in excitement as his eyes freely roamed her body, devouring it.

Moving her leg up between his thighs, she brought his gaze effectively back to hers, and jerked forward to catch his lips in a desperate cry for contact. He growled possessively back into her mouth and urged her to grant him entrance, pushing her back onto the pillow.

One hand tangling into the alluring horsetail, somehow she managed to squeeze the other between their forms; tracing down the soft cotton of his shirt, feeling it give way to the coarse texture of his jeans. She then inched her fingers up until the cool metal of the zipper registered in her heat-muddled mind, and tugged at it violently.

~ 11 ~

A small exhalation of air escaped her lips, and she stretched languidly, flexing muscles having seized up from the strenuous activity of the night before. She felt wonderful, refreshed - like she'd just run twenty minutes, and entered the shower to the cool feel and gentle massage of water drumming along her heated flesh.

She'd been with people before: lovers, if they could be so lightly termed; but none had left her feeling so completely filled before... so wanted. So loved. It was a night she wouldn't soon forget, and she looked forward to others in the future.

Matt had returned to his own bed - just to be safe if the Dixon's or anyone else decided to pop in unannounced in the middle of the night - after they'd cooled down somewhat, caught their breaths, and heartbeats had returned to normal; though not before spooning with her and basking in the afterglow. Content to let a satisfied silence settle around them. The tingling of a final kiss before he'd left still lingered on her lips.

Without him beside her Ally felt suddenly cold. So bereft without his warmth and touch. She told herself she was just being stupid - since he were only a few steps away in the other bed - but somehow... she didn't want to deny any longer that these feelings were supposed to be normal. That when you loved someone... it was okay to feel severed in half when they were gone. She didn't want to deny anymore, she didn't want to hide anymore, she didn't want to shield herself from her feelings.

It was okay to want.

It was okay to feel.

It was okay to love.

She smiled. A pure, innocent smile. The first time she'd smiled so truthfully since her mother's death.

The sheets rustled softly as she turned over to face him, her smile broadening. Matt was truly an innocent when he slept. Like he delved back into the years of childhood the instant his mind was released from the burden of the day.

Detangling herself from the cerulean sheets and covers, she stepped lightly onto the soft, cobalt carpet, and padded noiselessly over to his stolid form; completely oblivious to the surrounding world. It was then she noticed her state of undress.

She paused abruptly, blushing and moving to cover herself out of modesty. Then she shook herself and asked furiously what she was embarrassed for? The only person in the room was Matt, and she was quite sure he wouldn't mind in the least.

Reaching his bedside, she crawled over his form, and sat on his waist, struggling to restrain a laugh. Matt was *truly* innocent in his sleep. Hair everywhere, his face was peaceful, void of all lines or concern. His limbs were thrown out at odd angels, and in his sleep the covers had somehow become wrapped like shackles about them, preventing any further movement from the perpetrator.

A giggle managed to worm its way free of her pursed lips. She clapped a hand furiously over it, staring at him in apprehension, worried it would waken him.

But no, Matt seemed to be a fairly deep sleeper - he was probably one of those people who wouldn't awaken until they wanted to, or something blew up.

Watching him for long moments as his even breath constantly fanned a piece of stray hair hanging into his face; she carefully leant forward, and kissed him lightly. Her eyes fluttering shut as she gave into the feelings coursing within her.

Matt woke to the smooth touch of her lips, her hands cradling his cheeks gently to keep his face in place. One thought only passed through him mind as he gently returned the kiss, moving his arms up to her lower back to keep her from slipping off him. Feeling her naked body move rhythmically against his, warming him to the morning. *This is a nice way to wake up...*

What was that? The kiss grew steadily in intensity, taking its time; mirroring the waking mind.

He grinned, tightening his arms around her. *I should really try to restrict you from doing that... I said I wouldn't mind waking to this every day.* He opened his eyes, finding her already staring at him, and winked.

Count yourself lucky. This is probably just a one-time thing.

Well in that case- tomorrow I'll just have to return the favor.

Her smile growing, she released his lips and licked his nose, never breaking eye contact. "I'd like that."

"Good." Sitting up he captured her into his arms and proceeded to finish what she herself had started. Feeling her legs wrap around his waist and lock behind him at the ankle.

Submitting to him, she relaxed in his embrace. *Yes, I love him. I will love him until I die and beyond death.* To him, she asked, *Have a good sleep?*

Wonderful. Good morning.

Morning. Her arms tightened around his neck. After a while she asked, *We have to get dressed sometime - we'll miss breakfast. Then everyone will wonder where we are.*

The door is locked - what can they do?

Break it down for one...

Spoil sport.

I'm not a spoil sport - I'm the voice of reason.

Voice of reason my ass.

What was that?

Nothing. Neither could stop the grins or laughter that forced them to part for air.

Eventually they subsided, and Matt pecked her once more on the cheek before rising with her in his arms and headed into the bathroom to start the new day.

~

"A guy I know who golf's, one day bought a box of fifteen golf balls labeled *'They fly faster and straighter'*. But after only one day of golfing, he brought the box back to the store and asked, 'Do you have any labeled, *'They float'*?"

After a moment of silence, the table erupted with laughter, and Cody fell off his chair when he lost his balance from giggling so hard.

Wiping a tear from his eyes, Eric held up his hand, "Wait, I got more! A bear and a squirrel were fighting. Suddenly, a genie pops out of the ground, and says, 'I'll grant you each one wish if you stop fighting.' The bear thought for a moment, then said, 'I wish that all the bears in the forest were female... and that they liked me.' The squirrel folded his arms, and said simply, 'I wish he were gay.'"

Most people now had to clutch at their stomachs they were laughing so hard, so when Eric opened his mouth again, Miranda held up her hand, "I think that's enough, Eric. You'd better stop now before we burst."

Sadly, Eric complied.

Matt had to agree, he didn't think he could have taken much more - his chest was full of cramps and small pains as he laughed, and he looked around the table to see Cody banging his fist on the floor, tears spilling from his eyes as he laughed. At the sight, Matt had to hold his chest harder as he burst into a new wave of uncontrollable laughter.

Once everyone had calmed down enough to finish their breakfast, Dixon stood up at the table and raised his hands for silence, smiling at them all. "I think you've all been working very hard this year. So as a reward, the teachers and I have decided to take you all on a field trip-"

"Oh! Where too? I hope it's to the mountains; I've always wanted to go down a mountain on a sled! I've skied before though - have you Eric?

Is it true that Canada is fifty degrees colder than we are? Will we have to dress up like Eskimos? What are Eskimos-"

Cody ducked abruptly as a fork went whizzing scant millimeters above his hair. And decided to remain silent... at least for the time being.

Dennis cleared his throat, glaring at Jason as if daring him to try that again - though he couldn't deny it had achieved the desired results. He than continued. "As I was saying: we'll be having a field trip. Nothing fancy, just a day outing into Newport to see a movie. Any suggestions?"

Nobody really knew what was playing now at the theaters, so they all agreed to just decide when they got there.

Jason raised his hand, leaning back in his chair with an aloof manner. "One question: Can we blast the guy in front of us if he wont shut up?"

They all snorted, trying to stifle their laughter at the disapproving looks of the adults.

The twinkle vanished. Dennis frowned, "No, and that's something I wanted to talk to you guy's about." Jason groaned, his chair dropping back onto the tile with a *clack*. "There will be *no* open displays of your gifts - understood?"

They all looked up, startled. Never had Dennis been so stern, and they all nodded quickly in acknowledgement.

Dennis nodded back in affirmation. "Good." And his twinkling smile was once again etched across his face.

~

Once again Matt looked out to the horizon as the school disappeared behind him. It was just like the first time; save that unlike before, as Ally stood beside him, he could see her.

He watched as her hair fanned out behind her in the wind, whipping like a banner painted gold and tangerine by the rays of the morning sunlight. She turned to smile at him, and to his utmost relief - remained visible.

"WOW!!!" Cody was bouncing up and down at the rail, attempting to get a better look at the waves, Matt supposed. "Dolphins! Look!" he pointed, and Matt and Ally followed his gaze to see what they could count were four or five dolphins racing the ship. Staying just ahead of it under the water, the mammals were an awe-inspiring sight jumping the waves now and then for a breath of air.

It's déjà vu - with a twist. Matt grinned. The dolphin's, Ally; he even felt a strong desire to shove Cody over the rail...

"Are they bottle nose dolphins? I can't tell. Actually, I don't know other kinds of dolphins. Do you, Mathue? What about you, Ally? I wonder if they'd hurt me if I jumped in? Maybe I could ride one like the kids in movies-"

A sudden, unexplainable urge to be reckless washed over him, and Matt found himself wanting to do something drastic and exciting to get his adrenalin running. He looked over at Ally, and smirked, wave upon wave of avidity crashing over him. "Feel like pissing Dennis off?"

"You're on." She grinned back. And before the gaping chatterbox could comment, they both pulled themselves onto the rail. They balanced for a moment, delighting in the full force of the wind running fingers through their hair; then tilted forward, and dove into the great blue on either side of the ship.

The chill water hit her face like a stinging slap. Ally drifted motionlessly for a moment, relishing the numbing cold of the ocean around her; then her gills slit open along her neck and she drank in a life-granting breath. Her legs fused together and effortlessly propelled her forward.

Catching a streak of sapphire from the corner of her eye, she shot her gaze to her right and grinned over at Matt. *Race you?*

He smirked. *First one to fall back loses.* And with that he sped on ahead towards the haul of the yacht - already yards ahead of them.

It was always a different sight that met them from beneath the waves - light reflected differently below the surface. It shone down between different heights of the waves to shimmer around them like a multitude of starbursts or stage-lights. It wavered and brushed them gracefully before continuing on down to reveal the sandy ocean floor. The haul of the yacht was a dark brown against the bright blue of the surface. It left behind it a trail of bubbles and a jet stream that was difficult to maneuver in.

It was in that stream they swam, laughing silently as they were flipped over and rolled constantly in the water. Eventually they caught up to the boat, and swam beneath the propellers and from the jet stream to mingle with the pod of dolphins, swimming around and with them playing chicken with the Yacht as it motored after them.

Matt knew very well neither of them was about to fall back any time soon. This was a race for exuberance.

Her heart swelled in the maddening rush of excitement. An awkward flip of her tail sent her swimming just ahead of him, and the stream of bubbles caused by her maneuver flew back to pop in Matt's face. Ally smiled slyly, glancing back at him as he glowered and sped to swim up beside her - the slight twitching at the corner of his mouth giving him away.

They had to be going at least seventy - Matt mused - as they were matching the speed of the yacht dead on. Eighty was pushing it for them, but was perfectly plausible. The fastest they'd ever gone was sixty - this was pure elation. The speed wouldn't allow them to stop by twisting their tails beneath them as they would usually have done - and with the yacht behind them they dared not stop or slow to drift to a stop. When the time came they'd have to swerve out of the boats path and work from there - and even then maneuvering would be difficult and made with split-second decisions.

The thought was stimulating.

The dolphins talked and laughed in their amusing language of clicks and whines and whistles; gossiping about the two new additions to their group. Mermaids hadn't been seen in these parts for... eons. The fish were just as much a topic of interest to the dolphins as the mammals were to the mermaids.

Ally laughed into the water, her voice carried away on the currents. She lifted her arms out to her sides, like the wings of a bird. As this slowed her momentum - her arms usually plastered to her sides - she had to power her tail faster to keep up - but it made her feel lighter. Like she were flying through the water instead of swimming through it.

So swept away by the feelings of freedom coursing within them, Matt and Ally found themselves following the Spinner Dolphins like young ducklings; spinning and weaving ahead of the yacht in a mesmerizing dance. Thus it came as quite a surprise when the dolphins abruptly tilted upward, and crashed through the surface, flying into the air with grace and style. Gulping in deep breaths of air before splashing back into the water once more.

They rose up again, and Matt yelled in ululation as the warm air hit his flushed face. Feeling the water drip from his scales, the wind lift him up higher into the sky. He lifted his arms to pull himself upward, then brought them before him to break the surface as he fell back into the sea, his tail resuming it rhythmic movements that powered him on once more.

His adrenalin was defiantly pumping.

~

"Hey! Hey guys!"

"Go away, Cody."

"You guy's have to see this!"

Kim looked up from her Gossip magazine to stare over at him skeptically. "What is it now, Cody? A dragon escaped and is now flying over the boat?" she asked him with mock eagerness.

"No." Cody shook his head. "Better!" He shot his index finger towards the bow of the *Prowler*. "Matt and Ally are racing a bunch of dolphins against the boat!"

"They're WHAT!?" Dennis and Brandon jumped from their chairs as if electrocuted, knocking them to the deck; and raced with the other teens out of the cabin, and to the rail just in time to see Matt and Ally clear the water, accompanied by a pod of Spinner Dolphins.

"What the *hell* do they think they're doing!?" Dennis bellowed, leaning as far as he could over the rail to get a better look at Matt's blurry form beneath the water.

It was impossible to see Ally - her black scales camouflaging her perfectly against the dark green of the ocean. It was, in fact, only the to the credit of the light reflecting off his azure scales that they could see Matt at all.

"It looks to me like they're having fun." Brandon said wistfully, raising his eyebrows and leaning on the rail; watching the two as they spun around in the water, oblivious to their onlookers. They sped up again and splashed from the water, - Ally materializing from seemingly nowhere - enabling them to count six Spinner Dolphins, each grinning as if they hadn't a care in the world.

Cody was now positively springing up and down on the deck: looking for all the world as if he'd attached coils of mettle to the soles of his shoes. "See! I told you! I told you- oops- AHHHHHH!!!"

Somehow, - exactly how was a concept beyond comprehension - Cody had managed to jump himself over the rail, and into the icy, life-rendering water below.

~

She closed her eyes in ecstasy, using the feel of the water coursing along her body to keep herself in alignment with Matt. Stretching out a hand she caught the dorsal fin of the dolphin closest her, and clutched at it swiftly. Allowing her body to go limp, her arm felt for a moment as if it'd had a go on the rack; and she was suddenly yanked forward through the water.

Laughing in abandon, she was unable to stop the wave of giggles that hit her full force as a pair of strong arms embraced her firmly but tenderly about the waist; tugging gently. Still giggling madly, she released the fin from whitening fingers, and twisted about to latch her lips to his furiously as they floated down to the bottom of the ocean.

You cheated.

And your point is?

He winked. *You lose.*

She punched him lightly, and rested her head to his collarbone, sucking in great gulps of air through her gills.

Both hearts beating furiously, hearts thumping madly to catch up after the race; they sank down without a care or thought to the world; the weight of their upper bodies causing them to tilt until they were sinking head first - not that either cared.

Feeling the soft sand beneath him float up to tickle him softly as he hit, Matt twisted so his neck wouldn't snap, and allowed the rest of his lengthy body to twist and stretch out on the eroded rocks. Ally held to his breast.

Looking back at the haul of the boat and watching as it sped towards the rising rock in the distance, they both exchanged looks.

Should we catch up?

In a moment - just let me catch my breath. Matt smirked. *Besides, if Dennis has realized we're gone... I say giving him a few more minutes to cool down isn't such a bad idea.*

She smirked back, and focused once more on returning her heartbeat to normal.

Suddenly they both heard the unmistakable sound of something of fair size hitting the water. They jerked up in alarm to see Cody holding his breath with his eyes clenched shut, struggling furiously to swim up to the surface. Thrashing blindly as the water stung his eyes and befuddled his senses.

The two of them exchanged frightened glances. The way he was swimming, he'd hit the propeller blades.

~

Cody shrieked as he fell over the rail, flailing his arms madly for purchase. When he hit the water he felt as if an infinite number of blades had suddenly struck his body, piercing the skin, plunging into his heart. The cold numbed his body to where he almost stopped caring whether he lived or died - but then he wouldn't get to tell the others what it was like to be cut in a million places all at once; and so he swam.

Water streamed into his mouth and ears and eyes, choking him - stinging. He wasn't sure which way was up, but since it was obviously a lot easier to swim in one direction than the other - he used common reasoning and started to head for the surface.

He shrieked as something grabbed him violently about the middle - though all that came out were a couple hundred bubbles. And all that came in was probably - what Cody assumed to be - the entire ocean.

Something soft brushed his cheek, and he opened his eyes - snapping them shut again almost immediately. But that quick glance calmed his nerves tremendously. Now he would get to tell the others all about what it was like to be rescued by mermaids!

He felt the something that had him around the middle suddenly flex, and he was abruptly twisted in the water and flung gently onto the bare, broad expanse of what he could only guesstimate was skin - and therefore, Matt's back.

Water streamed by him. He started to slide off, and his fingers sought desperately for a handhold - they found one in Matt's neck and around his middle, and he held on for dear life. Clutching so hard he was sure later he almost broke something. At the moment, however, his mind was far more concentrated on the burning sensation in his lungs.

That annoyance was driven sharply from his mind though, when suddenly a greater and much more excruciating distraction presented itself in a searing shock-filled brush up against his legs. He screamed in abandon, the blistering pain that shot up his limbs nothing short of agony.

~

Ally acted rapidly, swimming up to catch the kid about the waist; holding him steady as his terror and panic-filled mind caused him to lash out and thrash viciously in her arms. Reaching over she brushed his cheek lightly, hoping to the gods he would calm enough for them to get him to the surface.

How long could humans survive without air?

It had been so long she'd forgotten. But they had to remind themselves: Cody was a sage, even at level three - that had to count for something.

Matt followed her swiftly and calmly. Gazing at Cody in concern, his mind racing, he told Ally simply: *Put him on my back.* Muttering into the water, "Fastest."

Nodding, Ally held the teen tighter as Matt turned, then pushed him onto her lovers back. Off Matt went, Ally following closely.

They were down fairly deep; the height from which Cody had dropped, the current, and the force the propeller blades caused in the water all combining to leave Cody at a dangerous depth - nearly thirty feet.

Streaming along behind them, Ally watched Cody closely in case he were to slip or slide off - but judging by the blue of Matt's face and the tightness with which he must be clutching his saviors neck... she judged it fairly unlikely.

Then something happened that nearly made her wish he *had* fallen off. As the surface grew nearer and nearer, the light growing brighter and more radiant as they climbed; Cody's legs - previously floating forgotten above Matt's form - abruptly fell as the mermaid darted upward, and brushed sickeningly along the sapphire scales that protected the entire lower half of Matt's body.

Blood burst forth into the water, a cloud of rust trailing after, marring the water with its symbolism. His jeans were shredded, parts floating away unneeded. Strands of flesh still connected, fluttered like bands in the water, trailing after the shell-shocked teenager. Still too frozen in remembered pain to do more than simply cling to the only thing he had left to save him. Terrified for the first time in his life.

Though sadly, it was far from the last.

The sight was so sickening - finally she was forced to advert her eyes.

They broke the surface with Cody still holding on for dear life, gasping and coughing the salt water from his stomach and lungs. Numbed by the pain, his mind in a standstill.

Slapping him on the back a couple times, Ally forced him to breath. Watched him critically until she was sure he was fine - at least in the air department. They'd have to get him back to the boat soon and healed, or he'd loose far to much blood.

Matt treaded the water silently, slightly tilted so he was still almost completely submerged. In this fashion he allowed Cody to be almost entirely exposed to the stinging chill wind - far colder than the water as it bit into his unprotected flesh. But he also kept his head well in clear access of fresh, clean oxygen.

He began to sob as feeling returned to his limbs - and with it the pain. He glanced down and felt the bile rise drastically in his throat at the sight of his mutilated legs, and swiftly looked away.

Glancing around, Ally nudged Matt silently, and they both made for the yacht - which had slowed to a stop a fair few yards ahead.

Lifting Cody from Matt's back, they both gently took an arm, and made steadily for the boat. Swimming carefully with Cody held as far from their tails as physically possible.

Brandon tossed the rope ladder over the rail as they drew near, gazing down at them with laughter in his eyes - as if pleased they'd gone and done something spontaneous to disrupt the regular routine. Clearly he hadn't caught sight of the pallor of Cody's face, or he would have frowned.

Ally left Cody in Matt's support, and tugged herself onto and up the ladder. Her arm muscles strained as she pulled her entire body from the water and up the ladder - until her feet could separate and help in the place of her tail.

Watching her closely, Matt waited until she'd disappeared from sight. Then he lifted Cody up from the water with his mind; wincing slightly as drops of red splattered onto his face. Keeping the limp form steady at the rail, he waited until he felt the gentle tug of Ally's mind against the thin thread of thought that connected him and the chatterbox - and surrendered him to her care.

Assured Cody wouldn't drop back down unexpectedly; he sank down into the comforting waves, and viciously cleansed himself. Coming to surface once more, he sucked in a deep breath, reached up, and slowly began his assent up to chaos.

As he neared the rail, Ally's blank visage met his eyes, and he took her hand without deliberation - using it to pull his exhausted form onto the support of the deck. There his gaze fell to Jason's inert form lying next to Cody's. He glanced to Ally for explanation, his eyebrows drawing to a narrow V.

Ally answered him carefully, her gaze drifting seamlessly from Cody to Jason and back again. *I brought Cody up fine - before I could heal him, Jason decided to be a hero and tried to do it himself... knocked himself out and did more harm then good. It wasn't 'just' loss of blood that caused Cody to faint.*

Kim walked over to them, then, scowling. Having not heard the transaction, she repeated to Matt what he already knew... simply with different wording. "The bastard tried healing Cody on his own. He was so weak he ended up knocking himself out. -And watching, Cody fainted. Idiots."

Matt's arm twitched, as if he were about to raise it to heal the two comatose teens - when suddenly a great booming voice shot across the deck and slammed into them viciously. It gave them an extremely clear idea of what type of mood Dixon was in...

"ALLY! MATHUE! GET YOUR ASSES OVER HERE RIGHT NOW! OR SO HELP ME I'LL-"

"Now just calm down Dennis, they'll be alright-"

"IT'S NOT THEM WHO SHOULD BE WORRIED!" Dennis screamed, spit flying, nodding over at Cody and Jason.

Ally swallowed thickly, more from lack of anything else to do than nervousness. Extending her hand, a wash of black light flowed seamlessly from her fingertips to surround both forms. The shreds of flesh hanging limply off what used to be Cody's legs, melded back into whole, healthy membrane.

Once Cody had stopped chattering about how cool it was to drown, Dennis whirled on Matt and Ally. Standing calmly at the bow, arms crossed, the two faced his fury unblinkingly.

My, he looks mad.

No- really? I'm sure it's just the light...

For a moment all was quiet. Then Dixon opened his mouth, and Ally braced herself for then inevitable blast of hot air.

"WHAT DO YOU THINK YOU WERE DOING! HAVE YOU *ANY* IDEA HOW RECKLESS AND STUPID THAT WAS!!! YOU COULD HAVE BEEN KILLED - YOU COULD HAVE GOTTEN LOST! IT MAY SEEM COOL TO YOU TO BE ABLE TO BREATH WATER BUT I ASSURE YOU IT'S JUST AS DANGEROUS AS AIR!"

That last comment having flown completely over their heads, they reveled in the small laps of silence as Dennis paused to take a breath. And then the relentless spiel started up once more.

"AND DON'T EVEN GET ME *STARTED* ON CODY! AND JASON, TOO! DID YOU REALLY THINK-"

Matt abruptly held up his hand, palm outward. Effectively and immediately cutting the lecture short. "It's all very well for you to yell at us for what *we* did. But you cannot blame us for what happened to Cody - he's been threatening to push himself over a ledge for a while now. And Jason? We had nothing to do with *his* stupidity."

Looking around Dennis, Ally saw Jason's visage grow dark.

Matt continued, "We have a fairly good understanding of our own abilities, thank you. We are well aware of the dangers of the ocean." *We were attacked by a shark, after all.* "We apologize for having a little fun, but there was no permanent damage, and as such - we'd appreciate it if you backed off a little." His gaze never wavered. He met Dixon's glower dead on, and never backed down.

Though Dennis' face was a bright red, and his mouth was still working furiously and soundlessly; he could argue only that Matt had a point. Finally, affronted the child had spoken to him in such a manner; he pointed over at the cabin, and told them to go and stay there for the remainder of the trip. Which lasted only the next ten minutes.

~

"So, what's it going to be?" Miranda asked them in her stolen voice, looking up at the movie listings from her position on the walk.

"*Stolen Hearts.*" Kim gusted.

"Eww." Cody scrunched up his nose in disgust. "I want to see an action thriller - like that one!" He pointed; it was a remake of Steven King's *The Shining*.

Alexandra shivered, "No way, too scary. Lets see..." Her eyes flew over the options. "That one!" She pointed up at *No One's Girl*, a movie about a girl who ran away from her drunken father one night after her mother had died, and had made a living by thieving with a group of boys who called themselves the 'Dark Team'.

Dixon smiled, "Not too mushy. Not too scary - but just right. All who agree to see it say aye!"

"AYE!!!" Shouted the majority, Kim still whining avidly about *Stolen Hearts*,

"Well that settles it then," Dennis smiled, and walked over to the ticket booth. The clerk in which, had been watching them with growing amusement whilst they argued.

~

"-Alrighty then. We're in row..." Brandon checked the tickets. "Seventeen. Pick someone you're least likely to punch, and find a seat."

With those words, there was a great scrambling to get to a seat as far from Cody as humanely possible. And when everyone had finally settled down, he was left sitting between Miranda and Dennis - who were just as displeased with this arrangement as he was.

Ally listened to the conversations around her in an abstracted sort of amusement before the movie started. Listened as Dennis tried to drill the meaning of 'lips shut' into Cody's un-abiding head, trying to make him promise not to utter so much as a cough during the production. She could hear Kim muttering fierce curses under her breath over at Jason, who was doing the same, the two of them together sounding like the berating winds of a gale. It was odd, to feel so content in the midst of so many - she'd always been an ochlophobic. Had always had an irrational fear of crowds. But for some unknown reason... she wasn't scared anymore - she was... calm. Relaxed for probably the first time in her life.

The lights dimmed, the crowd quieted, the movie started, and Ally had to admit - it was actually quite well done. She could hardly see the outlines of the people who reset the props after each scene, - or during scenes - nor could she see the strings that lifted the girl up into the sky at one point. And in all, she actually found herself enjoying the production.

Halfway through the movie, however, she had an incredible urge to lay her head on Matt's shoulder. And though this baffled her, as she wasn't tired or anything similar - the real reason she never acted on the desire, was for with Jason sitting right next to her; she thought better of the urge.

~

When the play ended, they left the dark theater for the blinding world outside. Stretching muscles seized from having remained immobile for so long.

Miranda bought them all an ice-cream cone or treat of their choice from the candy stall across the street, and ushered them quickly back onto the yacht. Sated as they all were; the speediness which was their leave, hardly bothered them in the least.

Matt felt the day had actually been worthwhile, he'd surprisingly enjoyed himself - even after the fiasco with the dolphins and Cody - and the play hadn't been half bad. Thus he was disappointed somewhat to admit the day was over.

At least the canister of toffee Cody had received from Dennis assured a peaceful interlude from the mindless chatter - for a time.

~ 12 ~

Brandon smiled at them, having waited in the cafeteria until the others had left. "I'm sure you'll be pleased to hear that your trip into the ocean today is going to be put on hold for a little review session I've set up for the two of you. It's basically going to test - in miniature - all of the skills you've thus managed to perfect.

"So if you'll follow me, we can get started. Then you'll have the rest of the day off." And with that, he spun on his heel, and led the way out of the lunchroom into the hall.

Following Brandon to the second floor left Matt and Ally speechless as they stared down the hall at what appeared to be a very plain, yet elaborate obstacle course.

Brandon stood before of them and grinned, clearly pleased with himself. "It took me all last night, but I finally got it all set. The course is simplicity itself - you basically have to blast all the glass jars from where you're standing, at the red line." He made a sweeping gesture at the floor with his left hand, where a red ribbon had been taped temporarily to the linoleum. "Then you get to move on - blast the moving targets, which I'll set off before you begin-" Matt looked around the assorted jars - stuck around the walls like iron shavings to a magnet - to some bull's-eye targets suspended from the ceiling by different lengths of rope. He supposed Brandon would 'set them off' by making them swing back and forth on their ropes. "-After you get past those, you'll find yourself in front of a metal barrier. You'll have to melt it completely to reach the next obstacle."

"Which is?"

Smirking, Brandon winked. "You'll see it when you reach it. Now since I can't just reset the course when you're finished - you'll both have to go at the same time. You're timed, so go as fast as you can without getting sloppy." He then made his way down the corridor, and swung each target back so they were weaving back and forth erratically on their ropes. Moving back to where the two were waiting, he raised his arm. "Ready... go!" he brought his hand down in a slash, mimicking the falling motion of the starter flag.

It took a moment for them to realize that they were supposed to begin, but they swiftly came to realization, and began to shatter the jars with systematic blasts of energy. Their aim was perfect, each orb of energy hitting the jars squarely in the center, causing them to burst in confetti like brilliance. The multicolored shards of glass smothering the hallway with tiny clinks and wind chime sounds.

Once all that were left of the jars were little bits of glass glued to the walls and ceiling here and there, they both dashed ahead across the mound of glass shards - careful, though, not to slip - to the next ribbon taped across the floor. There they set about dismantling the targets.

It didn't take them long to discover a small blast of energy wasn't going to do the trick. The targets were copper - but solid and at least thirteen inches thick. Making their orbs bigger, they tried again. The smaller the orb - the less damage, but the easier it was to aim. By making the orbs bigger, they found it much harder to actually hit the targets - let alone break them. The ordeal was made all the more vexing as the targets never ceased their gentle sway back and forth across the hall.

It took a while, and both missed their fair share of targets, before every last one had been reduced to worthless piles of scrap metal strewn across the hall.

Annoyed, but relieved, they then moved on to the barrier.

Clenching their fists to their sides, they began to heat it. Raising the temperature around it slowly - degree by degree, until the metal began to run in little rivulets down the wall to the floor. Pooling and collecting, the metal started to slump like butter on a hot day.

Matt saw it first; the hidden rope that was released as the metal withdrew from the wall and liquefied to the floor. His eyes looking ahead, he yelled a warning and lunged forward. Wrapping his arms firmly about Ally's waist he threw them both to the floor. Their breath knocked from their bodies, Matt was coherent enough only to vaguely realize something very large had flown clear over his head.

Ally, stunned, the breath stolen from her lungs as Matt flung himself onto her and shoved them both heavily to the linoleum; drew a sharp breath, and flipped herself over onto her back in time to see a huge metal log come soaring back at her, headed right for her face - and over her head as she lay on the floor. The whoosh of air pushed before it sounding like a hail storm to her shell-shocked mind.

Beside her Matt raised his head, then swiftly ducked it again as the log came soaring back. *What the hell!?*

My thoughts exactly.

What the hell is it?

Dunno - but it looks like the targets... at least, it continues to swing back and forth like them.

Waiting for the log to clear over them again, they stood, and faced it coldly. From this new position they could see it was indeed a log, about five feet long, a foot in diameter, and made of wood. As far as they could tell - some sort of hardwood. The log was suspended from the ceiling by four lengths of chain link - not easily broken by natural means.

The log came tearing back at them, the air whistling out of its path as it gained momentum on its downward fall. The two of them only stared at it with growing annoyance.

The log hit the air no more then a couple inches from their faces, and stopped so abruptly it snapped in half. The force propelling it, and the speed at which it had hit the shield; causing it to splinter, both halves dangling at odd angles on the chains. Swinging now erratically.

They gazed at it for a moment, than turned as they heard the sound of solo clapping coming from behind them.

Brandon made his way carefully though the mess of glass and clumps of copper now all molded together by the barrier; having run and melted into the mass, then cooled and solidified in the air. The hall wouldn't be something so very simple to clean. In fact - it looked quite impossible

"Well done, very well done indeed. Save for the loss of time gained on the targets; you both got a hundred percent. You did the course in just under ten minutes!"

Matt suddenly realized he was breathing hard, and forced himself to take calm, steady breaths. "What was the big idea with the log!?" he demanded. "We could have had our heads loped off!"

"But you didn't, did you?" Brandon raised his eyebrows. "It was to test your reactions, and reflexes. And I must say you passed. Now, since I doubt you're going to offer me any help with cleaning this up." he gestured down the hallway. "You can go and enjoy your day off."

~

Matt woke sometime early Saturday morning. Unwilling as of yet to let the few wisps of sleep escape him for the morning, he struggled to return to bliss. Eventually sighing in resignation, he moaned in annoyance and rolled over, his hair falling away from his face. Already the thin, fragile tendrils of his dream were leaving him for awareness, and the sounds of running water reached his ears. He opened his eyes to see light pouring in from the cracks in the bathroom door.

Yawning he pulled his arms over his head and stretched, attempting to draw off the inevitable for as long as he could. Sitting up he paused for a moment to let the spinning world right itself, than got out of the bed, and began the morning ritual of dressing and tying back his hair.

Clipping in his earring, he left the room and locked the door after himself, leaving Ally to herself. Making his way down to the cafeteria, he pulled out a chair and sat down heavily with a *fwump*. Putting his feet up he allowed himself to ease into the morning. Yawning still, he snatched a couple pieces of toast already set out for the morning, and smothered them with jam and marmalade - devouring them hungrily to break his fast and ease the rumbling down below.

He felt like being alone for the moment; felt like relaxing and relishing the silence.

Despite his hatred of the boring days spent 'searching' the ocean; his love for the water continued to grow. Making his way out of the oaken front doors, and onto the dock, he looked to where the Yacht was anchored out to sea just a way's from the castle, and another sigh passed from his lips.

He sat down on the dock and looked out towards the horizon. It was a cool day, and there was a thick layer of fog drifting lazily across the still waters. Backstroking across the waves.

Looking up into the sky he could see the pale-yellow sun's blurred image behind the thick clouds overhead. It was actually quite beautiful. He could see sparse pieces of the white sky hidden behind the gray clouds; it looked as if somebody had began to paint a picture but just hadn't finished yet.

He heard a distant rumble off in the distance, and he knew it would soon be raining over the school. Another rumble, and he looked off to the gray storm clouds flashing with lightning rolling in from the west - they were coming in fast, perhaps it would be raining too hard for them to go out today. Now there was wishful thinking - Brandon would sooner chew his own ear off.

Removing his boots and socks and rolling up his pant legs to his knees, Matt dipped his toes into the chill water below the dock. The iciness of it causing chills to chase each other up and down his legs until they were numb from the cold. His hairs stood on end - but he liked the feeling. It was wonderful knowing a human could die of hypothermia had they attempted this, but as soon as Matt let himself - his body would shift and take care of that problem for him.

He remained like that for a while, just sitting there and relishing the tingling feeling and numbness of his lower limbs. Finally he allowed his legs to relax, watched them carefully as they fused together, and watched as his feet grew flat and long; turning into his graceful sapphire fins.

He watched the scales inch up his thighs and around his waist - covering his pants - stopping just below his navel. Then he felt his shirt slowly dissolve into the thick air, his gills reacting to the cold mist. He blinked once, his vision becoming blurry, and slipped off the dock into the warm, comfortable waters below.

The dock was suspended about a foot above the water by twenty-foot poles driven into the sea floor to keep them anchored. It was always a surprise to see how deep the water was so close to the castle; it was like somebody had deliberately placed a mound of rock out in the middle of nowhere for the castle.

But this didn't bother Matt.

He gently drifted down to the ocean floor, and drifted along the sand on his back, using the underwater currents to propel him along. Once in a while flipping his tail gently to speed his momentum ever so slightly. Staring up at the surface, he could see little more then a few spaces of white. The density of the fog blotting out everything save a dull yellow globe where he assumed the sun was situated. He relished the feel of the water caressing his skin and scales; massaging him gently. Easing away any and all tension.

Turning back onto his front, he thrashed his tail once and sped off around the heap of rock. Once, twice, and again. Then he tore off in the opposite direction after a school of fish- catching up to, and passing them effortlessly. His heart singing in vivacious freedom.

Suddenly he stopped, drifting to a stop in the middle of chasing down a lone tuna. Something had caught his ear, and he floated back down onto the sand as he listened, straining his ears in the direction of the dock.

There it was again: "Matt..."

It was quiet, muffled by the waves and the fog. But the octave and note of longing in it were unmistakable.

Ally.

A smile blossomed on his face, and he swam quietly over to settle beneath the dock, looking up through the water to see her silhouette through the cracks in the wood. She was kneeling on the timber, snow melting at her touch to drip down through the cracks in the wood; peering over into the water. "Matt, are you out there?"

Still grinning, he swam over slightly to the left where he could see her face staring out into the water a little to the right of him, trying to make her normal eyes pierce the inky blackness that was haven. It was a futile effort - she couldn't see him. But he could see her perfectly.

Without a moments deliberation he flicked his tail, and sped up to the surface. Propelling himself forward just enough to be able to reach her wrists as he cleared the water; his fingers wrapping around her skin gently, innocuously, but with an unbreakable grip. Pulling her in with him as he dropped back down. Dragging her with him to the bottom.

Ally laughed uncontrollably as she struggled in his grip; trying to break free, to swim away. But Matt held fast, and soon she relaxed in his grip, allowing her body to drift down and meld with his, her face flushed from laughing. Her smile as broad as ever.

I suppose this was your idea of a joke?

Matt grinned. *In a way, you were just in the wrong place at the wrong time.*

Ally felt his tail wrap smoothly around hers, keeping her body pinned to his, and she leaned down so their faces were almost touching. *Well then I guess should count myself lucky.* She whispered, her lips barely brushing his.

Matt lent forward and kissed her deeply, his tongue probing for entrance. Pulling back after a moment, he asked softly, as if unwilling to disturb the silence and peace that lay beneath the waves. *What made you look for me out here?*

She gazed deeply into his eyes. *Matt, I'm your lover. I know things about you you probably don't even know about yourself.*

Such as...

Such as: when you wake up in a good mood - like today. You feel like keeping it that way. So in retrospect, you normally go off on your own to try and find some seclusion. Like, oh I don't know - the ocean?

He laughed. *Fairs fair, I guess.* He kissed her again. *Anything else about myself I should be made privy to?*

Her eyes twinkled with inner workings of mischief. *Well, you're also quite a lousy kisser.*

His eyes flashed and he pinched her mockingly, delighting in the small squeal of surprise that shrilled from her lips. Then set about proving her wrong.

~

"Tell me another."

"Alright, lets see." Eric put his finger to his chin in pretence of thinking. "Oh I know. In a hospital: the first Australian asks: 'Was I brought here to die?' then the second Australian answers, 'No, you were brought here yester-die'."

Alexandra and Cody both chuckled. Already they were red-faced, but they continued to beg him for more jokes.

"Another! Another!" Cody yelled, jumping up and down along the balcony - dangerously close to the ledge.

Eric grabbed a hold of his coat collar, and pulled him back with a sharp yank, remembering Cody's affinity for leaping over ledges and railings. "Alright - family story. My mom always hides the Christmas presents around the house in various places each year but... sometimes she can't find them. So about three weeks after Christmas, my brother's sitting on the couch playing a game, when he suddenly draws a package from between the cushions, and exclaims: 'Oh... a puppy!'."

It took a moment for the punch line to sink in - but when it did Cody fell down onto the snow, clutching at his stomach and laughing like it was the last day of Earth. Eric looked down at him and his lips quirked. Nothing gave him more pleasure than to see someone laughing at one of his jokes.

"More, more!" Cody giggled, regaining breath enough to speak.

He cracked a grin, he had the perfect one: "If at first you don't succeed... skydiving is *not* for you!"

Cody fell back onto the snow, almost crying in gayety.

Still grinning, Eric glanced over at Alexandra to see her stone-faced, and staring over the ledge.

"What is it?" He walked over to her, concerned. Not just for her lack of mirth, but her expression practically radiated anxiety

"Look." She whispered, and pointed.

Eric moved over to the ledge, and peered down at the rocks below, the waves crashing into them like brass cymbals. "I don't see anythi- wait..." Eric peered closer, his fingers grasping the rock.

Alex looked over at him, anxious. "You see it?"

"Yeah I see it. It looks sort of like a body-"

"COOL!" Cody bounced over and jumped up onto the ledge on all fours, staring down at the crumpled figure lying amidst the jagged rocks.

It really didn't resemble much save a black shapeless mass of what possibly could be assumed was seaweed; but the eyes of sages were sharp - and what *could* have been a shapeless mass to an ordinary human, resembled to a sage more closely that of a figure which stood upon its hind legs.

Yanking Cody back onto the safe side of the ledge, Eric reached over the side with both arms. "You're going to have to help me, Alex." He told her.

She nodded, and mimicked his stance.

Then they began to pull. Using the advice Miranda had given them; extending their minds down to the figure - it started to rise.

Cody - shaking with excitement - stared over the ledge at the rising figure, growing larger and clearer all the while. He wished desperately he could do that - but it was quite possible he'd overexert himself in the process; and for once, Cody let the others handle it.

Unlike Matt and Ally, who were powerful enough to do such trivial things without the support and guidance of their hands - level five sages found it incredibly difficult to lift things with telekinesis. The strain on their minds was severe, and their bodies suffered as a result. Eric was already suffering under the strain, and struggled to keep his hold. But when Alex fainted -slumping down into the snow - the figure, now undeniably human, almost at eye level; Eric grunted in pain, fighting desperately to keep his hold under the sudden addition of opposing force. The figure rose up in agonizingly small increments, but eventually Eric managed to lift it high enough for Cody to reach out and yank it over the ledge.

Staring blankly at the figure slumped over limply in the snow, Eric slid slowly down against the rock ledge. Sweat trickled steadily down his face, despite the frigid weather. His breath came fast and short: wheezing. Sweat ran into his eyes and stung, and he closed them painfully, trying to regain enough breath for speech. Eventually he hissed out, "Get, Matt.... Ally..." Before passing out from exertion, his head lolling onto Alex's shoulder.

Cody took one last look at the figure, than spun to his feet and tore off back into the castle.

~ 13 ~

Matt circled around Ally and embraced her into his arms, dropping small, sucking kisses onto her neck. Pushing her hair aside with his nose. Drawing in the faint sent of seawater mixed with the underlying aroma that was just Ally.

She leant back into his arms, her hands on his as they traced the thin line of skin revealed between the rims of her shirt and pants. Teasing, barely touching, moving slightly under her shirt. She tilted her head, exposing more of her neck, and he took the offer enthusiastically - nibbling suggestively up along her jaw.

He was glad no one was up yet. They'd been quite obvious on their way back to their room from the dock - what with him whispering words and promises of things to come, and her trying to suppress the resulting blush. Both off them landing heavily against the walls here and there; finding the task of reaching the privacy of their room quite demanding of attention they weren't willing to give.

Their heads shot up when a sudden BANG! BANG! BANG shrilled loudly at the door. Shattering the relative silence as effectively as a baseball through a window. They broke apart just as a frantic Cody burst into the room, gasping for breath and clutching a stick at his side. "MATT! ALLY! Boy am I glad to see you! You've got to come, right now!"

Though relieved beyond words Cody was apparently too exhausted to notice the flush mirrored across their faces, or the disheveled state of their clothing - the fact that Cody had stopped talking after telling them precisely what he wanted... had them considerably disturbed.

Matt turned his head, buying time to regain his composure. "What is it, Cody?" *We've got to remember to lock that thing.*
I thought you had.

I was slightly distracted by other... things... He shot a look at her over his shoulder, and caught her whipping her neck furiously - her blush returning in spades.

Cody swallowed, still gasping. "Just follow, me - no time to explain!" And he sprinted from the room.

Now they were scared. *Did he just... actually shut up without an explanation?*

He did... I'm worried. Ally glanced over at Matt, exchanged a baffled look, then the two of them ran out after Cody; now miles ahead of them.

~

Being the fastest one among them - catching up to Cody was no simple matter. In fact, they never did. They caught a few quick glimpses of him as he rounded corners - which kept them heading in the right direction - but other then that, it was apparent that if Cody didn't wish to be caught... he wouldn't be.

They reached the balcony just as Eric was coming around. He smiled as they made their way over, "Glad to see you two could make it to the party. As you can see, we've had *one* too many drinks." A hiccup would have been well placed - as it were, Eric could hardly lift his head from where it rested on Alex's shoulder.

Matt rolled his eyes, and helped him to his feet as Ally revived Alex; only then did they notice the figure lying in the snow.

"What the... Who's this?" Matt asked, looking over at the figure with interest and slight surprise. At first glance one could tell the man was fairly young, with downy blond hair, a little stubble, and a muscular frame; around thirty, he guessed, with a slight smattering of pale brown freckles across the bridge of his nose.

Eric shrugged, or... tried to. "We don't know. Alex saw him lying on the rocks." he twitched his head in the direction of the ledge behind him. "We lifted him up. Took more out of us then we'd have wanted." He grinned.

Ah. Thought Matt. *I guess that explains a few things.* He watched the man as Ally's ebony energy surrounded him, reviving him. Watched as he stirred, and exotic golden eyes snapped open. He then jerked into a sitting position, shaking his head, a hand to his temple.

Gazing at him a moment - as if assessing a potential threat - Ally strode over and knelt beside him in the snow. At her touch the white stuff melted and ran, leaving a dry patch of stone for her to sit on. This did not go unnoticed by the man; he stared.

Ally looked steadily into his eyes, wondering just what sort of character he possessed - and deciding to find out. "Who are you?" she asked him quite bluntly.

"Who are you!?" he demanded. His voice was rough, most likely the cause of disuse; and quite caustic.

Ignoring his rudeness, passing it off as fear, she answered him tersely, "My name is Ally. His name is Mathue," She pointed, "Eric, Alexandra - and the landed fish over there is Cody. Now I'll ask you again: Who are you?"

"I... don't remember..." He paused, his eyes crossing in apparent deliberation. Suddenly he exclaimed, "Wait! Yes I do! It's, Gregory - no! Wait a moment, I'll get it..." He scrunched up his face again. His voice had changed; still rough around the edges, but now there was a eagerness and kindness that hadn't been present before. "Yes, that's it! It's Darius- no... Yes it's Darius." He smiled broadly, nodding his head so furiously, Ally was afraid it might wobble off.

Behind her the others wore identical expression of skepticism and amusement.

"Don't you mean delirious." Eric whispered to Alex out of the corner of his mouth, and she hid a smile behind her hand.

Ally shot him a glare, but thankfully, Darius hadn't noticed.

"Darius Thorn, nice to meet you, uh... Ally." He shot out his hand, and Ally took it tentatively. Giving it a quick pump before snatching her own hand back as if she might catch something. Again, Darius seemed not to notice.

Suddenly the door to the castle banged open - smashing angrily against the stonewall of the castle - and Mr. And Mrs. Dixon - as well as a bemused Jason and Kim - strode swiftly out of the school; practically running towards them. Faces filled with what looked to be concern and fright mixed together and tied up neatly with apprehension.

Dennis knelt down beside Darius, and brushed off his wet t-shirt with a glove taken from his own hand. "Oh Mr. Thorn we are *so* sorry about your flight. Did it crash nearby? -Or did you have to swim a fair distance?"

"Come inside, you must be freezing!" Miranda scolded, and helped her husband lift the dazed man to his feet.

"Flight... oh yes! *That* flight!" Darius muttered as he was virtually dragged inside by the Dixon's.

The seven teens left out in the air stared at the shut door for a moment; utterly befuddled. Then Cody piped up, finally unable to hold his tongue any longer. (Though all things considering, for the amount of time he *had* remained silent - he'd accomplished something.) "What was that all about? I wonder who he was? Darius, I mean. I He sounded kind of important, the way Dennis and Miranda went on- hey! You guy's came with them!" He turned to face Kim and Jason, who were standing a fair distance apart. "Do you know what's going on? Who he is? I- murph!"

Reaching over, Eric slapped a hand over Cody's mouth. Looking over at Kim and Jason, he asked, "*Do* you guy's know what that was all about?"

Kim shook her head, "Jason and I were just talking outside the cafeteria when they ran past... so we decided to follow them. I bet we're more in the dark than you guy's are - who was that man anyway?"

"His name is Darius Thorn." Cody told her, shoving Eric's hand away indignantly, "But other than that we know nothing. It was so COOL! Alex saw him lying on the rocks down there and Eric told her to help him pull the guy up - so they did. Wouldn't it be cool to be lifted into the air like that!? Hey, Eric! Do you think you could do that to ME sometime? I'd be awfully good - I wouldn't move or anything! It'd be really neat to fly. Have you ever wondered what it would be like to- MURPH!!!"

Eric looked at them sheepishly, hand firmly clapped over the offending voice box.

~

When Matt and Ally got back to their room, the mood was unmistakably gone. Instead they curled up together on Ally's bed, and discussed silently this abrupt development. Darius was certainly an odd one. Hopefully he had nothing to do with them.

"Well, Dennis and Miranda obviously knew him. He must have been on his way here for a reason." Matt leant back against the headboard, running his fingers absently through the strands of chestnut hair.

"If that's true then why was he such a dimwit?"

"Maybe he was just pretending?"

"And why in the world would he do a thing like that!?" Ally tilted her head in his lap to look up at him.

"I don't know! It was only a suggestion. I'm really as clueless about this as you are."

"Well, whether he's really an idiot or..." She glanced up at him again, "really pretending; I doubt he has anything to do with us."

"Hmm."

"What?"

"Well I was just wondering... Dennis mentioned the guy's flight - I mean his *flight*! I bet his just a psychotic millionaire who's going to give them some charity or something. After all, this *is* a non-profit organization."

"Yes, that's makes sense..."

"Of course it does. Because *I* am a genius."

She snorted, but deigned not to answer. Instead she asked, "Yeah... It does seem slightly odd. Supposedly this *is* a non-profit organization, yet... they have to get their money from somewhere."

Matt was silent for a moment, his thoughts turned inward. That precise thought had been nagging him for a while now - where did Dennis get the money from? Had he not given Miss Gilbertson fifty thousand to give them a simple tour? It seamed more then only slightly farfetched.

Glancing over at the clock, he sighed, and pushed those thoughts aside for the moment. "It's about dinner time - what say we go grab some grub?"

She laughed quietly, and allowed herself to be tugged to the door.

～

But those thoughts weren't to be shoved away. No sooner had they walked into the cafeteria, than Matt spotted Darius sitting at the far end of the table with Dennis and Brandon. The three of which all conversing in hushed tones, serious expressions marring their faces. They stopped when they caught sight of the two when they entered the room.

Matt, however, had caught something of the end of Brandon's last sentence: "Though... do you suppose they're ready? I mean can they handle it?" Confusing as it was, he supposed it hardly concerned him; and shoved it aside.

Dennis stood abruptly as if electrocuted, and smiled at them as they sat down to the soup and salad - the twinkle mysteriously absent. "Matt, Ally; I believe you've already met Mr. Thorn?"

Matt nodded carefully, staring fixedly over at Darius. Ally pretended not to have heard - though listening closely.

"Eh hem." Dennis cleared his throat awkwardly, than smiled again. "He'll just be staying with us for a short while, and I hope you'll make his stay welcome."

Ally looked away, and spooned out some soup for herself into a bowl.

Matt did the same, though asked cautiously, "If you don't mind me asking, sir: Why is Mr. Thorn here?" He ignored the startled look Ally shot at him from behind her bangs, and stared unblinkingly over at the man in question.

Something in Dennis' eyes said he was taken aback, but his face remained neutral; "He's here to oversee the safety of this place - he'll give his okay, and head back to Oregon with the final report."

Sounded plausible enough. Matt remained staring at Darius for a while longer, before he - like Ally - turned to his soup, and made an effort to forget the entire ordeal. Something about it continued to nag at him from the back of his mind, though, and he was heard pressed to ignore it.

The something that continued to nag at him was made all the more infuriating because it seemed to have a point - there was something odd about this Darius - and not just the way he acted. No, it was something more... familiar.

It wasn't long before everyone else came in for supper. The temptation of food not nearly as tempting as were the answers to questions Dixon might be able - or willing - to satisfy. They were sorely disappointed. Dennis gave them all the same speech about being nice to guests, and asked them that - since it was Saturday - would anyone like to show Mr. Thorn around the school?

Cody's hand immediately shot into the air. "I will Mr. Dixon! I will!"

Dennis inclined his head. "Thank you, Cody." Before sitting back down at his salad.

"The perfect match!" Eric cracked. "The chatterbox and a crazy!"

Everyone laughed, Miranda scowled, and Cody was too busy eating to care.

~

The next day brought a new wave of dread into Matt's system, as Brandon walked over to them smugly at breakfast, holding out their communicators.

Beside him Ally went green.

With everyone watching, Matt put on a spectacular show of yelling bloody murder. Telling Brandon quite equivocally that they weren't even going to go *near* the ocean until Brandon finally agreed that he wouldn't make them spend the *entire* day out in the ocean - maybe only the morning. Then, reluctantly - with everyone still watching them speechlessly - they took the communicators from his open palms, and strapped them onto their wrists.

Finishing up breakfast without appetite, they followed him from the cafeteria, and out onto the warming dock.

~

Walking to the back of the yacht, they folded their arms over the railing. Watching the castle fade away as they sped off into the calm, open, blue. Brandon told them they'd be starting at the end of the trench again - and as a side note warned them to keep a close eye for sharks. It was a very long swim - it would take them at least an hour to reach the spot with the boat, and Brandon said they'd only have to go until midday. That gave them leeway of maybe three or four hours... which wasn't as bad as it could be.

Sighing, Ally leant forward, cradling her head into her arms; staring down into the white water formed as the yacht motored by. Her hair tied back for once in a braid down her back, to keep it from flying into her face.

Matt couldn't help but notice the change in the temperature, and his heart lightened considerably at the prospect of spring. Though the waters were still chill, and out in the pacific as they were they couldn't hope for anything as farfetched as summer; the snow on the castle turrets had begun to melt, and it was certainly better than winter.

Beside him Ally didn't share his buoyant mood. Her thoughts were still dark and revolving constantly around Darius; there was something about him... but when she dove over the side into the warm waters with Matt at her side, she couldn't help but let her thoughts get carried away by the soothing ocean currents.

Behind them lay the trench: dark and foreboding. But before them was a wide-open area of sand and nothing for miles. The sunlight filtered down through the water to cast rays of light dancing along the sandy floor, shadowed here and there only by a few sparse clouds and by the Yacht following them over head. It looked almost like an underwater beach - random mollusk's, and small hermit crabs, the beach-goers.

Suddenly feeling a rush of exhilaration, Matt flipped his tail and sped out into the open sea. Spinning and flipping through the water, Ally laughing beside him all the way, he eventually slowed to catch his breath; drifting down onto the sand. *That was fun.* He couldn't explain in its entirety just what had caused the spontaneous act - only that it somehow felt... right. Stopping completely he allowed himself to float down onto the sand, feeling the cool grains rise to kiss his body as he caught his breath.

He gazed up towards the surface seventy feet above with wonder resplendent on his face; awed beyond words at the knowledge they could live in such a blissful world.

Ally swam over to him, and flopped down onto him, her tail drifting over to brush his. Knowing this couldn't last for long - Brandon - after all - could see them on the monitor.

Despite the thickness and sheer strength of his tail: he could still feel the softness of hers. And - marveling at his own sensitivity - reached over with his arm and drew her close, kissing her on the cheek lightly chastely. They lay like that a moment more, then sighed in tandem, and swam off once more - slower this time.

After a while, though, of seeing nothing but sand, they both grew bored and detached. Thus were both beyond gratitude when they caught sight of the blue light flashing on their communicators, calling them to the surface. Switching direction on a dime, they tore for the surface and the rope ladder waiting for them.

Brandon smiled at them as they clambered over the rail, sympathizing - it seemed - with their malcontent. Handing them a platter of sandwiches, which they took gratefully and ate at such breakneck speeds, it was a miracle they didn't choke themselves.

Brandon sat down with them in the cabin as they finished and – thankfully - swallowed. "Now I know you've got to be fairly bored - nothing much to look at through this stretch. But I don't want to turn back until you reach the reef. You're almost there, maybe only a click or so further, so it won't take that long and-"

"Reef?" Matt looked up from where he'd been intently studying his nails. Raising an eyebrow.

"Yes, the 'Discuss reef'. And-"

"But, there can't be a reef here. We're nowhere near the equator, its far to cold!"

"That may be true, but remember that project they started in 2002?"

"Yeah… you mean the one about spreading ecosystems? Eco-Diversity2002, I think."

"Your memory is better than mine. Anyway - the reef you'll be coming upon is living proof they succeeded."

Wow. Matt blinked his eyes wide.

Ally smiled slightly; she was probably just as amazed - but knew the reef couldn't be all that Brandon made it out to be. It just wasn't warm enough up here to sustain such an ecosystem. They were too close to Canada…

They strapped on their communicators before getting up, then walked over to the rail, and dove over.

Crashing into the water with a sigh, Matt closed his eyelids and swam off after Ally; much less enthused then he had been before.

Knowing full well Brandon wouldn't let them quit for the day until they'd reached said reef; they swam on slightly faster then usual, though still taking their measured time. Streaking past fish and reeds for another mile or so, it wasn't long before they caught sight of a large undersea mountain looming up before them. Jutting up into the distance about thirteen leagues from the sea floor.

Wow. Matt looked up without raising his head, peering through his dark brown bangs at the rigged peaks and sharp overhangs formed by the natural rock. *Wow.*

Gazing from side to side along the rise, Ally watched the rock wall as it sped off in either direction. Never ending. She'd guessed it to be at *least* 200 miles long; it just kept going and going and going.

Wow.

You can stop saying that now!!!

Matt flashed her a grin, flipped his tail, and started the swim up the vertical incline of rock. Higher and higher. Swimming around sudden outcroppings and darting away from a rock that tumbled off a ledge when Ally bumped it.

Normally when they headed for the surface, they simply sped right up - now they were swimming perhaps as slowly as a human would; taking their time and admiring the natural formation. Maybe it was that usual swiftness which prevented them from ever noticing the pressure change in the depth of the water - Matt noticed it now. As they rose Matt could feel the decrease in pressure - his ears didn't pop, or anything like that. It was just a sudden realization that the water around them wasn't pressing down on them quite as hard. It was so strange. He knew that *regular* humans had to rise slowly and exhale as they ascended, to avoid exploding -that's what he'd heard anyway from Kevin. But he supposed the fish part of his body took care of everything on it's own.

Suddenly he became aware of something else. *Too high, it's much too high. Its going to* - Matt's head broke the surface. - *be much higher than we expected.*

They heard the breaking waters before the Yacht, and turned to see it stop just a few meters away from their buoyant position.

Brandon leaned over the forward rail, smiling. "And this is where we stop for the day. There's a cove just down there a ways," he pointed down the solid rock mountain; which rose another meter above the surface before finally deciding it'd gone high enough. "So boats can get through, even though I still have to be careful of submerged rocks and such. That's where we'll be starting tomorrow-"

"TOMORROW!!!" Matt and Ally both screeched, looking affronted.

"You promised us a five day break!" Matt spat, his face turning red from the effort of scowling so deep; his eyes looking as if they were about to pop from his skull.

Brandon started to argue, but the two held their ground - or, water; and finally he relented. "Oh all right - *all right*!" He half snapped, half sighed. His lower lip jutting like a pouting six-year-old. "You can have your break - but only four days! You hear!?"

They both nodded, satisfied, and made for the rope ladder hanging permanently over the side of the Yacht.

Brandon looked down at them, something behind his eyes suggesting inner workings. "You know, I've a few call's to make-"

"What sort of calls?"

Brandon seemed to blush. "That's none of your mind. The point is, if you two want to go say... exploring? I'm going to be maybe a couple minutes. If you'd rather not, of course, you can still come aboard." He forced a smile, then pushed off the rail, and disappeared beyond the hull.

Matt looked up at Ally. "Want to? We'll probably just have to wait onboard if we don't. At least this way we could have some... fun." he winked.

Her lips twitched, and she released the rope, allowing herself to drop back into the water with a splash. Surfacing, she shrugged, trying desperately to hold back her smile. "Why not. Do you want to go over?" She jabbed her thumb at the looming barrier behind her.

Matt looked up; they could easily climb over. It wasn't that high. And it didn't look *that* jagged... "Sure." He nodded, making for the wall.

He turned when he felt a hand on his shoulder.

"Not that way." She smiled. "We're not going to climb over..."

Matt's eyes opened wide, and he stared at her. Turning back to the rock mountain he gazed at it steadily. Sizing it up. "You think we can jump it?"

She grinned. "Only one way to find out." And dove back under the surface.

Matt rolled his eyes then allowed himself to sink after her. *This is suicidal...*

They dove down the twenty leagues or so, then switched direction before hitting the sand, and tore up towards the surface. Gaining momentum as they went.

Matt stared up at the surface determinedly. Watching the light as it became brighter and brighter. Though outwardly he was determined; inside his heart was shaking at the very pit of his chest. Trembling with the prospect of what he was about to do.

How do you know we won't just spill our guts all over the rock?
I don't.

Matt turned back to face upward. *Well that's comforting.* He missed her smile.

The surface grew ever closer, and suddenly they cleared the surface; breaking the warm water at top-notch speed into the chill air. Water sprayed away from their bodies, dripping down off their flukes as they flew up and over the wall.

Matt felt his heart leap into his throat as he neared the end of the rocks - they were going to make it! He'd forgotten just how high they could jump with the right speed. Then he clutched at his chest in pain, twisting, and hitting the water at an angle as he clutched his hands over his torso.

~

Ally flew over the wall with grace. Angling her body so she soared up into the open sky, then tilting downward to slip back into the warm embrace of the water. Hardly causing a ripple, let along a splash. Rising up to float a ways form the wall, she clenched her fists in triumph. *Yes! We did it, Matt! Matt?*

She whirled, her eyes darting. She spotted him easily, lying in a tight ball on the ocean floor quite a ways beneath her.

Concerned, she swam down towards him. *Matt...*

I'm ok, I just... Matt took his hands from his chest, and a crimson plume of what appeared to be smoke welled up and away; borne on the ocean currents. It didn't take three guesses as to what exactly it was. At the sight she drew a sudden, sharp breath. Abruptly Matt convulsed in pain, and clutched his hands over the gapping wound tighter than a tourniquet. Curling back into a ball of misery.

Ally hurried to his side, and pried his hands away from the wound. She only managed a quick glance - but what she saw almost made her wretch. Swiftly replacing the pressure with her own hand to stanch the flow of blood; she closed her eyes, and focused.

The wound was probably fatal; the rock had cut straight into his lungs... Coughing he chocked up some blood, and wondered if he should be feeling panicked. Though fear was the furthest emotion from his mind at the moment; feeling the wound close and the flow of bodily liquid ebb. All he felt was annoyance, really, as his tail uncurled from its spastic position to rest peacefully against the rock.

Feel better?

Matt opened his eyes and sat up to gaze at her - about to tell her he'd never felt better. When suddenly he looked passed her, his eyes and mouth opening wide and gaping in awe.

Ally looked at him in vastly returning concern. *Matt... what is it?*

In response, Matt lifted his hands, reached out, and took hold of her face. He then turned her head to face away from him, and her eyes bulged from her skull.

There, before them, was a sight matched by nothing Earth could conceive.

Ally gazed out speechlessly in wonder. Swimming up slightly through the water to get a better look. The reef sped off in either direction along the rock barrier, and out before them as far as they could see.

Wow.

~ 14 ~

After the original shock had worn off, Matt and Ally swam up closer and soon discovered why it was called the 'Discuss Reef.'

The only fish that could be seen, were discusses.

The reef itself was a beautiful array of colors. Coral and sea urchins, seaweeds and tube plants co-existed in harmony - but no other fish but discuses could be seen.

There were many of them. Large ones, small ones - some of them *extremely* small; but they were all of the same species.

Matt gazed around in open mouthed wonder at all the different colors flitting back and forth along the sandy floor. Through the reeds and coral, up through the water, darting back and forth - each a different color and design. Each just as awing and beautiful as the last.

With interest he watched a tiny discus that was probably no bigger than his little finger, was a bright neon orange, and seemed to be quite disoriented as to which way it wanted to go. It would swim up one piece of the bright pink Anemone it was hovering around; than change its mind halfway and dart back down again. Then it would dart around and into one of the tubes - a second later darting back out again. Then it began to swim around and around the Anemone with ever increasing speed - before it decided it was much too dizzy to continue, and instead floated down onto the sand for a moment - then it would start the entire process all over again.

He chuckled silently at its antics.

Ally twisted in the water, staring around with mixed emotions of wonder and confusion. *I didn't know there were so many different kinds of discus fish.* She wondered aloud, watching a red discus with orange and black stripes as it explored the tiny crevasses between the hard coral; searching for food, she assumed.

There aren't. Matt told her, his eyes now focused on a fish about the size of his torso; a dark green with purple stripes. *It's all unnatural - the fish, the reef... It's all man-made. It's not right.*

But it is still beautiful...

Matt had to agree; the way everything just blended... it *was* beautiful. But as he gazed around, he couldn't help but think something was terribly wrong - not just the fact that there was way too much human intervention here - but something paranormal. Something just wasn't right. It wasn't like when they'd sensed danger with the shark; no... he wasn't afraid. He was more... curious, like something was hidden from him. He felt close, as if it were right beside him, but cloaked - shielded.

And he wanted to find out what.

Though before he could ponder more on the subject, Ally swam from him, and out over the corral. *Strange...*

What? He asked, swimming up beside her. Still weary, looking down beneath him at the waving plants and fish.

The fish, they don't seem to care we're here...

Why should they? I mean we have fins too... right?

Ally looked at him with a critical eye. *Matt, we're predators. Mermaids eat fish.*

We do? Matt raised his eyebrows; this was news to him. *You don't say.* Looking back at the colorful twisting rainbow beneath him, he thought for a moment. Then a sickening thought entered his mind. He turned to her. *Raw?*

Ally shot him a smile that said clearly: 'Got a problem with that?'

Matt did his best to hold onto his lunch. *Did you... ever ...*

Eat a fish raw? Once.

Matt looked back over at her, his eyes wide and his tongue hanging out in an obvious attempt at a grimace. What it was actually, was comical. Ally had to physically restrain herself from laughing. Instead, she snapped: *Oh stop gaping! I was hungry, and in this form it looked... tasty...*

And was it?

Ally put a finger to her chin. *I really can't remember...*

Sure... Matt replied in a sarcastic tone; insinuating a falsifier.

I can't!

Matt rolled his eyes.

Ally charged.

She hit him lightly, but hard enough to send him flying back through the water over the coral garden. Flipping his tail he stopped himself before he could crash into the barrier. *Oh you are so dead!* And he was after her in a nanosecond and a stream of bubbles. Tearing around rocks, reeds, fish, and eventually cornering her against the rock wall where they had started.

Grinning uncontrollably, Ally tried one last futile escape by faking left and swimming to Matt's left. But he caught her tail at the last second as she raced by, and dragged her slippery, wriggling form back into his arms - that was when he noticed the blue light flashing on his band.

~

"What were you two *doing* that took you *fifteen* minutes to notice your bands!?"

Ally blushed guiltily and lowered her gaze, but Matt shrugged indifferently - hoping the laughter in his eyes couldn't be seen. "We were just so busy exploring the reef, we forgot to check it as often as we might have."

Brandon took the excuse without question - he'd seen the reef. Knew well the awe inspired by it. He continued, "That as it were - you had me worried sick. I was just about to call Dennis-"

"NO!" eyes popped and mirrored looks of horror etched themselves across their faces.

Brandon's lip twitched. "I wasn't too thrilled at the thought myself. So next time - check it a bit more often, all right?"

They nodded in assent.

~

That was close.

Matt watched the jagged barrier as it got smaller on the horizon. *Yeah...*

We should be more careful about what we do and where and around whom we do it.

Aw! But half the fun is never knowing when you're about to get caught! He cracked, flashing her a grin.

Ally shot him a smile from behind her bangs, and, giving his hand a reassuring squeeze; went back to staring out at the water. The mirrored expanse broken only by the Yacht as it sped across its glazed surface.

The waning day was already becoming warm and humid. And not long after their clothes had dried - their sweat had soaked them again.

Ally had long ago retreated to the coolness of the cabin, but Matt had remained at the stern. Staring out towards the horizon, his thoughts buried deep until finally he snapped back to reality, and turned and headed for Ally and the cabin.

Only at the first step did he realize the ache in his legs; he'd been standing still for far too long. Taking a moment to stretch out muscles seized, he made his way sluggishly over to Brandon. "How much further to the school?" He asked, wiping the sweat from his brow with the back of his hand.

"Not far. Just about another five minutes." Brandon replied, keeping his eyes trained on the small black dot off in the distance; flicking once in a while down to the binnacle.

Matt watched him for a moment; contemplating whether or not to lay down his proposal. Then he sighed, and asked softly, "Mind if I swim the rest of the way?"

"No, not at all. Just mind you don't mention anything to Mr. Dixon, he'd have my head if he heard I'd let you."

"Sure. Thanks." Matt told him over his shoulder as he walked back to the stern.

Climbing up onto the rail, he balanced there for a moment. Just gazing off towards to horizon. Watching the water as it frothed in the ships wake. Ignoring his hair as it flew out and whipped around his face. Then he tilted forward, and dove into the silent world below.

He maneuvered his body and hit the water at an angle - gliding into the depths with minimal impact. He held his breath as he went under;

allowed himself to sink to the bottom, slowly. Keeping his eyes clenched tight against the stinging salt.

He remained that way until the stinging in his lungs could be ignored no longer, and reveled in the feeling of the warmth encroaching up his frozen legs, towards his torso, and over his neck where he gulped in a grateful lung-full of air into his body.

Opening his eyes wearily, he blinked his other eyelids into place, and watched the haul of the *R.K. Prowler* as it sped away off towards the mound of barren rock in the distance. The blaring sound of the motor muffled by the water.

Knowing Ally wouldn't follow him, knowing she knew when he wanted to be alone, and would respect his feelings; he sighed and sort of wished she'd followed him... Moving his fins sharply, he sped off along the barren sandy floor of the ocean. Catching up to the Yacht in a matter of seconds.

Matching his speed with that of the boat tearing through the water above his head, he swam as close to the sandy floor as he could; felt the irritating grains as they brushed his body in a sensual caress as he passed.

He kept his eyes trained ahead at the mound of rock. Already he could see the poles that held up the dock - but there was something else too, something...human. Matt looked closer; there were many miniature beings off swimming clumsily around the dock and outer wall of the castle.

~

Kelsi dipped her feet into the cold water tentatively - afraid a fish would come up and bite her foot off. She sat alone on the dock, wrapped in a soft towel. She'd only come because Cody said he wouldn't leave her alone until she at least came. She didn't have to go swimming or anything, but she had to at least come. And when Cody says he's not about to leave you alone - drastic measures must be taken.

She was sure Jason or Eric would have just shoved him aside or locked him up in a cupboard somewhere - and she supposed she could have just ignored him. She was good at that. Or if worse came to worse she could have blasted him; but she was a peacemaker, even had she wanted to she doubted she would have been able to make herself do any of those things. And so she'd agreed to come.

Now she sat shivering on the not-yet-warm dock. Watching the others as they swam. She looked around abruptly, thinking of Cody. Where was the little guy? ...

Suddenly she heard the sound of crashing waves and an outboard motor getting louder and louder. She looked up to see the school Yacht come plowing across the ocean towards them, slowing as it neared the dock.

~

The Yacht coasted to a halt at its regular distance from the school, dropping anchor and causing waves to crash into the solid foundation of the castle - much to the delight of the swimming teens. Standing at the rail, Ally gazed down at them a moment in contemplation; wondering why they were out swimming in such chill waters. How they could stand such chill waters. And how in the world they'd managed to get Dixon to agree. She shrugged mentally, supposed that because of the new warm weather, Eric or Cody or someone had begged Dennis to let them go swimming. -Either that, or Miranda had recommended it; and without further deliberation she dove back into the ocean which had grown on her almost like a second home.

Looping in the water, she surfaced almost immediately. And noticed forthwith the sudden reaction to her as everyone backed off slightly. Above the surface it was fairly obvious she had a tail; perhaps that was the reason behind the irrational paranoia. Her eyes narrowed; need they be so condescending? And so blatantly obvious while they were at it?

Kelsi didn't really mind the 'water sage' form. She kind of liked it actually - found it quite interesting, entrancing and beautiful. Though she knew where the others were coming from, of course - Matt and Ally were four levels higher than Ivy at level six. Which was a large enough gap as it was. But they were then five levels higher then any of the level fives, (I.E: Eric, Jason, Kim, and Alexandra) which put them all in a spot of inferiority. And if truth be admitted - fear. Matt and Ally were too far separated from the others - they were different. They weren't to be trusted. And they were far too powerful to play around with - or tease. The only other option left? Hostility.

Kelsi, however, did not suffer from these same prejudices. Sure Ally and Matt were powerful - sure they were different; but weren't they all? Smiling over at Ally, who was returning the glares directed at her full force and was backing away from them ever so slowly; she asked sweetly, "Where's Matt?" She glanced up at the Yacht, expecting to see Matt dive into the water as Ally had.

Ally, still wary, deigned to glance her way. She gauged Kelsi's expression - and once satisfied the other wasn't simply baiting her, she answered disquietly, "He's around here somewhere. He swam the rest of the way back, so it's probable he got here before us and - ah. There he is." She waved her hand over to the left, maybe a couple meters out to sea, where there was a sudden splash, and Matt came pelting out of the water; straight up into the sky. His sapphire fins glittered and sunlight flashed from water droplets beading on his sapphire scales, causing them to glitter, before he flew back into the water gracefully. Leaving Kim and Ivy - the closest to him - showered in water.

He re-surfaced next to Ally, and shook his soggy mane from his eyes.

She crossed her arms in mock jealousy. "Show off." She muttered.

Matt grinned, and folded his arms behind his head. Tilting back he flopped down in the water and floated so his tail was visible above the water. "Yeah but what can you say? I've got talent."

"Yeah. Right!" Ally suddenly flipped around and pushed down on his forehead and sent him sprawling beneath the water. Having been breathing regular air at the time - the action caused him nothing short of a choking attack. Fighting for the surface, he coughed and hacked the water from his lungs. This took the time of a few seconds, and by the time he'd regained his breath, Ally was having an attack of a different sort - clutching at her chest and laughing so tears ran down her cheeks.

Well now Matt wouldn't have any of that. With a devilish grin he grabbed a hold of her tail, and dragged her under with him - kissing her briefly on the cheek before speeding off away from her.

You are so *dead!*

Those above the water could see well enough the blackened forms of the two as they raced with blinding speed around and around the school, the dock and them. Twisting and turning with amazing velocity and accuracy. The chase went on and on - neither of them tiring. Though no mater how fast Ally went or how hard she tried, she just couldn't seem to catch him. Like she herself had said; he was just faster.

The others watched with growing delight and enthusiasm. Cheering on and watching in wonder as the two spun around with such speed it was difficult to follow with the eye.

Suddenly Matt stopped, turned on a dime and surfaced a foot from Jason - to Jason's quite surprise and displeasure. Ignoring him, Matt looked up from the waves over to the west balcony high above them; at a small figure waving his arms to get everyone's attention.

Ally surfaced with him, and as she too looked up, everyone's eyes slowly turned towards the new distraction.

~

Cody continued to wave his arms and shout until everyone - even Kelsi - was looking up at him. "WATCH THIS!!! He screamed, his shrill voice carrying easily to the figures below. And without further ado he climbed up on top of the ledge, balancing precariously. He'd always wanted to do this...

He raised his hands over his head into a point; just like he'd seen the professional divers do on T.V. Then he tilted his body foreword, bending into an arched position.

"No, Cody! DON"T!" Kelsi shrilled from below.

Came a small voice from below - just some fan wishing him luck. PHST! Like he'd need it, he was the best! He'd done this a *million* times!

Pushing himself off with his legs, he jumped.

The others watched from eighty feet below as the small level three sage plummeted, head first, at a million miles an hour; towards the warm, smooth, glass-like water below.

It was thrilling!

It was exciting!

It was fun!

It was... it was...

Cody searched for a word, his vocabulary abruptly on leave. He watched the water grow nearer - suddenly he wasn't so thrilled anymore. He could see the rocks coming up to meet him at blinding speeds.

He found then, the perfect word: Stupid.

He shrank away, screaming. Flapping his arms wildly to slow his progress as his body built up momentum.

~

Matt watched in absolute wonderment. How could anyone be so stupid?

Cody looked fine until he was about halfway down the rock face; grinning like an idiot. Like this was an everyday sort of thing. Then he started to scream, and twisted out of his graceful dive into a mess of wildly flapping arms and legs.

He gave Cody credit for one thing: he'd never have had the courage to jump; even though he knew *he'd* probably survive. Cody, on the other hand...

Matt's eyes grew large and his pupils dilated, focusing wholly on Cody.

And suddenly - just as he was about to hit the first rock - Cody went soaring out to sea as if he'd just been hit by a giant, invisible fly swatter. Nine pairs of eyes watched as he flew out a hundred meters, then finally slowed, his flight curving so he came down with a splash into the icy cold water.

For a moment the water was still. Everyone was quiet. Then a head broke the glassy surface. A spluttering, coughing, but nevertheless grinning, head. "DID YOU GUY"S SEE THAT!? WOW!" Cody yelled over to them after his spasms had passed. "That was the absolute COOLEST! You guys have to try that sometime! First it was like: COOL! Then it was like: WOW! Then it was like AHHHHHHWEEEEYEEEEEE HAWWWW! - Common say it with me - WAAAAAAAAA-HO-HO-HOOOOOOOO!"

Matt rolled his eyes over to Ally. *Well at least* someone *had fun.*

Ally groaned and sank back beneath the surface into the silent, peaceful, Cody-less world.

"I want to go again! -Hey" He blinked suddenly, as if just noticing something. "Why are you guys all the way over there?" He continued to blink in confusion; then grinned in realization. "I know! You all swam away because you were afraid of the big splash I'd make - right? Right!?"

~ 15 ~

Supper that night was full of chatter.

From Cody.

All pleasantries aside - He just wouldn't shut up about his miraculous dive.

Matt putt his elbow on the table - narrowly missing his pasta dish - and rested his cheek in his hand. "You know." He mumbled across to Ally. "I'm thinking now maybe I should have just let him hit...Guts splattered across a rock; can't talk."

Ally wasn't listening. She had her hands up on the sides of her face; covering her ears as tightly as was possible. But still she could hear Cody's monologging from across the table; recounting his super spectacular dive again... and again... and again... and again - the story differing each time.

Even Eric was struck speechless. He'd fallen asleep into his lasagna; a noodle would fly out away from his nose every time he exhaled - then flop back when he took a breath.

Jason was attempting to send his fingers through the sturdy wood of the table; clenching so furiously he'd displaced the blood flow. His jaw was clenched just as tight, his teeth grinding so harshly Matt believed his teeth would break in a matter of minutes.

The teachers were reduced to witless shells; staring stupidly over at Cody as he tried to explain exactly how he'd flown through the air. Dennis himself was gazing at the chatterbox blankly, his eyes gazing straight through him to a time where kids were seen and not heard.

Cody himself continued to prattle on, completely oblivious to the lack of attention.

More time passed, and finally Kim snapped. She stood up so fast and so violently she sent her chair clattering to the floor. "Oh Cody for the love of peace - will you please SHUT UP!"

Cody's mouth snapped shut, staring up into her flushed face wide eyed and in apparent shock. It didn't take long though, for him to forget why he was staring at her. And he opened his mouth again, "You know, Kim. You should take some stress pills or something. Or maybe wear less blush - I had a cousin once who had too red a face, very terrible, very sad. Doctors say there's no cure. I think it's called 'Mad Syndrome' or maybe 'The Crazies'. You should get Brandon to check it out, or maybe even Dennis - hey! Dennis, did you ever get a medical degree? Are you a doctor-"

Kim let out a wail of exasperation and sat back into her chair - which wasn't there - and ended up landing quite heavily on the floor where she lost her temper completely.

It took Jason, Eric, and Alexander to hold her back from a still yapping Cody. But Kimberly was quite a bit stronger then her lithe fame suggested; fighting against their restraining grip, biting anything she could reach, clawing desperately against exposed flesh in an effort to reach the small chatterbox who was now backing up politely. Eventually the boys gave up, and Matt was forced to knock her out with a small orb of energy. She was revived later by Ally in a separate room.

Dennis sent Cody to bed.

All in all, no one could argue against the fact that it had been an interesting dinner.

And Darius had been completely whipped form their minds - no one had seen him since that morning at breakfast. And no one had heard anything about him thus.

~

Ally shut and locked the door behind her, turning in the dim lighting to smile seductively over at Matt.

He grinned, and in two strides had reached her, hoisted her off her feet, and sent her flying with a slight squeal to land with a *flump* on his bed. Stifling her laughter she tried to crab walk away from him as he crawled over to her on all fours.

~

Eric fell back onto his bed; laughing so hard his chest was liable to burst. "Great look for you, Jason. It may even become popular one day!"

Jason slammed the door behind him and stormed over to the mirror. He touched his tender cheek gingerly, looking at the three red scratches across his cheek and forehead. One was even bleeding, causing a small trickle of blood to run down his cheek and dribble lightly onto the carpet. Glowering at his reflection, he snagged a tissue from the box on his bedside table, and attempted to stanch the flow.

Still laughing, Eric attempted to quell his curiosity. "Let me guess, you tried to hit on Kim again."

"Shut up." Jason muttered, dabbing lightly at the cut.

"-And she - once again - said: FORGET IT!" Eric did an exact likeness of Kim's tough, yet still feminine voice; pulling his hair back to imitate the bandana she always wore.

"Shut up!"

Eric continued as if he hadn't heard. "And then you decided to try to persuade her by putting your hand down her pants, and she: *hiss*!" Eric hissed like a cat and slashed at the air with his bitten nails; mimicking a clawing motion.

"SHUT UP!!!" He hollered. Whipping around, Jason abandoned the tissue and fired a marble sized ball of ruby energy straight towards Eric. Who ducked just in time.

Ssssssssssss….

Eric turned around slowly to look at the burning hole in the wall that divided their room from the one over. It was about as thick as an eraser, and went clear through the wall right where his head had been only moments before. Jason's aim was pretty good. Eric swallowed.

Jason stared, he hadn't meant to put that much power into the blast - had that hit Eric… well; he'd probably be banging on Ally and Matt's door right about then.

He was just about to mumble a small apology and return to his wounds - when he heard something that made him pause, and looked closer at the hole he'd made in the wall.

Yes, the wall divided their room from the next; which happened to be Matt and Ally's. But he'd thought the walls would be much thicker than what they apparently were - his blast had gone clear through. His ears pricked and he heard it again; a small anguished moan.

Before he'd completely thought through the action, he'd taken three strides to the wall and plastered his ear to it; listening intently. Again he heard it, but now the indistinguishable sound was clearer - it wasn't anguished, it sounded almost... needy? Pleasurable?

Eric - having remained seated, stunned against the wall - now stood, his eyes widening further. "What are you doing!?" He hissed. Lowering his voice subconsciously as if some part of him was now fearful of being overheard. He yanked on Jason's arm, trying to pull him away from the wall.

"Eavesdropping. What does it look like?" He tried to shove Eric off, but Eric held fast.

"C'mon, man. Let's just go get Dennis or someone to fix it-"

Jason pushed back against the annoyance with most of his mind focused on what he was hearing. Suddenly he stopped trying to shove Eric off, and stood perfectly still against the crimson wall; staring blankly at nothing in particular.

Noting the lack of resistance, Eric tugged again. "C'mon-"

"Shh!" Jason hissed. "Listen!" He moved away from the wall, and shoved Eric forwards.

Eric put his hands up to stop his face from colliding rudely with the wall, turning his head to prevent his nose from meeting the same fate. The suddenness of the action caused his ear instead to rest by the hole. He was about to push himself away and start yelling at Jason again, when a sound caught his ear that forced him to pause and listen intently. Slowly his eyes began to pop.

He pushed himself from the wall as if burned.

Jason was grinning from ear to ear, the slashes across his face all but forgotten.

Eric looked at him with an expression of clear astonishment. "They're making out!" he hissed.

"Matt and Ally sitting in a tree. K-I-S-S-I-N-G. First comes love, then com-"

Eric suddenly placed both hands on either of Jason's shoulders and shoved him back so fiercely Jason hadn't time enough to react. He landed sprawled on the floor, and looked up in shocked amazement at the other. Eric only glared. "Not a word of this. To anyone!"

"And why the hell should I listen to you?"

"Because if either of them found out we heard them - heard them, you know... They'd probably be pretty pissed. Wouldn't you?"

Jason didn't look too happy about this statement, but he caught what Eric was getting at - Matt would probably flay him alive if he found out Jason knew. He didn't even want to think about what Ally would do.

Eric raised his eyebrows, still glowering. "Not a word." He turned and made for his bed by the far wall.

Jason watched him with swiftly narrowing eyes. "Are you a virgin, Eric?"

Eric stopped short, than continued on as if he'd never heard.

~

Matt woke in the dark shadows of night.

He knew where he was. Knew precisely what had happened. And as his eyes grew accustomed to the dark, he looked down at the sleeping beauty by his side.

She'd wrapped her arms tightly around his waist and shoulders, clutching to him desperately even in her sleep as if afraid he might leave. Her legs were tangled around his and in the sheets. Her hair was cast along his chest. Her breath ghosted across his exposed flesh.

He recognized the need to return her to her own bed; what if Dennis or Miranda came in to check up on them in the night? He had no proof they did - on that same thought, he had no proof to say they didn't.

She sighed softly in her sleep, and snuggled deeper into his embrace.

He tightened his arms around her, his heart bleeding with emotion.

No. For just one night he wanted to remain with her. Completely.

He stroked a strand of hair away from her face; tucked it behind her ear. Reaching down he tugged blankets back up to cover her venerable form, and drifted back into the hazy, restful world.

~ 16 ~

"Ok guys! Up! Rise and shine! It's time to go!"

Matt sat up groggily, rubbing the sleep from his eyes with a hand. Yawning, he glanced down at his watch; his eyes popped. "It's only five in the morning!" He groaned.

"I know." Brandon replied cheerfully, (Much too cheerfully for five in the morning.) placing his hands on his hips as Ally struggled awake in her own bed behind him. "But we have a long drive ahead of us today, and I want to get an early start."

Matt remembered. The ocean. He fell back into his warm covers with a moan; burying his head beneath a pillow.

Brandon headed for the door, calling over his shoulder, "We're leaving in an hour, be ready!" - before shutting the door behind him perhaps not as softly as he could have.

Ally growled and turned over in her covers, scrunching herself into a ball.

~

"Brandon if you ever, *ever* wake us up that early again: I'll introduce you to unbelievable – *excruciating* - pain." Ally told him as she climbed aboard the Yacht; ignoring the hand Matt offered. Swinging herself over the rail she stood glaring at him defiantly, her arms folded across her chest as if *daring* him to contradict her.

Brandon waved a dismissive hand, and held out their communicators. "Remember, check them regularly." Then he turned and made his way towards the cabin, where he revved up the engine, and started to move the boat gently away from the dock.

"He doesn't really mind pissing us off... does he?"

Her eyes narrowed. She glared daggers at Brandon's back a moment longer, before spinning on her heels and leading the way to the stern where they usually stood.

~

By noon the both of them were extremely fed up and bored entirely out of their wits... Even more so than they would have been had they been swimming at the time. At least under water there were things to look at... occasionally.

It was so early, only the first rays of sunlight were peeking over the water; casting a blinding brilliance of light darting across the waves that eventually forced Matt to turn his head, his eyes still too weak to adjust properly to the brightness. Six was just too early.

Brandon remained indifferent for most of the ride; though after an hour or so of nothing, even he was relieved to see the rock barrier come into view. Heaving a great sigh and whispering a 'thank you' to whatever deity may have been listening. And before they knew it, they were over the reef.

Without saying anything to Brandon or each other, Matt and Ally strapped their communicators to their wrists, and dove over the rail.

Ally couldn't explain her urgency. She lowered her eyelids before she hit the water, and even as she pulled up out of her dive, her fins had sprouted from her feet. She was changing faster than usual. Typically she would have taken her time. After all, they did have all day. But something was pulling her on, urging her to be swift - and she had this incredible desire to find out what. And fast.

She glanced down at Matt; saw him chasing a school of black discus fish out of a clump of seaweed, and she smiled. He looked up at her as they darted away from him. *What's wrong?* He swam up to her.

She removed her gaze from his. *Nothing. Let's get going.* And she swam off northward.

~

The reef was huge - and I don't mean 'football field' huge: I mean 'river' huge. It just stretched on for miles and miles with no apparent end. It even grew up the sides of the barrier in places.

The discus fish were all swimming carelessly - darting around and exploring. As if nothing mattered but play.

As big as it were, mind, and as boring as it was to swim over miles and miles of virtually the same coral and weeds: Ally had to admit it was better then swimming over a barren utopia of sand. There were things to look at: the reeds, the rainbow of fish, the coral... And it was unequivocally beautiful.

Ally had expected her feelings of urge to dissipate - or at the very least dim a bit. But they only increased. Growing stronger and more urgent as she swam on.

She began to accelerate, flipping her tail wildly but still gracefully behind her as she tore off above the coral. Faster and faster she swam until Matt shouted at her to slow down, and something about 'blasting her clear out of the water if she didn't stop real soon'. But she didn't stop. Nor did she slow or wait for him to catch up. She just tore on. Plowing through the water as a jet might soar through the air.

Soon she was straining herself; forcing her tail to move still faster. She was getting close... it pained her to move, but she couldn't stop now. And then, all too soon, she stopped.

She almost caused a two-mermaid pileup, stopping so fast. Matt had to swerve wildly to avoid swimming straight into her when she pulled up without warning. Her own built up momentum causing her to swim backwards just to keep herself from coasting forward another ten meters.

Matt shook his head as he swam back to her. *What's the big rush? We're only going to have to go farther if we go faster. And it's not like we have anything else to do today, unless you-* Ally suddenly placed both hands on either side of his face, and turned it around to face the other way. His jaw fell open with audible gasp.

Lain out before them was a giant chasm.

The corral reef just suddenly ended - as did the ocean floor.

Matt looked down to see the wall disappear into the darkness. Straining his eyes to pierce the ink, he could see it. Faintly. The sandy bottom at the end of the black. But it was still extremely far down.

The real eye-opener, however, were the mines.

Helium filled, spiked, steel balloons rising from the ocean floor where they were nailed or anchored into the sand and rock in some manner. Clip one of those and you'd be blown to kingdom come.

But beyond the fifty or so mines before them, they could see nothing.

Nothing but black, at any rate.

Matt turned his head partly towards Ally; his eyes still focused out towards the living bombs. *Uh... you think now might be a good time to tell Brandon we found something?*

Without answering, without averting her eyes from the awesome sight; Ally hit the purple button on her communicator. A few moments passed, then the blue light began to flash in response.

Matt spared the mine field one last, lingering glance; before rising up with Ally for the surface.

~

"What did you find?" Brandon called down. He had to yell for it was now raining heavily upon the water, the large drops splashing erratically around and on them as they bobbed on the rapidly rising crests of water. Lightning flashed and thunder rumbled. The sky was dark and glowered at them fiercely; clouds rolling in as the gale picked up force.

"Something spiky, with a short temper." Matt mumbled through the rain, his voice completely inaudible for the tumult. It wasn't overly creative, and through the howling wind he wasn't even sure if Ally had heard him.

If she had, her face remained stoic. "A minefield!" She yelled concisely.

Brandon nodded once, then disappeared from the rail. Within a moment he returned, his short hair plastered around his soaked - though grinning - face. They couldn't for the life of them figure why he was grinning in the midst of such bedlam.

"Continue on, and be careful." He shouted through sheets of driving rain. I" know you could easily survive through an explosion if you accidentally clipped one of those mines - but try not to all the same, all right? I'll call in and see what the coast guard knows about it."

They nodded in assent and dove swiftly for the calm beneath the waves.

They never noticed the knowing grin spreading to encompass most of Brandon's features. He watched the surface of the water for a moment - made absolutely certain the two were on their way. Then went back into the relatively dry cabin.

Watching the two red dots on the monitor for a moment, he reached for the two-way radio attached to the ceiling, and drew it down to his ear. "They're coming." He said, to whomever was on the other line in a cold, feeling-less voice.

~ 17 ~

Matt was instantly relieved as he accepted the shelter of the water once more. He may have already been soaked - but rain hammering onto his skull like some mad toddler wasn't his idea of pleasure.

Under the waves the storm was muted - in both volume and feeling. The currents of the ocean were slightly rockier than usual, but otherwise calm and soothing as ever.

The two slowly allowed themselves to sink back onto the ledge separating the beautiful - yet creepy - reef, from the dark, gloomy, and creepier nothingness beyond.

Matt allowed himself to drift straight down onto the ledge, where he sat with his arms folded across his chest, staring out towards the black, iron curtain. He tilted his head to look up at Ally, found her staring determinedly yet emotionlessly out into the void. *Shall we?*

She looked down at him. *Do you find none of this odd?*

How so?

How so!? She sighed and ran a hand through her hair, allowing herself to sink down onto the ledge beside him. *This reef, for starters-*

Brandon explained that. You remember the project just as well as I.

Fine - then this minefield. A random minefield in the middle of the Pacific ocean? Doesn't that seem slightly odd? People vacation here all the time - cruise ships drive over... Have you any idea how easy it would be for a rudder to accidentally set one of those off? She gestured wildly out towards the field.

I see your point, but-

Ally hastily cut him off. *And Brandon - now there's an interesting topic. He and Dennis and Miranda for example. They answer our questions well enough when its about sages or our powers - but when we ask about the castle, or what we're doing each day swimming aimlessly in the ocean, their responses seem a little... lacking. Don't tell me you haven't noticed.* She gazed at him steadily, daring him to look away.

He met her gaze and held it, knowing the truth in her words. He'd just always put it off as adults believing them unworthy of the information - or some such meaningless reasoning. He mimicked her earlier sigh. *You're right.*

She blinked in surprise.

You're absolutely right. Something's just not right...And I intend to find out what. He looked pointedly out into the void.

You're not suggesting-

I am. I have this strange feeling - like whatever lies beyond that darkness... might be the answer to all our questions. Besides. He grinned at her. *Nothing else we can do, right?*

She smiled, her own curiosity just at its peek. Taking his hand softly in hers, she pushed off the ledge and swam with him out into the dark waters towards the mines.

~

They couldn't exactly tell the time under water. But Matt could have guessed they'd been swimming for at least a half hour; slowly winding their way around the chains that kept the mines from surfacing, before they saw something that was definitely out of the scenery.

There, down at the ocean floor, nestled between the chains and rock and dead corral; was a small rectangular building, only about a couple meters wide.

A diver floated by what Ally assumed was a door, made completely out of steel - as was the rest of the shack. A small red light above the door indicated a camera that slowly turned in their direction as they drew near.

To keep himself from sinking without a struggle, the diver had locked himself onto a metal rail soldered to the side of the shaft using a small amount of regular bike chain. A joke compared to the chains used to hold the mines; the links of which were easily a foot long and at least two inches thick.

They swam closer still, and the diver suddenly became aware of their presence. Turning to face them, he didn't look at all surprised by their appearance, only slightly awed. This brought them both back to full alert.

Staring at them explicitly for a moment, he gestured at the door to his right, nodding at them carefully - never taking his eyes from theirs.

They've been expecting us. Matt said simply. *I don't know about you, Ally - but this place gives me the creeps.*

Ally said nothing in return, and swam on towards the door.

As they stopped before him, the diver nodded again, a stream of bubbles escaping from his mouthpiece. Finally be broke eye contact to turn and open a metal cupboard that had been fixed to the direct left of the door.

The man pushed a combination of five numbers or symbols on the keypad revealed behind the box. Ally couldn't be certain as to what exactly they were, as she'd only caught a scant glimpse behind the man's hand. Then suddenly - so suddenly Matt swam back a pace - the door opened. The two plates slid away to the sides into the doorframe with heavy clangs to allow them access to the chamber beyond.

Grabbing a hold of Matt's hand - despite her misgivings - Ally tugged him through the door into a tube-like chamber. The two halves of the door screeched shut behind them.

For a moment she couldn't see, then a light suddenly flared in Matt's palm, and she saw he was holding a small orb of energy. Glancing around, had she been expecting something extraordinary she was sorely disappointed; the tube they were in was smooth, small, and quite empty.

Well this is nice. We're two fish trapped in a- whoa!

Suddenly the chamber gave a lurch, and the water began to drain from it to who only knew where.

Matt felt his fins brush the bottom of the tube, and hurriedly began to change back - less he be landed in this strange, foreign place. His fins collapsed and melded, shaping his sensitive bare feet; which he placed swiftly onto the cold metal to keep his balance, as the water receded to his waist. He almost toppled over then, when his tail suddenly split asunder, his legs formed, and his pants appeared; followed shortly by his tank-top turtleneck. The loss of his gills, and the blurring of his eyes completed the transition. The orb of light never ceasing its strong glow in the palm of his hand.

As the water completely drained, trickling out gently, the other side of the tube suddenly gave a heave, and the wall began to slide away. Once fully agape, the tube opened up into a long, barren corridor revealing a man in a blue and white uniform. A small gold medal in the shape of a fish was pinned beneath his right shoulder. He motioned to them with a grim face, and they followed warily down the hallway.

A short dark passage, lit only by two dim lights - the hall seemed to echo and clang eerily with every step they took. The man turned abruptly down a stairwell they hadn't even noticed for the enclosing shadows; and from there through another code-locked door, and into a spacious chamber teeming with activity.

Ally looked around in surprise, though none of her emotion betrayed her outward features. There were computers all around the room on desks littered with paper. Telephones and radios affixed to the walls beside large posters of different people and maps of the undersea world - along with the coasts bordering the Pacific Ocean.

There was a large three-meter wide television screen attached to the far wall, but it was blank at the moment. On another wall - a door embedded in it's center - there were shelves upon shelves of machine guns and harpoons as well as a small assortment of hand guns. This, more than anything, drew their attention.

As Matt watched, one of the taller men talking in a huddle by the guns noticed them. Cutting his conversation short, he made his way unerringly towards them; his men following in his wake.

Observing him as the man drew near, Matt could tell he was a man well into life. Close to around seventy or eighty, judging by his weathered features and graying, close-cropped hair. An assortment of gold and silver medals were pinned to his uniform - a black work suit with a red tie and stripes.

He came to a halt not four feet from them, and saluted with his left hand. His face almost angry in the way he held it. But his eyes were kind - if somewhat dark and foreboding.

Confused, his eyebrows arched to his hairline. Then, when nobody made a move or did anything, Matt raised his right hand, and saluted back. If somewhat weakly. Ally did the same.

A sharp nod. "General Volkar welcomes you to the United States Aqua Base." He said, snapping his arms to his sides.

The man that had escorted them leant down slightly to whisper into Matt's ear. "Or the 'Under Sea Armed Bastards', as some have come to call us." He grinned, then returned back out into the dark chamber - supposedly to his post. The door clanged shut behind him.

That last statement, for some reason, sent chills of warning up and down Matt's spine.

The general continued, acting as though he hadn't heard his subordinate. "Mr. Kenith radioed to inform us of your arrival. Now if you'll follow me, I'll lead you to the missile room, where we will discuss our next attack position." He turned, spinning professionally on his heel; and began to head off towards the door on the opposite end of the room.

Attack position!!! Matt's eyes flared. His heart jumped into his throat. *What have we gotten ourselves into!?*

Ally made no movement to suggest she'd heard. She made no move to follow General Volkar, either. Instead she spoke up, her voice strong and hard. Her eyes betrayed her feelings only; burning as they were with mistrust and hatred. "What do you mean by 'attack position'?" She asked.

General Volkar turned. Appearing only slightly nonplussed. "Why, did Dennis not fill you in-"

"How do you know Dennis?" Matt demanded. "And you had better 'fill us in' right now, because as you will shortly find we have extremely. Short. Tempers."

One of the men bent down to the General. "Are they supposed to act like that, sir?" He asked in a stage whisper. One that carried easily and that Matt and Ally could clearly hear.

Matt's eyes flashed, and his hands clenched into fists by his sides.

The general turned his attention back to them. What he said was quick, ruthless, blunt and to the point. He told them definitively that the USAB was the main cause of terrorism in Canada. That Matt and Ally were supposed to help them to start a war. Supposedly - with them on their side - the U.S. couldn't lose.

Ally's lower lip curled in distain. "And you expect us to just go along with this?"

The general grew worried then; or - at least his brow drew to a V between his eyes in apparent bewilderment. "Of course." He said, sounding as though this were the most obvious thing in the world. "You are programmed to obey. You cannot refuse. Even if - by some miracle - you decided you didn't want to. For a machine, however, that is quite-"

"Machine!!!" Matt exploded. His face red and his fists raised. "We are living, breathing, human beings, same as you!!! Though after that *little* speech it's heard to believe that of you.   And if you expect us to just - just go along with the demolition and complete destruction of ten entire cities along the pacific coast - you, you can just BURN IN HELL FOR ALL *I* CARE!!!" He couldn't believe that such mass murder could be committed simply because the U.S. president willed it. –No, that wasn't entirely true. According to General Volkar - not even the president really knew what was being done in his name.

The man who'd spoken before once again spoke to Volkar. "They're not... androids, sir?" His voice was shaky and off-kilter. Clearly this new revelation was startling - if not slightly frightening. Mr. Kenith had delivered regular reports of the Androids achievements and growing prowess; the men knew well what the two were capable of, and if they were working completely of their own volition...

"Of course they are!" Volkar snapped. "They've just been re-programm-" but the general never completed his sentence. He cut off mid-word, and stared down in a soundless daze at the bloody stump where his right arm had once been. Shakily, eyes almost appearing traumatized rose up to glare back at Matt. Watched as the blue glow in his eyes slowly dimmed, and the cobalt irises were visible once more.

Ally glanced at him from the corner of her eye. To say she was shocked would be a gross understatement. Slowly, though, she came to the realization that if Matt hadn't done something - she most definitely would have. And it would have been a lot worse than one missing arm.

The general fumbled with his left hand for the gun that resided in the holster on his right side. Pulling the slide back awkwardly with one hand, using the top button on his uniform, he pointed the .T70 over at Matt; who scowled deeply. "Not so easy to pull the trigger with the wrong hand, is it?"

It was the general's turn to scowl.

Ally's eyes opened wide in realization. *'When he saluted...'.* "Matt!" She screamed, not bothering with telepathy. "He's left hand-"

BANG!

Matt jerked as the bullet entered his heart, passed from his back and was left smoking in the wall behind him. He hadn't expected the General to be able to do it. Hadn't even raised his shield.

His breathing shallow, he touched his chest gingerly, and his fingers came away with dark, crimson blood. The bullets of a .T70 were small though powerfully manufactured; they could slide through solid rock effortlessly. He looked up at the general; saw the satisfactory smirk stretching across his face.

The only sound in the room the loud, echoing sounds of liquid dribbling steadily onto the floor.

Then the pain hit. He doubled over, and in agonizingly slow motion fell to the floor. A widening pool of blood spreading around his inert form.

Ally looked at him, rage welling in her to incomprehensible amounts. She then shot her gaze back to the general, whose gun went flying from his loose grip, and into the head of one of his men. Her eyes radiated darkness, and in an instant the cold, unfeeling eyes of the general had grown wide, staring blankly at the ceiling overhead. The beam of energy that had passed through the very center of his chest faded, leaving a smoldering hole in the mans torso.

He was dead before he hit the ground.

It had happened so fast it took an extra second or two for the men in the room to snap back into action.

"IN ARMS!!!" Someone bellowed. In an instant every man in the room had trained his gun on her. They formed a tight circle around her, each man closing the gap. There was no escape.

A volley of bullets rang out in the room. Little clinks echoing as each one hit her shield and fell harmlessly to the floor. Still smoking.

Trying hard not to think about Matt, - whom she knew would be fine - Ally trained her attention fully on the remaining men. Closing her eyes she waited patiently for the onslaught to cease. For the men to come to terms with their doom, and accept it silently.

One by one the men lowered their weapons, realizing how futile it was to shoot at her.

Her lips quirked in what could almost be assumed was a grin. Raising her arms she interlaced her fingers above her head so the digits pointed out above her like a steeple. In awe the men watched as her ebony energy sparked from her fingertips; darting back and forth and crackling like lightning. Slowly the energy strengthened; the fragile sparks melding together to form long weaving tendrils of energy. These tendrils danced around her enthrallingly, falling down around her. Stretching and flattening until she was enclosed in what appeared to be a darker, more visible version of her shield. Though still broken at the very top where the energy continued to crackle and spread from her fingers. Continuously strengthening the shield.

It was impossible for any of the men to come to a reasonable conclusion as to whether this girl was human - or indeed, a machine.

Now she opened her eyes, and stared down directly at Volkar's corpse. "See you in hell." She whispered unpassionately.

The sphere around her suddenly seemed to flare. Mirroring her fury. It then blasted out in all directions, bombarding men with a multitude of streaks of energy - killing them instantly. Throwing their corpses up against the walls. Smashing the computers and machinery around the room. Exploding through the walls.

Her eyes blazed mercilessly.

The water gushed in.

~

"Hah! Go fish!" Cody grinned. Standing up on his chair to get a better view of his opponents.

Jason snarled, and leant forward. Stretching his hand for the pile of cards in the center of the table.

"Sit down, Cody." Ivy mumbled calmly from where she lay on her bed; green quilted, like everything else in the room. She hadn't really agreed to this, but since it was hers *and* Alexandra's room... she hadn't exactly had a choice in the matter. So now she lay, watching the others as they played for lack of anything better to do with her time.

Jason was rapidly becoming more entertaining than Eric and Cody put together - the way things were going...

He picked up another card, and sighed aggressively in annoyance as he got another - Ivy could only assume - bad card. He turned to Kimberly, who sat beside him at the circular table. "You got any sevens?" He asked, his teeth grinding.

The table had been dragged into the room from a storage closet Cody had... found, when sneaking into the kitchen last night for a late night snack.

Whatever reason he had for figuring the kitchen was on the second floor...

Kim flashed him a smirk. "No." Her grin widened at the inevitable twitch of his eye signifying the oncoming rush of abrasiveness. "Go fish."

Jason let loose a howl of outrage.

"So," Kelsi said, in an effort to conversation. "Any idea where Matt an' Ally are?"

"Probably back out in the ocean." Eric spared her a glance. "Why?"

Kelsi blushed and averted her eyes. "Oh, just wondering." She focused her attention back to the game.

It wasn't long before the turn returned to Cody. He looked to Jason with the widest, broadest most aggravating smile in the universe. "Got any sevens?"

"ARRRRRGGGGGGH!!!" Jason leapt onto the table - sending cards, snacks and beverages flying - and lunged for Cody. Hitting him off his chair the two crashed onto the floor, where Jason set about squeezing Cody's cocky little voice straight out his throat.

While this wasn't entirely a bad thing, Ivy felt she had to do something. Mrs. Johnson had taught her a new talent yesterday, and - she being the most powerful sage in the room at the moment - was longing to try it out.

She lazily drew up erect in her bed, and removed her leather gloves. Pointing each one of her eight fingers straight towards Jason's back, she concentrated.

It took her a few moments. But just when Cody's face was starting to go purple - and Eric received a vicious punch in the jaw from Jason when he tried to tear him off the feebly thrashing little chatterbox beneath him - her green-tipped appendages each stretched, and snaked away from her hand. Growing furiously towards Jason, where they wrapped themselves around his arms and legs, rendering him immobile. She then lifted him from Cody, swinging him roughly onto the other bed where he landed with a muffled *whump*.

She smiled crookedly as her fingers slurped back to their regular proportions.

Cody – unfortunately - caught a glimpse of them just as they returned to normal. "Wow! Did you guys see that!?" He exclaimed. Immediately forgetting his ordeal with Jason - who was glaring at Cody from the bed, but had decided - in part thanks to Kim glaring at him murderously and Ivy's stationary position on her bed - to stay put. "That was so *cool*! I've never seen anything so bloody brilliant! Will you teach me-"

Ivy rolled her eyes as she tugged her tight, concealing gloves back onto her hands. Tugging them up to her elbows she glared at them in distaste. She hated them, that was irrefutable. But after what she had done to that girl... just by touching her... Well, let us leave it as she'd rather be in discomfort then sacrifice another innocent life.

She glanced around and saw Kim slap a hand over Cody's megaphone.

~

As the ocean gushed into the room, Ally hastily created another sphere around her. Not an offensive sphere; but her shield. And she watched through the transparent walls, as the water flooded the room. Washing away the bodies, and shoving the broken remnants of tables and machinery around the room with unbelievable force.

She wasn't interested in the damage, however. Her eyes were frantically scanning the wreckage for something else. Something she couldn't bear to lose.

A glimmer of blue off to her left caught her eye, and she swam swiftly towards it. Her tail working furiously just to keep her on a straight bearing. She gasped when a beam fell and smashed into the water moments before her, then breathed calmly in agitation, shoving the beam aside with her tail.

She saw him. Lying motionless on a part of the foundation still intact. Stifling another gasp she glided swiftly down to him.

His shirt was gone - as were his pants. Replaced by his strong sapphire fluke, and broad, even chest. Even in his semiconscious state, his body transformed in reflex.

His chest rose and fell, but slowly, strenuously. Relieved as she was to see him breathing; the small hole at his heart was seeping blood at an alarming pace. Clouding the water a dirty, rust red.

She knew that - even as a sage - he would die.

Though not if she could help it.

Raising her hands over his body, she forced herself to ignore the furniture smashing up against her shield, and instead focused on the growing glow at her palm. Forced it to spread and encompass his entire form. Strengthened it until the horrendous wound had closed, and Matt's breathing had returned to normal.

His eyes fluttered, then opened. The first thing he saw was her; bending above him with worry written all over her face. He grinned. *You didn't think a bullet would do me in. Did you?*

Her mouth drew to a thin white line, though a smile still managed to make itself seen. Shaking her head incredulously at his ludicrous take on the situation; She leant down towards him. Pulled up abruptly however when suddenly another beam crashed down onto her, hit her shield, and was blasted away through the water at fifty miles per hour. Watching it fly, she glanced down at Matt. Both of them returning sharply to reality.

He swallowed, and clasped her hand in his. Swimming swiftly away from the collapsing base, heading in the general direction of the reef. *I'm not even going to ask.*

They tore off, winding their way erratically through the maze of mines. Listening absently to the sounds behind them. The rushing of water, the crashing of random objects… They were almost at the reef - were in sight of at least some semblance of alleviation- and were already out of the immediate danger; when Ally glanced a look over her shoulder. She saw something then that nearly made her heart stop all together. *Raise your shield!!!* She screamed, and flung herself onto Matt's chest. Clutching him hard as she generated her shield around them both.

Matt - reacting off her frightened actions - clutched her to him tightly, and risked a glance back in time to see the wooden beam that had hit Ally's shield go careening into a mine.

BOOM!!!

The shock wave was incredible. One by one setting off all the other mines in the field.

The two intertwined beings were launched away towards the ledge bordering the reef faster then either of them could ever hope to swim. And they kept flying until they hit the stone barrier that divided the reef from the open ocean beyond.

Rock and metal hammered their shield with amazing force. Ally was clutching Matt's neck so hard he was sure she'd have broken his windpipe had he not loosened her embrace.

Finally the sea calmed once again, but looking out towards the reef, Matt could tell it would be a while before anything grew there again. It was all covered in debris. Now just a barren field of rock and scrap lumber and metal and nothing but.

He looked down at Ally; plastered to his chest, her tail wound around his back. She was staring blankly out over the deceased reef. A lone tear rolled from her eye, and into the water barely noticeable.

Suddenly she clenched her teeth in firm resolve. Her hands tangling into his hair. *We have to warn the others.*

He blinked at her. *Why?*

Ally turned to look up at him. *Don't you get it? They're using us to win a war they're going to start by using us! You know what would happen then, if they succeeded? We could destroy an entire state in an hour - just the two of us. And if you gave us half an hour of sleep in between each destruction, that would mean the total destruction of an entire country in about a day!* Her eyes were bleeding pity. The inner pain welling up and flooding into the ocean.

But, we wouldn't - they *wouldn't - We're just not like that!*

So what if we're not? I'm sure they've thought about this, you know, like some sort of drug, to keep us in line. Please, Matt. We have *to warn them.*

Matt bit his lip, looking out over the rubble. After a moment she returned to her pleading stare. Her piercing, captivating blue eyes. Sighing, he pushed away from her and took her hand. *Alright. But we'd better hurry, I'm sure not even Cody could have mistaken that explosion for what it was. Brandon will know, and if you're right, he'll try to stop us. He may have already radioed in to warn Dennis...* He let the sentence drift unfinished. Neither of them wanted to think of the 'what ifs'.

So they swam.

And swam... and kept on swimming. Pushing themselves to their limits and beyond. It was like before; that driving force that kept Ally from giving into her desire to stop and rest. Except now, that driving for was their own.

It wasn't long before they reached exhaustion. Every stroke of their tails causing pain to arch through their bodies. Their tendons throbbed, and their lungs burned. Though it wasn't for naught: they'd made it more then halfway back, and only had another hour or so of full-till, power swimming.

They didn't know how fast the Yacht *could* go. Nor did they know how long it would take Brandon to react when he realized they weren't coming back up - or even moving for that matter. They weren't stupid: they'd left their wristbands with the tracking devices back behind in the rocks and rubble now coating the Discuss Reef.

Risking a while of sleep, curled up together in the sand; they pressed on. Forcing their bodies further and further past their limits, straining with all their being to get back as soon as possible. Who knew what Dennis had already told them? Some lie... probably...

Swimming at the very floor of the ocean - just to be safe - they could hardly feel the coarse grains brushing their skin for the speed at which they were traveling. As they were going about a hundred clicks, it also came as no real surprise when the both of them had to swerve widely in opposite directions to avoid crashing pell-mell into the stone foundation of the castle.

Matt careened to the left, darting off and around the dock. While Ally streaked upward, swerving up out of the water to break her forward momentum. Crashing back she floated down onto the rocks and clutched her chest, wheezing and trying her darnedest to ignore the throbbing cramp in her tail.

Re-surfacing after a moment, they both pulled themselves up out of the water and onto the dock. Breathing in the cold, the wind, and the rain dampened air. Already they were soaked through: the heavy downpour persisting relentlessly in lashing bouts of rain and wind.

Finally Matt pushed himself warily to his feet, and pulled Ally up beside him. She lent on him, too tired even to support herself. And he was reduced to practically dragging her into the castle.

There, in the dry entryway, it came back to Ally what she was there to do. With that remembrance, reserve energy flooded into her system, and she took off determinedly for their rooms - the first place having entered her mind of where the others might be residing.

She'd never been one to care for other people; Matt had changed that. And now she was heading off to save - or at the very least warn - eight other people. None of which she really found herself thinking of as friends, let alone people of whom she owed. They were just people.

Despite that - she still had to warn them.

What Dennis was trying to do couldn't be allowed to happen. She *had* to do something. Interfere in some way.

Matt pulled up beside her, and they both stumbled into the hallway that led off to each of their rooms. There they were confronted by all eight of the people they'd come to warn. All of them pulling out of one of the bedrooms along the hall; Alexandra's and Ivy's, if they recalled correctly.

They pulled up when they caught sight of Matt and Ally; drenched but standing still and stern in the hallway.

"We have to leave. Now." Ally announced quietly. Something in her eyes causing an urge to back up.

Eight pairs of eyebrows arched in unison.

"Why?" Jason asked, folding his arms across his chest. He most likely believed them crazy; standing there dripping wet and passed exhaustion, almost to the point of collapse. Maybe they were.

Matt took a step forward, causing Jason to take an involuntary step back. "Dennis and Brandon - maybe Miranda, we're not sure - have been training us not for our benefit, but for theirs. They're going to use us to launch an attack on Canada. They're going to use us to kill millions of people! We- UNGH!" Matt's head jerked back, his eyes widening, then drifting shut. His body went limp and he pitched onto the carpeted floor. Besides him, Ally slumped down against the wall. Two identical feathered shafts protruding sinisterly from the backs of their necks.

Denis and Brandon stepped into the light, each of them cradling an identical tranquilizer gun in the nook of his arm. Brandon looked grim. "They were both hit by some falling rock on the way back." He informed them succinctly, looking up with the self-same fake frown painted across his face. "They began to think we were going to kill everyone in Canada, or some such story like that. Anyway, they became a danger to themselves and those around them. We are sorry to have used such an inhumane way to stop them - but they'll be better in a week." He smiled grimly, then both men knelt to retrieve the bodies.

Ally moaned softly, but was safely out. The sedative worked swiftly into her blood stream; immobilizing all bodily functions. Matt only nodded sleepily, as they were borne from the hall.

Once they were alone, Jason looked over at Kim and raised a skeptical brow. Kim returned his gaze. Both had been brought up in the households of soldiers. They were quite well informed when it came to silencing another party, and something about Brandon's story rang false. Quite a few things, actually.

Dennis had been far to quiet; remaining in the back ground while Brandon did all the talking. Knowing Dennis' character, he normally would have jumped straight into explanations. But just then, it seemed as if he simply didn't have one to give. Also, that amount of drug in such a young system couldn't take more then perhaps an hour or two to wear off.

Neither Kimberly nor Jason liked being left out of the loop. They were going to get to the bottom of this.

~ 18 ~

Matt woke abruptly to find himself perfectly dry, and not at all where he should be. He looked up to see a ceiling suspended a good fifty feet above him, the translucency of which suggesting at either a glass or plastic make. Blinking, he glanced over to see the all too familiar rock pile over in one corner of the room.

Propping himself up on his elbows, he looked around and confirmed his suspicions. He was in the tank. It was drained, of course, but it was still the same tank where he'd learned he was a water sage; that he could turn into a water dwelling being at will.

Looking beyond the glass walls of the tank, he saw what appeared to be blurred figures standing together in a loose circle. Blinking a couple of times, they became clearer. Though thanks to the muffling effect of the glass, he could only make out parts of what they were saying:

"Well- Mr. Dixon... it took you- enough, but- finally di- it... lations."

"Thank- ou, general Admar- will- soon." It wasn't hard to make out Dennis' slightly mussed head of hair - that same head tilting with his response.

"We- now I suppos- ... begin to test- them, do you... ... ... long?"

"Oh very- ...I hope-"

Matt felt movement to his right, and shot his gaze over to find Ally lying beside him slightly buried in the sand. She twitched again, and gave a mumbled moan, before raising a hand to her temple. Her eyes fluttered.

Matt thought quick - if Dennis knew they were awake... *Don't be startled. We're in the tank-*

That had the opposite effect of what Matt had initially intended. It certainly got Ally moving; she jumped to her feet and stared wildly around the room. Frantically searching for any means of escape. Her eyes flicking constantly back to the plug sealing the top of the tank.

Suddenly the chatter and discussion outside the tank subsided, and Matt got warily to his feet, watching as Dennis and a young man - in about his late thirties with dark brown hair - came closer to stare through the glass. They were accompanied by Miranda, Ileena, Joanne, and two other men wearing black uniforms like General Volkar had worn.

Matt's scowl deepened. Just the sight of the men made his teeth clench.

The other 'general' - as Matt supposed he was - looked them over with mild curiosity through the glass in the tank. After a while he nodded, and turned from them back to Dennis, who saluted. Then turned to nod at Miranda.

Only then did Matt notice the black remote Miranda was clutching to her chest. At least a foot in length and width; it took both her hands to support it. She placed it on the floor - where Matt could more clearly see the varying assortment of buttons, switches and knobs - and hit a large green button near the right-hand corner of the box.

The tank suddenly gave a weird rally of tiny clicks and booms. It lurched, and suddenly from the floor of the tank, water began to flow.

Clean, untainted, salt water straight from the ocean.

To a normal person in this predicament: they'd be dead as soon as the tank was completely filled. And though Matt and Ally could easily transform, Matt knew that's what Dennis probably wanted them to do. He hated not having a choice. Clenching his fists he glared out at the spectators beyond the glass. They only gazed back steadily.

How long can you hold your breath?

Matt's eyes shot over to Ally in surprise. *You actually think we can get out of this without showing them-*

How long can you hold your breath! It was no longer a question - now it was a demand.

Matt could see the determination in Ally's face. She knew it was hopeless, knew they couldn't hope to survive more than a few minutes in the filled tank without changing. Though despite that she still wanted to fight. To remain dignified until the bitter end.

That's what he loved about her. That's why he'd die for her.

About a minute, I'm not entirely sure. It's not like I've ever tested myself. Matt shrugged. He knew the people outside the tank could see him; but he was passed caring. Right at that moment he knew what it was like to be an animal at the zoo; locked in a small pen with people ogling and pointing at you... It was sickening. He wouldn't put up with it - didn't have to. He would defy them for as long as that were possible. And then he would curse them until he was out of breath.

Reaching the slim curve of their waists, the water was cold and bone tingling with their combined fear - not of the water, but of the people.

The water reached neck level and they began to tread. Kicking their legs and waving their arms. Keeping their mouths just above the surface. They'd forgotten how hard it was to swim without a powerful fluke to keep you up; and went under several times. Just barely making it back to the surface as lungs began to ache.

The waterline met to the top of the tank.

Taking one final glare at the people outside the tank, Matt blinked, took a deep lungful of air; and shivered as he felt the water close in around his head.

He was trapped.

~

Beyond the containing glass walls of the tank, one of the uniformed men gasped when he saw the water start to flood the cage, and grasped at Dennis' arm. "You... you're not going to kill them!?"

Dennis scowled and shook the man off like a person might shake off a pestering dog. Ignoring him completely.

General Admar, catching this from the corner of his eye; turned his profile toward him. "What *are* you doing, Dixon?"

Dennis smiled, the old twinkle surfacing with a hidden mischief. "Just watch."

The men and women around the tank all looked on with either apprehension, or complete confidence warring on their faces; as the two teenagers treaded water frantically as they fought against the rising suffocation.

The two were staring out at them through the glass however, despite the stinging salt. And were glaring at them with a murderous vengeance outmatching any human emotion ever felt or shown.

They were animals trapped in a cage. Putting on a show. And these *humans*, this different species; were the caricaturist audience.

Dennis' grin broadened as he watched Matt convulse, his body yelling at him for air. Then he curled over, and began to sink – rapidly - towards the tank bottom.

Gasps of awe and surprise echoed around the room as Matt's legs fused together slowly; his feet flattening and stretching; becoming the beautiful sapphire fins that glimmered in the light refracting into the tank.

Then his shirt seemed to dissolve, and six slits opened up along his neck; three to each side. His face relaxed, and he no longer struggled with the need for air, his chest rising and falling rhythmically. But he'd been defeated, and he curled up into a ball miserably on the sandy floor. Clutching at his powerful tail in anger, almost crying in frustration.

Above him Ally still fought. Clutching at her chest frantically, her body screaming for oxygen. She lost her stance and curled over in the water, twitching. Her mouth opened in silent pain, bubbles erupting from that gapping orifice in a wide flurry towards the top of the tank; where a carbon bubble formed. And remained. Unable to escape. As were the two beings below.

She convulsed once more, forcing herself to live another second without air. Then slowly - very slowly; as if even now she refused to give in - her legs became one long, shiny black tail. Her feet flattened out into the wondrous fins. Her shirt became one single buff tied tightly around her breasts, and her gills opened up along her jugular.

She sank away slightly from the top of the tank, her tail flipping lightly to keep her erect. Her eyes opened, then flared.

Dennis looked on in triumph.

~

Ally turned over in the water, and gazed out at the humans behind the glass. Observing her as a scientist may observe some fungi beneath a microscope.

Her eye's grew dangerously dark, and the next second a beam of black light had shot from her irises and gone straight towards Dixon. What happened next happened so fast no one really knew quite what transpired: the beam shot out, hit the glass, rebounded, and came pelting back towards Ally all within a heartbeat.

She had only enough time to widen her eyes in surprise before the beam struck her in the chest, causing her to roll over erratically in the water. She was slammed into the opposite wall, the breath knocked from her body.

Coughing, she brought herself back up almost immediately. The blast had been meant to shatter the glass - not to cause bodily harm. That kind of attack was reserved for later, when she had Dixon struggling in her grip.

Darting forward, she came up right before the men beyond the wall of her cage. Charging her energy, her eyes widened once more: she fired. The beam - as predicted - shot back at her from the glass, hit her shield, rebounded, hit the glass, rebounded, hit her shield again, and exploded. All happening so fast it was a blur.

~

Beneath her - still curled into the sand - Matt couldn't help but notice the flurry of activity in the water. And he raised his head from where it'd been resting on his tail in time to see Ally fire again; this time charging so much energy it hit the glass of the tank, flattened and spread out across it, then exploded with such furry it sent her flying back across the tank.

Coasting to a stop near the rock pile, she sped forward and prepared to fire again. Her eyes radiating now murder, anger, frustration and hate.

Matt swam up, darted before her, and caught her around the middle in mid-fire. The latest blast hitting his own shield and dissipating as he held her close. She fought him; pushed against him and struggled to break from his grip and resume her meaningless attack. Ignoring a wild slap to the face - and the resultant stinging of his left cheek - he began to slowly force her over to the pile of rocks, and to the slight concealment offered there.

There he held her tightly against him. Let her vent her anguish in less diminishing ways. She punched him fruitlessly, pounding her small fists into his upper torso; knowing she was hurting him but at the same time caring little. Little by little her anger lessened, and soon she was reduced to a hiccupping mess clutching silently to him for support. Sobbing haphazardly into his shoulder. *Why couldn't I break the glass?! Why? Why!? WHY!!!*

Matt had been wondering the same thing. Why *couldn't* she break the glass? She'd smashed boulders into smithereens with the slightest of effort - melted pure steel... Why?

He gazed down at her, confusion engulfing his own gaze. *Maybe a force field?*

She looked up at him angrily, tears blurring her vision. *Don't be stupid! We don't have that kind of technology yet! Force field.* She tried to shrug it off; laugh at the ludicrousness of the idea. But she couldn't. She could only resume her sob-fest into his shoulder.

Maybe we do... He never removed his gaze from her face. Puffy and red now from her anguish. She didn't reply.

~

"And that gentlemen, is how we will win this war. We start it, finish it, conquer the northern hemisphere, and come out on top within a week with hardly even having deployed any valuable resources. *Then* we'll talk about Brazil."

"Very good, Dixon. Very good indeed. You've done well - you shall be promoted for *sure* this time!"

Dennis' exuberance dimmed somewhat.

"But how in the world did you get these kids so bloody powerful is what I would like to know." General Admar continued. Glancing conspicuously at Dennis from the corner of his eye.

Dennis coughed. "Yes, well. Ha ha, that's something that may take a little explaining - heredity and all. I'm not the head director of Genetic modification for nothing you know!" He clapped the general on the back, and proceeded to lead him from the room. Still yattering on.

Behind him Miranda looked downcast. Glancing down at the black box in her hands, she shot the tank one last pitying glance, before following her husband from the room. Voices floated back from the hallway:

"When will they be ready?"

"Give us a week. And they'll be yours."

"Excellent. I'll expect a full progress report - anything about those two we should know? Recklessness? Loyalties?"

"No, no. The new darts will take care of all inhibition and disobedience. They'll be dolls - and yes; I'll have the reports completed and sent off at once."

"And what of the other eight?"

"They're still quite novice. But I do believe we'll have some use for them..."

As the voices faded, there was a sudden flurry of movement behind an air duct high above the tank. There was what sounded like a hushed - though heated - argument; then three figures swiftly made their way from the scene.

~

Matt continued to hold Ally until her body had relaxed, her sobs lessened, and she'd finally allowed herself to drift off into oblivion within the shelter of his arms. Only then did he allow himself to fall prey to slumber. Allowed the soft folds of worriless-ness to close snugly about him.

~ 19 ~

Ally woke with a start, shocked to find herself submerged. Then the memories flooded back. She scowled, and pushed herself lightly from Matt's lax embrace. Drifting around weeds brought back with the return of water, she swam up to look out through the glass.

When she was positive beyond second guessing no one was there to see her, she swam up to the top of the tank, and pushed firmly on the lid. It couldn't have been more adamant. That having failed, she swam down a few feet, and fired at it a couple times. To the same aggravating result.

Suddenly she became aware of movement around the door.

Thinking it to be Dennis, Brandon or someone she'd rather not face at the moment; she turned to glare out at the room beyond. Instead of Dixon, she saw a brown blur with deep blue eyes staring at her from just behind the doorframe. Then the blur was gone.

She blinked.

~

"They're in there all right. Or, at least Ally is. She was firing energy orbs at the plug in the top of the tank. I don't know where Matt is, though. I couldn't see him."

"He's in there. We saw what happened." Jason said grimly, exchanging glances with Kim and Eric. "Let's do this." He started into the room.

Suddenly Kim leaped forward and grabbed his arm, dragging him back into the vacant - for the moment - hallway. "Wait!" She hissed in what could be assumed was a whisper. "Are you absolutely *certain* no one else is in there?"

Cody nodded. "Uh-huh. No one but Ally - and I guess Matt too, he's got to be in there somewhere... Hey! DO YOU THINK HE ECASCAPED-"

"SHHHHHH!!!" Eric leapt forward and shoved Cody up into the wall. His hand slapped over his mouth. "For once in your life, Cody." He said through clenched teeth, exerting all self-control just to restrain himself from yelling or slapping the kid senseless. "Keep your damn-mouth-shut!"

"Ok, ok. When do we-"

"SHHHHHH!" Everyone held their fingers up to their lips, and Cody – finally - shut up. A hurt look in his eyes as he chewed his lower lip to distract himself from all the wondrous things he wished to say.

"Besides." Jason ran a hand through his hair for the umpteenth time. "We know that if Ally's still in there, most likely Matt is too. Matt wouldn't leave without her - I doubt Ally would either." At a glance from Eric he left his comments there, though it was obvious something just behind his tongue was straining to break loose. Leaning forward he glanced out into the room, a sigh escaping his lips. He saw Ally, floating a few feet from the bottom of the tank. She was gazing steadily at the doorway, but wasn't moving other then the occasional flick of her tail.

He took one last glance around the room. Confirmed all was clear, then motioned to the others to follow him, and made his way cautiously into the room.

~

Ally watched as Jason entered, followed closely by Kim, Eric, Cody and the others. All of them looking around as if they expected some guy with a knife to jump out at them at any moment.

Matt! Matt wake up...

Behind the mound of rocks, Matt's eyes jerked open. His first thoughts revolving around Ally, he glanced around for her frantically, and saw her floating a few feet from where he lay. Her face was carefully emotionless, facing the room beyond. His eyebrows drawing to a point between his eyes, he swam up swiftly towards her. Movement beyond the tank caught his eye, and he turned his head to see Jason and the rest enter the otherwise empty room. *What?...*

I don't know. But neither Dennis or that general is with them... that has to be a good sign.

Yeah... Matt looked out at the teens, now lined up evenly along the front of the tank. Staring in at them through the glass. Matt couldn't help it, he bristled. He hated being on show like this; unable to hide or defend himself.

~

Giving Ally a once-over, Jason found himself admitting that she *was* beautiful - if you ignored the little fact that she was extremely dangerous. Mind you, his thoughts never once wavered from Kim. He shook his head, cleared his mind, and turned towards Alexandra. "Ready?"

Alex glanced down at the heavy round box clasped tightly in her hands. "Yeah." She placed the box down on the floor, and held her hand over a small black switch in the middle of the box. Looking up at Matt and Ally, she caught them staring out at her from inside the tank. She couldn't help but notice how much they seemed like animals, trapped in an exhibit for all to see. Swallowing, she pushed a clump of her hair behind an ear, then looked back down at the box. "Let's do this." She flipped the switch.

~

Ally's hands shot out to her sides when suddenly the tank gave a great lurch. Matt had likewise done the same - time honed human reflexes a habit not easily broken. Both gazes shot to the plug in the top of the tank when it lurched again. Then very slowly and - surprisingly - very muted, the large plastic plug keeping them trapped in the tank started to lift away, providing a small crack of freedom growing ever larger.

Beside her Matt allowed himself a grin, and darted up towards the space between the lid and the tank - towards his freedom. Ally swam cautiously with him. It seemed a tad easy...

Together they pulled and squeezed themselves from the tank, and with small suction-like *pop*s; managed to land themselves safely on the ledge that ran around the edge of the tank. Breathing harshly more from relief then from the effort.

Slowly their tails melded back into legs, their regular attire manifested itself, and their breathing returned to normal. They took their time getting back to their feet.

Below them Alexandra flipped the switch back again, and thick, clear cables they'd never noticed before; lowered the plug back onto the tank. A soft *schwoomp* telling them it had sealed.

Matt shivered violently. "I never - ever - want to spend that much time under water again." Ally smiled weakly, then started down the steps towards the other sages clustered around the front of the tank.

Matt watched her, then jumped right off the ledge, straight down the last forty feet ten times faster then she. He grinned back up at Ally. *Hey, it was faster than your way.* He winked.

"Show off." Ally muttered from the corner of her mouth, much too quiet even for Alex's acute hearing to pick up. Slowly she made her way down the remainder of the staircase, then lifted her eyebrows at Jason. Evidently expecting some sort of explanation.

Jason swallowed, though he met her gaze unwaveringly. "You were right." His voice cracked ever so slightly, so he tried again: "You were right. Dennis, Brandon... they were just using us. We-" he gestured at himself Kim and Eric. "We heard everything they said yesterday... everything. We saw what they did to you two..." He shook his head, then brought his gaze determinedly back to hers. "We're leaving. We decided to take the yacht - it can't be that hard to drive. Alexander said he's driven motorboats before so... yeah."

Kim spoke up. "You guy's can do what you want. You can come with us, or you can stay - or you can escape on your own. We just realized we needed to get you guy's out of there. Like, I know you wouldn't go and destroy an entire country of your own free will but... well, we did what we could." With that she turned away.

"After we saw what they did to you, and after we heard with our own ears that you two were telling the truth: Cody went and stole that control panel from Mrs. Dixon. Kind of shocked us when he turned up all happy and eager for a rescue mission. We came up with a reasonable plan to get you out." Jason concluded.

Matt raised a brow. "In other words: Cody did all the dirty work, and you guys figured you'd wait until the coast was clear, press a button and everything would work out dandy?"

"Yeah. Problem?" Kimberly's eyes flashed.

"Nope. Just making things clear."

It was quite obvious Jason and Kim were not used to conversations of this nature. They just wanted to get out of there, and fast.

Ally held her head high. She wasn't used to accepting help - didn't like charity; but in this case..." I'll go with you." She risked a swift glance over at Matt.

I go with you. I always will.

She nodded, striving not to let her extreme alleviation show on her face. "Right. Lead the way."

Jason gave them both a ruthless grin - a reflection of his former self - then turned, and led the way from the room.

They'd made it only to the entrance of the cafeteria however, when the front doors banged open, and twenty men flooded in to confront them. Each of them bore an identical, deadly looking gun. Tranquilizers.

The men apparently weren't expecting them to all be waiting for them nicely in the front hall; it took a moment for them to go into action.

Before they could, however; Kelsi took matters into her own hands.

"Run!!!" She hollered, and everyone tore off in separate directions. Pelting down the corridors as if their lives depended on it. Which - in a sense - they did.

Ally ran. Though a year ago she would have stood her ground and fought, she knew it was hopeless; she'd get hit by at least one dart before she could do much damage. She dashed into the cafeteria, and hit the doors leading to their rooms. She could tell she was being followed, and that at least a few of the others had accompanied her. She prayed Matt was among them. But she didn't stop, she never slowed; she just kept on running until she hit the solid stonewall at the end of the hall.

Then she stopped. Cursing under her breath she whirled to face ten of the men closing in on her with their darts trained on her, Jason, Eric and Cody whom had all crowded in swiftly behind her.

She heard ten identical, soft *clicks* as the men each turned off their safety. But she didn't let them get any further. Creating an orb around herself, Jason, Eric and Cody, she distracted the men long enough to charge up a phenomenal amount of energy. Thinking only of getting out of the predicament as fast as possible without harming herself or the three boys with her: she screamed at the top of her lungs, and sent energy flying out in all directions. Just like she'd done at the USAB.

Above and around them, the walls were blasted, shattered. And began to crack and break.

~

Matt followed Kim's purple skirt as it streaked out ahead of them - man that girl could run! They flew off down the opposite end of the corridor, off towards the spiral staircase ahead. The sound of their pounding footsteps echoing off the walls like an army.

After Kelsi's frantic shout of 'RUN!', the kids had all split off into two groups under a split-second decision. Some of them flew off into the cafeteria, and the rest tore off down the hall after Kim. He hoped to God Ally and the others met back up with them unscathed.

Behind them they could hear the explosive blasts of air as the men fired dart after dart after them. Some hit the walls, the rest flew passed them with high-pitched whistles. One or two struck Matt's shield, but he didn't risk a glance back to see if any of the others had fallen. He just kept on running after that purple skirt. How could she even *walk* in that thing!?

He hit the staircase three steps at a time, and blasted Kim the rest of the way up when he neared the top to find her slowing. Pushing herself up with her arms she shot him a lethal look.

Ignoring her he moved aside to allow the others passage, when suddenly he felt the floor beneath him shudder violently. He looked up in terror to see the ceiling begin to crack and break all around him: *Ally!*

"Everyone to me!" He heard above the sudden noise of rock crumbling, shifting and smashing. No one argued, and dashed over to him in a panic, slipping slightly on fallen debris.

Not bothering with a head count - as he had no idea who'd even followed him in the first place - he swiftly shut his eyes and devoted himself completely to generating a large a shield about him and the others as he could - just before the ceiling gave out.

Kim and the others who'd made it into the shield, looked up and watched with mixed emotions of horror, fear, and astoundment as rocks and rubble rained down upon them. Boulders; sections of the castle hit the shield, and bounced away - only to be replaced by more and more. One rock having been repelled off the shield; hit another slab of stone not four inches away, rammed back against the shield and exploded into thousands of tiny pebbles. This causing Kim to dart back in a hurry to get closer to Matt and the very center of the shield.

Matt himself was starting to waver under the strain. Making a shield as large as he had, with an entire castle intent on crushing it... Constantly he was forced to exert more energy to strengthen the continuously depleting shield; to fix breaks and cracks caused by the falling rock.

At one point the floor beneath them cracked, split open, and they went crashing down at least five feet before they hit solid rock and stopped. Bruised, yet alive only six feet down from where the top floor *used* to be.

"ALEX!!!"

Matt thought he'd heard someone scream. But with all the noise of the falling rocks around them, it was hard to tell.

About another ten minutes later - give or take - the rocks ceased to fall. Or at least they couldn't hear any more if rocks were falling elsewhere - for they were encased in a solid tomb of stone. In the dark and - worse - unsure as to how many had survived.

Matt forced some energy to form in his hand - like he'd down at the base - and took stock of their situation. Ivy was standing next to him, looking up at the rocks pressing down on the shield, and beside her Kelsi stood doing the same. Glancing up himself, he was pleased to note the shield would hold - at least until he decided otherwise. It was easier now to maintain it without the constant battering.

Kim was there, looking around and scratching her head as if in marvel. And when he looked down into the far reaches of the sphere, he caught sight of Alexandra. Curled into a ball, weeping into her knees.

Dropping his orb to the floor - where it continued to glow cheerily - he stepped slowly over to her. "It's ok, Alex. I'll get us out of here. It's not like we're trapped forever." It was awkward; he'd never spoken to her before, and wasn't sure exactly what to say. He was about to reach out to pat her back - offer her some sort of comfort - when she abruptly lifted her tear-streaked face towards him.

"It's not that it's- it's... oh Matt!" She suddenly - to his complete and utter shock - launched herself at him and clung desperately to his jeans. "He- he got hit! He was outside your sphere. He just- the rock- he didn't see it, I- oh!" She burst back into a fountain of tears, unable to continue.

Bemused and unsure, Matt took a hold of her by her shoulders and shook her gently. "Who, Alex? Who was outside my-" Then his breath hitched. He swallowed and shut his eyes. That frantic scream - Alex... Alexander. If he hadn't made it into the shield... then he'd... he'd been crushed.

Alexander was dead.

~

"Wow!" Jason looked around at the rock around them. Crowding them. Though stopped and held at bay by a frantic shield generated by an even more frantic Ally. "If that didn't stop them, I dunno what would!"

Ally ignored him, much too engrossed in her own thoughts to listed properly: She knew he was all right, but even so... she wished Matt were there beside her.

Her hands still outstretched - though cramped from bearing the strain of keeping the barrier in place while the castle died around them - She swallowed, than opened her eyes. Instantly she grew angry, finding the three boys staring at her. "Well what was I supposed to do!? Let them shoot us!!!" She lowered her arms to her sides; satisfied the shield was stable now the rock had stopped falling. And worked her shoulder muscles to ease them back into working order.

Seeing Jason about to retort, Eric hastily interjected. "No! We're glad you did what you did. We were just wondering how you planned to get us out of here." he gestured around at the rock.

Annoyed at the sarcasm Eric couldn't keep from his voice, Ally huffed and turned from them. "Well if that's all... Hold on." Facing the wall of rock in the direction she was sure the old stonewall had been before she'd destroyed the castle, she raised her right hand. Praying she was correct - and that she wouldn't cause another sudden collapse of the already once-pulverized rock - she forced a small amount of energy from her body to form before the palm of her hand. Then released it.

No matter how many times he'd seen it done; it still amazed him to watch. The ebony orb shot away from Ally's hand just slow enough for them to follow it, and crashed into the wall of rock encasing them. Blasting a hole the size of an average family car out to where they could see the ocean. Glittering brightly in the fading sunlight. A few more rocks rained down around them, but - thankfully - the remainder of the castle stayed intact. Instead they harmlessly clattered across the floor, or dropped into the sea with small *plook*'s.

She sighed, gazing out into the sunlight. "That good enough for you?" She called over her shoulder.

Eric grinned. "Not exactly perfect, but I'm not one to complain." He moved forward toward the opening, and looked down. He whistled shrilly. "Lots of rocks over here... but we can jump into the water right there." He pointed at a small pool of water where no rocks were present.

"What about the others?" Cody piped up - and for once said nothing more on the subject.

Ally smiled weakly, keeping her gaze averted. "If they were with Matt, I'm sure they're fine." Her throat constricted, her voice cracked, and she made her way hurriedly over towards the opening.

Jason followed her every move, his eyes glittering evilly. His hands stuffed in his pockets. "I bet you wish he was here, don't you?" He grinned at her maliciously.

Eric mouthed at him to stuff it.

Ally whirled, her eyes glowing dark. "What's that supposed to mean!?" She demanded.

"Don't you want to hold him, to kiss him, too- khaaa!" In an instant he'd been thrown up against the rock, a small protruding boulder digging harshly into his back between his shoulder blades. Jason could breath enough to talk, though, and interpreted her next question before she could open her mouth. "That's right. Me and Eric caught you two snogging a week ago-"

Eric gave him a glare that clearly said: *leave me out of this!*

Eric needn't have bothered, however. Ally was more then capable of weeding out a lie. Her eyes flaring, Jason suddenly found himself thrust up harder against the rock; the boulder bruising his skin to the point of breaking. He cried out in pain, though struggled to maintain eye contact.

Ally's gaze grew fiercer still, grinding Jason against the rock as harshly as she could. Then, quite suddenly and without warning, she released him. He fell to the remnants of the floor heavily. The impact jarring his legs so they couldn't hold him, and instead dropped him mercilessly. Coughing, he sighed wearily in relief.

Ally glared at him a moment longer, trying desperately to get her rage under control. Different thoughts and emotions chased each other around her head, warring with her for dominance. She hated Jason for having intruded on their private moment, for talking about it so bluntly. While at the same time, she really couldn't have cared less. Finally she turned from him, made for the ledge, and dove expertly into the water not five feet below. Expertly avoiding the rocks that threatened to impale her.

She surfaced in time to see Eric and Cody follow her into the water with identical splashes, followed shortly by Jason. Who refused to even look her way.

This suited her fine.

Eric was about to ask smartly what exactly they planned to do next, when-*BOOM!*

Ally looked up to see rock burst from part of what was left of the west balcony. The boulders, rocks and small pebbles flying away from the initial blast to go showering into the water eighty feet below. Erratic waves stemmed from the impact on the surface to rush over to the four of them where they tread the water close to the castle. Breaking over them and swirling them around like foam in the surf.

~

Matt comforted Alex as best as he could. But as time wore away he began to grow anxious, and a little antsy. Eventually he sent Kelsi to try and calm Alex somewhat. Then turning to focus on the wall of stone before him, he charged up a large amount of energy and held it in his palm. Glancing behind him to make certain everyone was out of range, he focused forward again and blasted straight through the wall. Sending rocks showering over the edge of what was left of the balcony.

Grinning, he then motioned for everyone to clear out. He looked back after Kim stomped out onto the balcony - grumbling about idiots - and saw Alex was still crumpled in a corner. Grief-stricken and weeping insuppressibly into her knees.

Not bothering to subdue her, he bent down and lifted her into his arms. Bearing her solemnly from the breach in the rock after the others.

Kim stared down over the damaged - though still remaining - ledge of the balcony. Glaring at Jason who was smirking up at her in a way that made her want to punch him. Reluctantly she pushed herself away.

"How're we going to get down?" She asked Matt pointedly as the teen deposited Alex on a flat slab of stone.

Glancing up at her he left Alex to gauge the situation for himself. Seeing Ally gazing up at him from the water caused an irrepressible feeling of relief to stem from his being and escape him in a sigh. His eyes overflowed with feeling, and he would have cried; but it didn't seem to be the right time.

Do you have the others? She asked him silently. Not really concerned, but impatient to get moving.

Yeah. But... Ally, Alex's dead.

But I saw you carrying her out of the castle? Allys' brows knitted together in confusion.

Not her. Him.

Oh... Her eyes grew wide as the information penetrated into her mind. He watched as Ally relayed the information to the three treading water behind her. Watched their reactions: Jason shrugged as if death were something you lived with. Eric floated on his back, tears running silently down his cheeks into the water. And Cody, a minute ago chattering a mile an hour, now as subdued as a kid who'd just been told there was no such thing as Santa clause.

Ally herself remained emotionless, her head lowered to the water; though he knew secretly she was inwardly mourning for the kid.

He shook his head, clearing his eyes of the tears he hadn't noticed, and repeated Kim's earlier question. *How will we get them down?*

Telekinesis? Ally shrugged.

Matt rolled his eyes; what else? Turning to the girls standing behind him, he fought to repress a smile. "Right, who wants to be first?"

"How're we getting down?" Kim repeated, slight anger making its way smoothly into her visage.

Matt turned to her in ever so slight annoyance. "Me and Ally will fly you down one by one. And don't worry, unless you tick me off it'll be a safe ride." He winked cheekily.

Kim glowered.

"Alex should go first." Kelsi said, standing from the girl's side. Her hand remaining on the girls shoulder, offering continuous comfort.

Matt didn't argue. Immediately he focused on the grieving girl, lifted her gently, and sent her slowly and steadily over the ledge.

~

Below, Ally took Alex carefully from Matt, and lowered her softly the rest of the way onto a pile of rubble close enough to the water for the girl to jump.

Then came Kim, then Ivy, then Kelsi. Each one just as cautiously lowered as the last.

Cody at one point had decided he'd like to try that sometime, and proceeded to tell them all about it quite loudly. Though a quick, decisive comment from Eric shut him back up:

"It would be awfully fun to do that! Not having to worry about the landing! I wish I could do that - I'd probably be the best! Hey! Have any of you guys ever gone skydiving - my dad took me once. It was loads of-"

"Cody." Eric said quietly, his fists clenching beneath the waves. "If at first you don't succeed... skydiving is *not* for you." He was evidently recalling that fateful day Cody had decided to leap off the west balcony, and splatter his guts all over the rock below.

It wasn't exactly the remembrance of the incident that shut Cody up so soundly - it was more the look on Eric's face. Straining and looking like the teen would explode at any moment. Actually, they were *all* under stress. It was just... Eric never looked serious. And it freaked Cody so much he'd decided it would be much safer for his health if he didn't push it.

After Kelsi was safely into the water, Ally looked up to find Matt standing on the ledge of the balcony, grinning down at her. Her eye's popped. "Don't-" She screeched, not bothering to speak telepathically. Her scream causing the other seven to glance up in surprise. But before she could stop him, he'd jumped. Feet first he shot towards the sharp rocks below.

~

Matt concentrated, his eyes focused. Aiming for the space in the rocks that should allow him to enter the water without impaling himself on the rocks first. And if he did - by some cruel fate - hit the rocks, Ally would be able to heal him before he died... Hopefully.

All he knew was they were wasting time. Dennis could be upon them at any time. And he would much prefer to avoid him and the rest of his 'men' for as long as he remained breathing.

As he plummeted he changed. His legs fused together, his feet flattened out to form fins, his shirt and pants disappeared and his gills slit themselves up along his neck. Already his form itched from the need for water, and the air was so warm it was almost intolerable.

But he never even made it to water.

Ally stopped him with a hand just before he hit, and he hung suspended over the rocks and rubble. His tail flipping uselessly in her grip, just grazing the surface and taunting him with the cool refreshingness of below. He moaned and looked over at her in annoyance.

She smirked at him, tilting her head and raising her eyebrows as if to say: Nice try. But better luck next time.

From behind her came the familiar shrill voice they all knew and loved: "WOW! I wish I could do that!" Startling Ally enough to drop Matt less than kindly into the ocean with a *splash*.

~ 20 ~

While the others spent a few moments on the rocks up close to the castle - resting up and devising their escape plan - Matt and Ally floated down onto the sea floor, and curled for a moment into each other's arms. Silent. Just grateful to be together.

The slight change of plans made it so the others were going to be relying on them a lot more. There was still the option of just swimming off into the Pacific alone to leave the others to their fates; after all, they'd done what they'd intended. They'd warned them, what more was to be expected? However, they couldn't just leave them stranded. One: Dixon might capture them, and seven sages at lower levels could be just as destructive as two higher-level sages. And two: it just wasn't ethical.

Ally sighed and opened her eyes, gazing up towards the surface where she could just make out the shimmering forms of the others as they sat and bickered on the rocks. Though they were all aware, they really only had two choices - either stay where they were and surrender, or escape into the ocean with naught but their own limbs to assist them - and while the ocean *was* getting choppier and choppier as a storm blew its way in from the east; it was obvious which course of action they would take. Despite this, however, everyone seemed completely bent on getting in the last word. And thus the argument tore on.

As the storm grew in velocity, winds forced the water into crests that were already a meter high and were getting higher. But despite the surface gale, the water below remained still and calm and quiet as always.

Ally sighed again. *Matt...*

Yeah?

Jason and Eric... and Cody they, they know about... us."

Matt's eyes fluttered open; he gazed down into her shining blue irises for a moment. Then a smile broke his features. *So?*

So? Ally spun around in his arms. *You don't care?*

What made you think I would care?

What I... I don't understand...

I don't care. He repeated, gazing at her steadily. *As long as I'm with you, I don't care what people think of me - of us. They can know all they want, but I won't give a damn.*

Ally smiled, and kissed him. It was slow. Gentle. Hardly intruding, she just wanted him to know that, in her own way; she really didn't care either. How could she have thought it would matter? How could she have thought it would have changed anything?

It didn't matter what people thought. What mattered was she loved him, and he loved her with an equal passion.

~

Jason wasn't really listening to the further debate raging on behind him; he'd gotten his two cents in. Nor was he concerned for the moment about the increasing storm around them. He was more intent on watching the two figures below the surface of the water. It was an understatement to say the two were difficult to see - in fact, he couldn't see their tails at all. He could however, make out the light glinting off their human halves. And as soon as Ally reached to kiss Matt, he went and shook Kim so roughly she flung around and slapped him.

For once Jason didn't retaliate, he only grabbed a beyond-shocked Kim's hand, and pulled her - practically dragged her - back to the ledge of the rock slab they were currently residing on. There he pointed down into the depths were Ally was still cuddling into Matt. "There! See, I told you!" He spat.

Kim stared, trying to pierce through the choppy waters. When she finally caught sight of them, her reaction wasn't quite what he'd been expecting. "So what, Jason?" She rounded on him. "What do you care if they're going out? It's not like *you* haven't ever kissed a girl before!" And she stormed off back towards the others, beyond annoyed to have been disturbed for *that*.

Jason glowered after her, then turned back to stare through the water once more.

～

Ally - opening her eyes as she felt a shadow cross over them - caught a glimpse of him out of her peripheral vision, and moved from Matt to glare at him.

She paused for a moment in thought, considering all of what had just come to light. Then when Matt started to turn his head to see what she was staring at, she came to a quick, decisive, decision. Grabbed his head with both hands, and turned his lips back to hers.

Jason glared even more vehemently.

Then she opened an eye, and he tumbled into the water with a yell and a sudden *splash*!

And as he pulled himself back onto the rock - coughing and spluttering for air - Kim came over – laughing - and shoved him right back in.

～

It had been unanimously decided for lack of any other course of action to take. They would swim for the coast. And pray to whomever may be listening they survived.

They swam and swam and swam some more. Under normal circumstances none of them would have even *dared* to swim for so long without resting - and the fact that they were nowhere *near* shore didn't help matters. But since there were two *very* experienced swimmers directly beneath them… they really had nothing to fear; and just kept on swimming.

Alexandra had stopped crying, but still she found it hard to keep up with the others while her thoughts continued to wander back to him. He'd been so nice to her. No one had *ever* been so nice - not sincerely anyway.

And the tears started up again. Welling up into her lashes, then flooding over and down across her cheeks to trickle silently into the water.

Beneath her Ally watched the girl choke and splutter, and looked over at Matt with a small, pleading smile.

Matt rolled his eyes. *Oh all right. No need to bring out the puppy-eyes...* And he flicked his tail towards the surface where he emerged a few feet in front of Alex. "Want a ride?" He asked her softly, cautiously; afraid of triggering another deep emotion.

Alex stopped swimming for a moment, treading water silently; then slowly she nodded.

Matt sighed, relieved not to have to deal with more anguish; and moved closer to her, turning around to show her his back. "Just hold onto my shoulders, and concentrate on keeping your feet away from my scales." He told her softly, keeping his eyes trained on the horizon.

Alex knew better than to ask why, and took hold of his shoulders tightly - wrapping her legs around his upper torso to avoid getting her legs slashed like Cody had done a while back.

Looking back to make sure she was on, Matt suddenly flipped his tail, and tore off ahead of the others. Not so fast that he'd unseat her, or leave the others behind - but far enough for Alex to think and come to terms with Alexander's death without interruption. Besides, he had to concentrate on keeping her head above the surface, and that made swimming slightly complicated.

~

"Lucky!" Cody exclaimed when Alex tore passed them on Matt's back. "I want a mermaid ride! I'm tired too!" True, they had been swimming at a relentless pace for at least a half an hour without rest. But none of the others were really tired... yet. It may have just been for Cody's level of power, or lack there of. Or it could also have been because-

"Well I wonder why!" Kim snapped, spitting saltwater from her mouth. "You've done more talking then swimming this whole time!"

"Easy, Kim." Eric played peacemaker. "The last thing we need now are tempers."

Suddenly Ally rose up before Cody, and showed him her back. Effectively putting an end to all conversation and complaints.

"YIPPIE!!!" Cody squealed, and made to jump on.

"Wait..." Ally stopped him, grinning. She glanced over her shoulder at him with an unreadable expression. "What did we learn the last time one of us gave you a ride?" She asked of him in a falsely sweet falsetto. Referring - of course - to the time Matt had rescued him when he'd 'fallen' over the side of the Yacht.

Cody's mood dropped a notch or two. He was reminiscing also. "Not to touch the tail." He recited as if in class being chided by the teacher.

"Right." Ally then smiled forcefully at him, turned back to face forward, and Cody - squealing in delight - jumped from the water with a loud, "BONZAI!!!" to land heavily on Ally's back. Sending them both sprawling beneath the waves so abruptly that when Ally finally surfaced the breath had been completely snatched from Cody's system. Along with most of his enthusiasm. Glowering and mumbling incomprehensively to herself, Ally swam off slowly after the others. Ignoring the choking, spluttering, much abashed kid seated on her back.

As Ally pulled ahead with Cody - though remained with the others to give Alex the space she needed - Kelsi abruptly pulled up short in the water. She clutched frantically at her wrist. The results of said clutching obviously not rendering pleasing results; she proceeded to grope along her entire body. Her efforts becoming ever frantic as to whatever it was she was searching for refused to turn up. Glancing up, she bit her upper lip. The others were already quite a ways ahead of her... She didn't want to hold them up. Turning around she began to backtrack, trying desperately to remember where it was she'd lost it. That watch *did* mean the world to her. It had been the only thing... the only and last thing her grandmother had given her before she'd passed away. Besides, she mused logically, as she scoured what she could see of the ocean floor from above the ever-rising waves, the watch had been a bright, neon pink. Wherever she'd dropped it, it should be easily spotted.

Pumping her legs and working her arms, she front-stroked across and over the waves. Her eyes on constant alert: ignoring the stinging salt.

It wasn't long before she'd lost sight of the others completely. The sun was blotted from view by the dense, angry storm clouds over head. And it didn't take Eric to point out sarcastically that she was completely and hopelessly lost.

Flopping onto her back, trying desperately to stay afloat and catch her breath at the same time. She struggled to keep the tears from her eyes.

Getting panicked now wouldn't help her in the least. She'd given up on finding her watch; now she'd be happy if she could just find somewhere to lie down, rest and think.

Then the tears started to flow, running down her cheeks and chin in steady rivulets.

She never even noticed the eerie shadows closing in on her from all around.

~

Another hour or so of non-stop, fairly demanding, swimming; everyone was undoubtedly starting to reach their end. (Except perhaps Ally, Matt, Cody and Alex…) It was then Matt came tearing back towards them.

"Where's Alex?" Ally asked, genuinely concerned this time.

"She's fine." Matt told her as he coasted to a stop near the front of the group. "We found a small underwater mountain that has at least a meter of rock out of the water - we can rest up there. Alex is there now."

Kim sighed and looked up towards the heavens, mouthing as if thanking some god.

They all doubled their efforts.

Ten or so minutes later and the small mound of rock came into view. Pushing themselves harder they all finally heaved themselves out of the water, and flopped boneless onto the desolate isle. Wheezing and concentrating only on catching their breaths.

Matt and Ally exchanged identical crooked grins, before climbing from the water themselves.

The undersea mountain - as Matt had said - only extended little more than a meter above the water line. And was only just large enough for them all to squeeze onto in varying states of comfort. It was hardly luxurious, but it meant rest - if only for a while.

Looking around at the others in turn, the two of them suddenly felt the irresistible weight of responsibility placed upon their shoulders. And - after checking with the other - dove in unison back into the water.

"Now where do they think they're going." Jason mumbled sleepily, dropping his head back onto the rock in exhaustion.

~

Matt swam a wide radius around the mountain as fast as he could, searching. He didn't have to search long. There, floating and drifting along the sand - probably washed in from some remote island - was a piece of driftwood more closely resembling the leg of an elephant. He grinned.

Grasping it around the middle, he heaved up the piece of lightweight material; and tore off swiftly back the mile or so towards where they'd left the others.

~

"I don't know if sages can catch hypothermia but, this'll help if we can." He grunted as he heaved himself from the water. Pushing the waterlogged log out in front of him towards the shivering group of teens huddled together against a ledge of rock.

"And how the hell is *this* supposed to keep us from freezing to death!?" Kim snapped, her teeth chattering so frantically that she shut her mouth in annoyance.

Matt grinned. "I thought Ivy could help us with that." He said, twisting his head to look over at said person.

Ivy already had her hands focused on the log and - quite suddenly - a beam of light gushed from them towards the log. Sunlight, Matt remembered. Turning his head and clenching his eyes. The others too had averted their gazes, having no such desire to go blind.

The log began to dry, rapidly. Then it began to smoke, and finally it burst into flame; crackling merrily and warming the isle and its temporary inhabitants considerably.

~

Ally swam through the water with a mission. Her eyes piercing and searching the inky water for her prey… There! A school of them just off to her left.

Grinning wickedly she tore after them with speed born of hunger. Overtaking them effortlessly in a matter of minutes.

They tore frantically away from her, but she was faster by about twenty clicks. Soon she'd rounded on the largest one, and dug her nails sharply into its slippery hide, killing it rapidly with a static shock through its thick armor. Grasping the limp body in her hands she turned fluidly and raced back off the way she'd come.

The survivors of the ambush thankfully flitted away in the opposite direction.

~

Matt was just reviving Ivy when Ally splashed ashore. Dragging along with her a large and - very dead - fish. Supper. He smiled at her. Someday he'd have to get her to teach him how to hunt like that…

Matt roasted the salmon over the flame carefully, turning it with his mind over and over in the flames. Once or twice his control slipped and he accidentally let it flop onto the log. But despite a few ashes attached to it here and there - it was eventually cooked. Perfectly tender and juicy and - most importantly - sustaining.

Ally split the fish open, and they each dove in. Prying out the tender meat with their hands and stuffing it into their mouths as quickly as they could. Swallowing and sighing in fulfillment.

It wasn't the gourmet cooking of the school chefs - or anyone, for that matter. But it was food. And boy were they hungry.

Only as Alex was finishing her fifth helping did she notice the abrupt decrease in numbers. "Where's Kelsi." She asked quietly. Glancing around at the others as if expecting the perky little brunet to pipe up and apologize for something she was never blamed for in the first place.

But Kelsi didn't speak up.

She wasn't there to do so.

~

They dove back into the water and began to search. Not knowing where to begin they headed back off from the direction they'd come. Retracing their steps. Hoping against hope she had just gotten turned around - maybe she'd fallen behind and simply lost sight of them.

But four leagues away from the rock and they knew they'd not see Kelsi again for a long, long time.

Maybe it was the lingering smell of blood in the water, or the feeling of dread creeping up the backs of their spines. But when Ally found the soft pink material brushing across the sandy ocean floor; ripped on one side and bloody on the other. It was fairly obvious something had gotten her.

They just knew.

And when they returned to tell the others, Matt couldn't help thinking: *From ten to nine, from nine to eight… Who's next?*

~

They finished the trout in silence and sat on the rock as close to the flame as they could get without scalding themselves, trying not to think about Kelsi or Alexander.

The sky had stopped lashing at them with thunder and lightning, and the sun was starting to peek through the cloud cover - late as it was in the day. But the wind remained. Howling around them and causing the waves to rise considerably high.

After a brief, concise discussion, they agreed they'd get nowhere with the waves twice as high as they'd been before, and would wait it out. They'd be rested; and besides, what was the worst that could happen?

The log had soon burned down completely, and Ivy could only keep a small fire burning on the ashes and bare rock for so long. It got to the point where eventually they had to give in and huddle together for warmth. At least the rain had stopped, and they were relatively dry. But chill wind blowing at sixty miles an hour was no mild breeze. It chilled them almost - if not just - as effectively as the rain had.

Matt and Ally had gone off again - in search of more fish? Jason doubted it. He had a hunch as to what they were doing. He was proven irritably wrong mind, as soon they returned. Each lugging a large pile of fresh weeds ripped up straight from the ocean floor along with them.

Matt pushed his bundle up beside Eric and the boys. Ally to the girls. Each group determinedly clustered together to keep warm - and to keep Kim and Jason apart. None were in the mood to handle escalated tempers right at that moment.

There was one good thing about the cold however: Cody's teeth were so busy chattering, he himself had no chance to talk. And when he did nobody could understand a word he spoke anyway.

"Here." Matt told them as he shoved the mound of seaweed towards them. "It's probably quite fetid to you. But it'll keep you warm... and hidden." Something in his voice suggested an omission, but they had no chance to prod as he and Ally dropped back into the water, swam around towards the other side of the rock, and pulled themselves ashore.

This was no easy thing to do, since each of them weighed two hundred pounds on land at the least; and neither transformed back onto their sturdy legs. Instead they pulled themselves up onto the rock by wiggling their bodies as a snake might, and pumping their arms as if they were doing push-ups, until they were fully settled onto the rock.

This act baffled the watching teens, and especially Ivy who came over to kneel beside them. "Why don't you turn back?" She asked, hugging a blanket of seaweed around her body. Though it did stink, it also warded off the cold - as Matt had said it would.

Ally - breathing hard after the workout, and trying to get comfortable against a jutting stone in her lower back - twisted to look up at her. "We want to be fully able to slip into the water quickly and quietly if needed... You should go tell the others to be ready to hide or move if we tell them." She looked away, her face surprisingly drawn.

Ivy couldn't help asking: "Why." Her face a mask of concern as her wild brown and green hair whipped out around her in the gale.

Ally looked to Matt for support, then back at Ivy. "When we were gathering that seaweed, we spotted a Yacht. And not any Yacht but *our* Yacht: *The Prowler*. And if that's not enough to bake your noodle - imagine about fifty armed men aboard with those annoying tranquilizer guns they seem to like so much; along with another twenty men in the water, divers holding nasty looking harpoons with nets attached. Apparently they intend to catch us." Ally's visage suggested indifference, even amusement.

"They were headed this way." Matt grunted, his eyes on the water. "But with these high waves we're hopping they'll pass us by."

"And if not...?" Ivy couldn't help but press.

Matt grinned down at Ally. "We figure we can slow them down a bit."

Ivy knew better than to ask for elaboration. Instead she made her way back to the others, and briefed them with everything she'd been told.

After that they all remained silent. Straining their ears against the wind in a futile and hopeless attempt to locate something... anything. The creak of timbers, the splash of the divers. The shouts of Dennis if he were with them... Anything. But with the storm ranging around them ceaselessly, it was near impossible.

They were so paranoid, even Cody had inherited a shifty eye. Peering from side to side in fear. Clutching the seaweed comforters tighter around him for warmth and concealment.

Ally and Matt however, remained calm and poised ready to dive; as they knew they'd have to.

Suddenly out of the blue came a shout slightly muffled by the wind: "I SEE THEM!! THE TWO FISHES!!!"

"THE OTHERS!?"

"NO SIGN OF EM'!"

Looking off into the haze of the mist swirling off the water, they caught a glimpse of the *R.K. Prowler*. The boat that'd become more of a home to Matt and Ally in the past year than either of their foster homes had ever been.

The boat now looked like a ghost ship: emerging from the fog with only shadows and silhouettes as passengers. It was an alarming sight, and Matt immediately dove for the shelter of the water.

Ally paused only long enough to hiss a warning at the seaweed-cloaked figures behind her. "They haven't seen you yet! Try to keep it that way." Before following Matt into the surf.

They were far more clever then the men thought them. Instead of swimming straight for the haul of the yacht they darted around the mountain, and skirted the boat before coming at them from the rear.

Glaring with glimmering eyes at the unprotected backs of the divers, Ally shot Matt a fierce grin, and the two of them darted forward completely unnoticed.

~

The group of teens left on the rock huddled together in apprehension, watching the Yacht as it came closer.

Though they knew they couldn't be seen in their camouflaged-seaweed, and that Matt and Ally would soon have it all taken care of - they hoped - they all felt the need to hide and the irresistible urge to run. None of them wanted to risk putting Matt and Ally in danger by charging the craft themselves, and though it shamed them to admit it, none of them would last very long even in a group if they decided to do just that. They couldn't generate permanent shields like the other two - they'd have no hope of defending themselves. And so they waited.

Jason acted first, his patience finally giving out. In a fierce whisper he shouted orders to the others through the wind. "Into the water! We can float away like a drifting clump of weeds - they'd never suspect it was us!"

"Oh yes they would." Kim mumbled, but with the high waves, mist and fierce winds; she too thought it unlikely. And followed Jason as he led her and the others slowly into the water. Dropping in with splashes muffled by the weeds. At once they were lifted high with a wave, then dropped back into the trough with startled shrieks.

Calming their frayed nerves, they floated so that their heads just broke the surface. Treading water just a ways from the rock, straining to keep the Yacht in sight, and themselves out of it.

They went behind wave after wave, coming up again and again to see the yacht and the men on it all still scurrying to figure out what was going on. Then abruptly, when they were once again hidden by a steep wall of water; an explosion sounded from out ahead. And they cleared the next wave to see the Yacht in flames, slowly sinking into it's ready grave. Men jumping into the waves and swimming for the small rock they'd previously occupied. Already a few men were mere yards from where they'd thought they'd be safe.

They watched the burning wreckage, floating in shocked silence unable to wrench their eyes from the awesome sight; when they noticed something moving swiftly in their direction. No not swiftly, it was motoring towards them at such a speed their hearts missed quite a few important beats. It was a motorboat; none of the men could move *that* fast in the water, even the ones with flippers.

Jason started to edge them slowly out of the things path, pushing on Eric's back and kicking frantically to move them from sight. When he noticed the figure at the front of whatever it was. "Matt!" He yelled, completely forgetting himself in his sudden relief.

It was indeed Matt, and he was towing what looked like a large piece of metal by a rope melted into each of the front corners. Lying on top of the makeshift raft was Ally, furiously trying to detangle herself from a net that was coving her entire bottom half.

For a moment Jason thought she was just being stupid. It looked to him like she could merely slip from the net like any ordinary fish - then he noticed the long metal shaft lodged through the net, through the top half of her tail, and out her other side. He blinked in horrified fascination. Blood was trickling steadily from the wound, down along her scales onto the metal. From there it melded with the water and rain and washed from the raft into the ocean. Clouding the dark water.

When Matt was but a couple of yards from the clumps of seaweed, he pushed his tail forwards and forced himself and the raft to a stop.

Behind him Ally grunted in pain, and rolled herself from the platform and into the water with an awkward splash.

Jason and the others watched as she floated down through the water until she hit the sand below. Wrestling with the harpoon's broken shaft all the way. Trying furiously to wrench it from her body with force. But though broken, the harpoon still retained most of its barbs, and pulling it back through her body was going to be difficult - if not impossible and incredibly painful. And if she didn't get it out fast... the loss of blood and the puncture of at lest one of her major organs was going to kill her.

Without a word Matt removed the rope from around his waist, and dove back under. He swam down to where Ally lay in a forced calm, and told her sternly not to move.

Ally released the harpoon, and struggled to stop her twitching. Relaxing down against the sand as best as she could, she reached back and clutched spasmodically at a rock jutting from the base of the underwater mountain. Shutting her eyes in readiness of pain.

Swallowing, Matt then took a hold of the end of the shaft, and pulled it as hard as he could, swimming upward with all his might.

For a moment nothing happened, the shaft remained imbedded strongly in her flesh. Then, with a sickening tear, the shaft ripped from her body, and blood gushed forth into the water.

Ally gasped in shock and pain, her eyes widening past normal standards. Then she slumped down motionless onto the sand, her tail flopping onto the rock.

For a moment Kim actually felt herself fearing for the girls' life.

The sudden release of backward pull caused Matt to spin whimsically away through the water. Breathing strongly in relief while at the same time snarling in annoyance, he hurled the detestable shaft away from him in scorn before darting back to Ally's side. Never missing a beat, he raised his hands over her leaking chest, and a gush of blue light spilled forth to envelope her form.

The organs healed, as did veins and arteries; and finally the epidermis closed over the nightmarish wound.

Ally took a few more shuddering breaths. Her chest heaving as her body tried to figure out just what had happened - one minute it'd been about to breath its last, the next it was as good as new. Most people would have gone straight into shock, but Ally only allowed a smile to gently cross her lips, before glancing up at him with nothing short of pure love and gratitude. *Let me rest for a moment, you go on ahead and inform them.* Her eyes drifted shut again, and she released her strangle hold on the rock.

Knowing better than to argue, Matt nodded and quickly rose up towards the surface.

As soon as his head poked above the waves, Eric - free of the seaweed - swam hastily over to him. Spitting out sea water and chocking as he swam. "What happened?" He asked frantically, glancing down conspicuously at Ally. She'd shrugged the remainder of the net easily from her body, and was now heading slowly for the surface, her former strength returning rapidly.

Matt was busy hooking himself once more to the large piece of metal. He looked over at them with a tired stare. "We were really just going to disable the rudder, but one of the divers noticed the light behind him, and turned and fired at us. He got Ally completely in the net but the harpoon missed her by a mile. When it became obvious she'd be free in a matter of moments, another shot the harpoon at her: it hit most of her scales, and bounced off. Then she was hit from behind by another - this one hit her skin. It happened too fast for either of us to react properly.

"They began to fire at me but I- I panicked and blew up the ship in their faces. Most of them are dead now." He said this without emotion; the same tired expression marring his features as he glanced over at Ally when she surfaced beside him. He continued. "After that I noticed a piece of metal floating by the boat. I melted the rope into it, and pushed Ally on. Then tore out here, you saw what happened next."

"Anyway now that we have this, we can get out of here faster." Ally was back to herself, the same forthright, domineering, teenaged sage they all knew and had grown to depend on. "So hurry up and get on before Matt an' I leave without you!" She snapped, slipping under the rope with Matt and fastening it about her waist. He smiled at her, then quickly looked away when she shot him a 'What-are-you-looking-at' glare.

The others complied without argument. Swimming forwards in a hurry to clamber aboard the metal plate - which was hard to do, as the rain made the surface slick and they all slipped off once or twice before finally remaining together steadily in the center of the handcrafted vessel.

Matt glanced back only once to see if they were all set. Then nodded sharply to Ally, and they both dove beneath the waves and took off as fast as humanely possible from the malevolent scene. Dragging the raft behind them.

Behind, the fires crackled merrily on as the *R.K* took its time sinking into the briny deep. Spitting and hissing angrily as the rain hammered from above and the water lapped at it from below. And the screams of panicked horror from the men followed them well into the night and beyond. Haunting them forever in their unguarded moments.

~

Having long ago pushed themselves to their limits and further, neither found it too difficult to reach that again; and before long land was in sight. Rising up from the water to meet them like a great deity of hope come to deliver them from their nightmare.

Matt pulled up along side the rocks as Ally climbed up out of the water. She was followed closely by the others as one by one they slid off the metal sheet, and slowly climbed up the rock behind her.

Matt followed soon after, but not before he'd taken great pains to hide the raft under a landslide of rock.

Pulling himself up the sheer - though short - cliff, Matt looked up to find Ally smiling down at him, a hand extended. The rain and spray off the waves had soaked her to the bone. Her hair clung to her back and cheeks, and her eyes held an exhausted, haunted look in their depths. Sighing in gratitude he took the offer and used it as leverage to pull himself over the glossy rock face.

As one they looked around at their chosen landing. It was a large peninsula of extremely flat rock - so flat it looked like someone had taken a steamroller to it. It *was* connected to the shore, but it looked to be a *very* long walk to the sandy beach, and all any of them wanted at that moment was to flop down and sleep.

Eric shook out his soggy mop in an effort to remove the strands from his vision. He - like the others - looked well passed exhaustion. Bags hung under their eyes, they were soaked almost passed recognition, and they were slumped over in varying stages of tiredness. Kim had even sprawled herself most unladylike on the rock. Well passed caring how she looked or appeared to the others.

Now they were unsure as to what course of action to follow next. They were free of Dixon, it seemed. But where to now? Before any of them could ask though, a blinding flash of light illuminated to dark sky around them, and intensified. Growing to such radiance even Ivy was forced to finally shield her eyes lest she be blinded; throwing up her arms in defense and falling to her knees as her legs suddenly gave out.

~ 21 ~

Standing beside Ally a slight distance from the others, Matt had thrown himself over his lover to protect her from whatever new threat had presented itself. Shielding her with his own body as well as his energy. Forcing it to branch out and protect the others as an after-thought.

Opening his eyes so they were barely slits in his face, Matt forced them to adjust to the light. Then he cautiously widened them ever so slightly as the vividity began to dim. The darkness and rain soaring back to close in on them like some forgotten antagonist.

Slowly he straightened back up, keeping his arms protectively wrapped around Ally as she mirrored his stance. Looking around they were confused - to say the least. "What... just happened?"

"I'm not entirely sure..." Matt withdrew from her slightly, looking around, trying to pierce the dense sheets of rain for a sign of whatever it was that had caused the light. Then he heard it, the thunderous beating of a pair of great wings. Like a hawk, save these wings suggested at a six-foot wingspan - or greater.

His gaze shot skyward, and fixed incredulously on the figure descending towards them. Its decent slowed by a pair of giant wings nearly as big as the figure itself.

A voice echoed through the night. "Hi kids, remember me?"

Something about the voice caused Ally's own eyes to widen in recognition. "Darius!?" She exclaimed.

The man - for they could see now it was indeed a man - folded his great appendages to his sides and dropped the last five feet to the ground, his landing surprisingly soft; marked only by the faintest rustle made by his wings. He looked up at them and smiled - no, he smirked. A knowing, conniving smirk. And Matt now recognized him. The downy blond hair and pale complexion of the castaway they had rescued... how many long months ago?

But this Darius was different. He had a strength about him that hadn't existed before. A scheming knowledge the flitting, almost senile Darius they'd met that day on the balcony hadn't possessed. His inhuman amber irises seemed to glow threateningly. And the wings... the wings most definitely hadn't been there before. And they were hard to miss, extending from his shoulder blades to almost a full ten feet when opened - they brushed the ground when folded as they were. Each of his feathers were a black matching no other black in nature. As dark as a starless night yet darker. Shining with an unholy light all their own. Each feather groomed and shinning to perfection as if they'd only just been opened.

"He's an air sage." Ally breathed beside him in openmouthed wonder.

Darius' smirk broadened. "I apologize for my default. I would have been here sooner had Dennis not insisted he could capture you without incident. Clearly he was wrong - one should never underestimate the power of a sage."

Eight pairs of eyes widened at this statement, understanding dawning horribly on their rain-lashed faces.

"De-fault being ours for not realizing this sooner!" Eric hissed angrily from the corner of his mouth. No one laughed.

Completely ignoring the others, Darius stared malevolently over at Ally and Matt. "Now I don't want to make this difficult, and I'm sure neither of you wants to get hurt; so if you'll just wait here calmly with me, Dennis should be here in a while to pick us all up. I have already informed him of your capture."

"Well you can retract that information." Matt snapped. "We're *not* going back."

Darius leveled a deep, booming laugh that sent the rocks themselves quivering. "You think to fight me? I'm stronger than you'll ever be, Mathue Adonis!" He spat the name as if it burned him.

Matt's eyes widened, and all anger he'd felt went flying with the wind. "How do know that?" He whispered slowly, his body becoming uselessly limp.

Having ignored everything up until this point, Ally suddenly interrupted with a soft whisper. "Matt... *'Every twenty centuries, ten are born'*!" She quoted, gazing up at Darius with sudden realization. Clutching his arm she continued. "He's an air sage... but only *ten* are born every twenty centuries..."

She needn't have continued, he finally understood. She was quoting Dixon; he was the one who'd told them all their history before they started their 'training'. He'd told them how ten others had come before them and, presumably ten before them - though none could actually prove that, as there were no records dating far enough back. So Darius was one of the ten sages born before them. The last? Or were there nine others hanging around somewhere?

As if interpreting his thoughts, Darius intruded on them. "Yes I am the last of the original ten. And the most powerful. One by one I killed off my brethren, my only true opponents. And now you are the only one's who once again stand between me and the dominion of *my* world!"

"*Your* world!?" Matt spat, his anger returning in spades.

"But if you *are* one of the original ten..." Ally ventured. "Then - then you must be at least two thousand years old!"

"Two thousand sixteen years, to be exact."

"And yet he doesn't look a day over twenty. I *must* get the number of his beauty agent." Eric cracked dryly, neither his face nor his voice mirroring any of his mirth.

Darius - still pointedly ignoring the other six - focused back on Matt. "I knew your mother. I was there when she died, when she had you!" His eyes flashed in loathing. "Now as much as I promised Dennis I'd hold you... I really can't let you go off to get stronger, now can I?"

It happened so fast Matt had hardly blinked and it was over. The sardonic smirk was back on Darius' face as his obsidian eyes slowly faded back to normal.

Beside him he heard Ally choke and he whipped his head to the side.

The streak of energy had struck her soundly in the chest. Passing through her skin, organs, and bones with ease. Bursting soundlessly from her back to leave her with a gaping black hole in the middle of her body.

Her nervous system too shocked to fully comprehend what had happened, she lurched, and stared down in denial at the wound. Her hand coming away drenched with blood. She lurched again, and looked over at him. Tried to speak though only dry air escaped her parched lips. Her knees gave way.

Forgetting Darius. Forgetting the rain and the others. Forgetting everything except her. Matt twisted and lunged for her body, catching her as she fell. Sinking with her onto the rain-lashed stone. Blood ran freely out between his fingers, soaking through his jeans and running away across the peninsula.

He didn't cry, he knew she'd be alright. Blocking everything from his mind he moved his hands over her chest and focused completely on reviving her.

A freezing, pale hand gripped his wrist. "No..." Ally mumbled, struggling to talk though nerves threatened to send her into a quivering mess. "No." She repeated more firmly, though still far too soft for anyone save Matt to hear. She clutched his wrist harder and forced him to stop.

Matt gazed down at his hand in horror, watching as the soft blue glow began to fade. "Ally." His voice cracked. "Ally what are you doing?"

"Nngh!" Ally convulsed as her nerves became aware of the wound, her eyes rolled in her skull and he clutched at her desperately. "Ally don't *do* this!" Slowly her spasm passed, and her eyes drifted back lazily to his. "I'm sorry." She mumbled.

Matt began to get panicked. "Sorry for what? For allowing that sick bastard to hit you!? Don't worry, I'll heal you and we can get rid of him together! ALLY DON'T DO THIS!!!" and the tears came, spilling over his cheeks and mingling with the blood.

She offered him a weak smile. "You know as well as I do - if you heal me, neither of us will be strong enough to fight back. He'll- NUYN!!" She struggled to catch her breath, to ignore the pain, and continued haltingly. "He'll kill us both. At least - at least this way one of us... one of us will-" Her knees suddenly jerked up in pain, she cried out in agony. Her voice piercing the night and slashing the rain. Slowly she brought herself back under control. "Matt, he'll massacre the entire planet if we - if we don't stop him here! Now... you- uhhuh- NYUHH!!!" Her limbs twitched and her eyes shut to blot out the pain. Her hand clutched his spasmodically and was suddenly awash in light.

Matt stared down at his wrist in horror, unable to stop her. She wouldn't let him. A slow, gentle smile crested her lips as the light intensified, growing darker and more radiant as more of her blood pooled around them on the stone.

"No…" He moaned, helpless.

"Listen to me, Matt." She sobbed, her own tears trickling steadily over her cheeks. "Kill him. Promise me you'll - kill… Nugg! Him!"

His own energy flared at his wrist in an attempt to push hers back, but again she wouldn't let him. Pushing harder she continued to force him to absorb her energy. All of it until slowly the ebony glow began to fade, the sapphire consuming it in its entirety.

Ally slumped down weakly in his arms.

He barely registered the feeling of refreshingness that raced throughout his body, the feeling of having just woken from a deep slumber. He was aware only of the body in his arms, still alive but barely.

Blood gushed freely now from her wound, creating a starburst design around them in a horrific reminder of human mortality.

She convulsed again, this time almost gently. Her nerves losing the strength needed to retaliate. Her next breath drawn thin as it ripped from her chest. "Ngnn!" She choked, and blood splattered from her mouth. "I love you." She whispered, so softly it was almost stolen by the wind.

She tried to say something else, but no sound beached her blood-flecked lips. She shook again, almost wearily. Then her head went limp in his arms, the fingers clutched about his wrist grew slack and her hand dropped sharply onto the rock. Her eyes gazed sightlessly up into the heavens, never to see them again.

Sobbing uncontrollably he buried his face into her hair and screamed out his anguish. Clutching her chill body to his desperately as if he would drag her back himself from the plains of the dead. But he could do nothing. He could only sit there and sob and beg her blearily to come back.

For the longest time he remained that way, just rocking back and forth slowly with her in his arms. Sobbing silently into her hair.

Eventually he drew back in the slightest. "I promise." He hissed into her clinging strands. Leaving one last lingering kiss on a cheek that would never be warm again, before taking in a shuddering breath and gazing brokenly out into the sea. He raised his voice so the one behind him could clearly hear it through the storm. "You never told Dennis…

did you? You never told him we were here. You wanted all of us to yourself from the start. The president never even had anything to do with this, you were behind everything!" He whipped his gaze around to meet the cold, unfeeling one he could sense burning into his back - and met that glare with equal force. His anguish swiftly being replaced by a burning, consuming hatred that threatened to burst forth and destroy anything unlucky enough to find itself in his path.

Darius said nothing, only continued to stare at him thoughtfully with the self same smirk still annoyingly present.

Whipping his head back he closed his eyes tightly in an effort to stanch the flow of tears running steadily down across his cheeks.

Taking another shuddering breath, he lay Ally onto the rock, then stood slowly from her form. Rising into a stance the others knew only too well. Matt was angry, and he was about to stand up for himself. His fists clenched at his sides - suddenly erupting in blue flame; crackling merrily and dancing along his knuckles in eagerness.

His eyes shot up blazing with hatred.

His own eyes darkening, Darius shot another beam towards Matt. But this one was deflected effortlessly off a clear, rippling wall surrounding the other. Matt's gaze intensified. "I made a promise." He mumbled. "And I intend to keep it!" He yelled, launching the flame straight towards Darius.

Unprepared, Darius took the brunt of the attack in his lower torso, but nevertheless remained on his feet. He smirked studiously. "I look forward to it. I haven't had a proper fight since-" He never got to finish his sentence. Screaming with uncontrolled fury Matt launched at him an onslaught of attacks. Hardly giving Darius time enough to dodge, let alone counter attack.

Finally raising his own barrier about him, the last three of Matt's attacks ricocheted off the air around Darius and shot back to explode mere inches from Matt's face.

Matt hardly flinched.

Darius smirked. "And what a fight this should be."

Matt only intensified his glower. No less then sixteen orbs materialized in the air before him.

Darius remained quite laid back. "I marvel at your talent."

"Yeah? I wonder if you'll marvel at your own rotting corpse!" And the orbs were all shot collectively towards him. Flying so fast they appeared only as small blurs of bright azure light to the watching sages left huddled together on the sidelines.

The dark sage only laughed. With a great rush of air, his wings exploded from his sides and he dexterously avoided the attacks. Soaring up far overhead before twisting angelically and darting back down.

His eyes narrowing, Matt charged more orbs and sent them one after the other towards Darius. And one after the other Darius dodged. Laughing manically as he twisted and swerved, flitted and danced around in the air. Looking to all the world as if he weren't in a battle at all, but merely enjoying himself in the rain. Indeed, the whether seemed not to affect his performance in the least. The rain seemed only to bounce from his feathers and ease his fevered muscles.

Snarling in annoyance, Matt tried again, only to have his attacks wasted. Growling with hatred he snapped and bellowed into the rain. "Coward! Come down and FIGHT ME!!!"

His eyes glittered. "Coward? Why, I was only having a little fun. I guess you do want to die after all." Tilting his great, expansive wings, Darius shot for the peninsula and the figure standing at its center.

They met head on. Energy crackled as their shields met and struggled to throw the other off. Eyes flashed and teeth bared. As the shields continued to repel each other as would magnets of the same pole, the two combatants within the shields traded blows with ever increasing ferocity. Matt's fists had become flaming, sapphire torches once more, and now he swung them wildly at every inch of Darius he could reach. Pounding into his flesh savagely, wanting only to hurt and not caring what became of him in return.

Darius exchanged punch for punch, his wings slapping furiously whenever he could find an opening.

Suddenly they stopped, poised in stasis when suddenly there was an angry crackle. The two shields crackled again, appearing as lightning where the two halves met. Then there was a sudden *pop* and both Matt and Darius were flung away from each other. Each flying to opposite sides of the peninsula and beyond.

Darius spread his wings and went soaring back into the bickering sky, but Matt had no way of stopping his flight, and instead went tumbling head over heels and crashed into the raging surf.

Pulling himself out of his plight, Darius sped off and began to circle the waves, urging his eyes to pierce past the inkiness that was darker than his own soul. But all he could see were the waves, breaking and crashing into each other and the rocks that made up the shore.

For the longest time nothing happened. Then without warning Matt came flying from the water, his tail gleaming, his eyes daring. His mouth wide as he bellowed out his defiance for the other. His arms stretched forth before him, an orb glimmering brightly in his palm. And reaching eye level with the other he blasted him clear across the sky.

Unable to stop himself, Darius flew down and smashed back into the peninsula. The angle of the impact causing him to lurch off the rock and land again in a crippled heap.

Though he couldn't defy gravity, Matt still grinned at his accomplishment as he dropped back into the waves; the impact stinging across his bare back and chest. Spinning over in the water, he paused for a moment to catch his breath, then tore off with renewed energy for the shore.

~

"Oh hell no..." Eric mumbled, as Darius straightened to his feet. His smirk completely whipped from his face now, and replaced with a deathly white line that only enhanced his murderous visage.

"Just *die* why don't you!" Alex screeched, then shut up immediately as Darius whipped his gaze to her.

Before he could even think of removing them from his sight however, there was another thunderous splash and Matt came flying once more from the water, this time heading not for him but for the shore. His momentum causing him to fly up a good twenty feet before his arch began to head for the ground. Changing swiftly, he hit the ground in a roll and pushed himself to his feel. "So you're alive." He said succinctly. *I thought for sure that last blast would do him in...*

"Yes. Surprised?" Darius asked him through a false smile.

"Not at all." Matt lied.

Before Matt could even think of getting back on the offensive, Darius suddenly threw up his hand and configured his energy into what looked like a long, black switch.

Apprehensive, Matt began to back up. But Darius wouldn't give him an inch. With a sudden flick of his wrist the whip came lashing down and snapped Matt's shield cleanly in two. Before Matt could react, the whip came down again through the break and lashed sharply across his left shoulder, sending him crashing to the ground with a cry of surprise and pain.

Darius fingered the whip fondly, and took his time stepping over to Matt's abused form lying prone and sprawled ungainly across the rock. "Like it? There's a lot you can do with energy - more then just simple energy orbs. Those are probably the more elementary of attacks." He flicked his wrist and the whip came down again, this time across Matt's back, leaving an angry red welt where switch met skin.

Matt cried out and attempted to return to his feet - but another strike stopped him and flattened him to the stone once more.

"You're too weak." Darius continued. "You're used to battles that are over quick - a hit and run scenario. You've never been in a lasting bout with an opponent of equal or greater power before." *Whoo-psh!* The whip came down again, rendering his shirt useless. Matt bit his lip harshly, struggling to withhold his cries of agony. "You can't handle it." *Whoo-psh!* "You're done." *Whoo-psh!* "You're dead." Darius raised the whip in the air, aiming to decapitate and end this pathetic excuse for a battle, when suddenly Matt's left hand shot forward and wrapped itself about Darius' right ankle. A sudden shock raced up the limb and throughout his entire form, and the whip suddenly flickered and evaporated in a wisp of smoke; the concentration needed to keep it in essence suddenly broken.

Matt grinned and removed his smoking hand from Darius bloody ankle. Jumping to his feet he whipped around and blasted Darius away from him with a flash of insubstantial energy. Dropping back to his knees, he suddenly lost the energy needed to stand. "I'm not... not beat yet." He hissed, watching through his drenched bangs as Darius rose back to his feet.

"Tricky one aren't you? I shall enjoy taking your life." He would end this quickly. As one himself he'd learnt long ago sages could be crafty in a sticky situation. If this battle were to go on for much longer... Matt could possibly find a way to best him - or at least disable him enough for the other six to finish him off. He'd already greatly tired him out. He hadn't anticipated needing to use this much energy just to finish the little upstart.

Moving his arm out before him, he tilted his palm skyward, and began to charge up the energy required. "You fought well I'll give you that. But I cannot allow this to continue."

"Why? Afraid you might lose?" Matt choked, making certain to keep his right hand hidden behind his back. It would probably be smarter to use both hands - but his left was currently useless. He cringed as he glanced quickly at the burnt and smoking appendage. That last attack had nearly done him in. Ally had taught him how to perform static shocks - but only for smaller creatures like fish. The energy needed to shock Darius had been much greater, and even then the amount he'd used hadn't been enough to kill him.

Ally... he glanced over at her body, feeling the sharp tongs of regret clench around his heart. Fighting the tears rising in his eyes he looked back sharply at Darius, watched him charge the attack that would end his life. He closed his eyes, feeling the tears leak out over the rims. *For you Ally... At least I'll bring him with me.*

"I'd ask you if you had any last requests - but I wouldn't grant them anyways so I really don't see the point." He smirked sadistically then tilted his palm so it was now facing him, the orb centered in it glowing brilliantly with an unholy light and the promise of his demise. And without further abeyance Darius hurled it towards him.

Yelling under the effort, Matt brought his hidden hand from behind him and threw his life's energy out to meet the oncoming attack. Bracing his knees beneath him to keep himself upright.

The attacks met in midair, collided and paused. Neither able to move forward.

Darius' eyes widened in astoundment. The sight that met his eyes completely unbelievable. *Where did he find the energy to...*

Focusing on his orb, Matt poured more energy from his eyes to strengthen it, his arms both utterly incapable. It was difficult, keeping himself upright whilst pouring so much into an attack already meant to kill, but he wouldn't give up.

They were even.

Completely.

Utterly.

He could win - at the cost of his life. And with nothing else to live for, he was willing to pay that price.

Pouring out the last amount of Ally's energy into the orb - the energy made from his own life - Matt blinked and stopped the flow. Watched in grim pleasure as his orb slowly overtook the other.

Realizing his folly, Darius struggled to take hold of his orb - give it more energy. But he was much too late. The small amount of energy he managed to pass forth was no match for the combined energy of two sages who could - together - easily overcome him. He watched in horror as Matt's orb slowly began to consume his, and soon it was completely enveloped. With nothing holding Matt back, the orb shot forward and blasted through the two-thousand-year-old sage; consuming him and sending him into oblivion with a shriek.

When the light had died, nothing was left to suggest Darius had ever been.

"Face it Sage." Matt muttered through blood-caked lips. "You're beat." He struggled to get to his feet: succeeding only to waver, stumble and drop back to his knees. He grinned into the sky, relishing the refreshing feel of the rain as it drummed lightly on his exposed flesh. *I did it, Ally.* He took one last shuddering breath, and gazed around him at the damage they'd caused. *It's over.* Then he pitched forward, his eyes closed before he hit the rock.

He could see her, standing calmly in the light resplendent cloud before him, smiling peacefully at him. He smiled back and made his way towards her. Taking her hand in his, intertwining his fingers with hers, they walked away.

From their worries.
From their pain.
From nothing.

~

They watched as Ally died, watched as she refused to allow Matt to save her, watched as she passed on to him the last of her energy. They saw all the sorrow, anguish, and bitterness well up and explode forth from Matt, saw the hatred well up in his eyes. They sat silently as the two sages fought, remained quiet as the shields rejected each other, waited noiselessly until Matt triumphed.

And did nothing as he fell slowly onto the rock beside Ally, never to rise again.

They were all crying, even impetuous Jason who simply allowed the water to flow down his cheeks in sparkling rivulets. Washed away almost immediately by the rain. Alex crying hysterically into Eric's shoulder; Cody and Kim offering silent support though clasped hands.

It was over, though they'd paid a terrible price.

Nothing was worth the life of another - and certainly not two.

They cremated them, right there on the peninsula in the rays of the dawning sun. Watching their ashes as they blew out to sea in the breeze and calm that had come about after the storm.

Then and there they made a pact and swore to help anyone - ever - if they needed assistance, in respect and final parting to Matt and Ally, who had showed them at the very end that nothing is more sacred then life. Proving that in the last moments of their own.

They left the peninsula, somehow evaded Dixon and his men, and started out anew. Using the storm to wipe their slates clean of everything that had transpired out in the Pacific Ocean - known as the ocean of memory.

They chose not to forget, but they chose to live on.

We are sages. We are not evil... Not all of us.

About the Author

C.D. Schrieber started writing when she was twelve, finding the imaginary worlds she could create through the use of pen and paper to be intoxicating in their endless possibilities. Residing in Alberta Canada, her fondness of reading is comparable to her joy of writing, and she is currently at work on the sequel to *Soul of Power*.

Printed in the United States
47114LVS00003B/85-171